The Deaths of December

ABOUT THE AUTHOR

Susi Holliday grew up in East Lothian. A life-long fan of crime and horror, her short stories have been published in various places, and she was shortlisted for the inaugural CWA Margery Allingham competition. She is the author of three novels in the Banktoun trilogy, *Black Wood*, *Willow Walk* and *The Damselfly*. She is married and lives in London.

You can find out more at www.sjiholliday.com

SUSI HOLLIDAY

The Deaths of December

MULHOLLAND
BOOKS
HODDER

First published in Great Britain in 2017 by Mulholland Books
An imprint of Hodder & Stoughton
An Hachette UK company

I

A CIP catalogue record for this title is available from the British Library

Paperback ISBN 978 1 473 65936 0
eBook ISBN 978 1 473 65937 7

Typeset in Sabon MT 11.75/14.75 pt by Palimpsest Book Production Limited,
Falkirk, Stirlingshire

Printed and bound by Clays Ltd, St Ives plc

Hodder & Stoughton policy is to use papers that are natural,
renewable and recyclable products and made from wood grown in
sustainable forests. The logging and manufacturing processes are expected to
conform to the environmental regulations of the country of origin.

Hodder & Stoughton Ltd
Carmelite House
50 Victoria Embankment
London EC4Y ODZ

www.hodder.co.uk

To my darling siblings: Abs, Ash and Keir . . .
with whom I have spent many happy Christmases and
managed not to kill

There's an art to taking the perfect photograph.

It's too easy now – all those camera phones, those built-in filters. People snapping pics of their artfully arranged lunch, taking selfies in changing rooms – all twisted and pouty, angled down so you can't see the chins, overexposed so you can't see the wrinkles.

That's not art.

Art is real. Art is the lines around an old woman's eyes that tell a story without words. Art is sitting on a freezing cold bench in the darkness, waiting patiently for the sun to rise. Grabbing that photo when the clouds are sitting softly, in perfect formation.

Art takes effort.

I still use a 35mm camera. I know they say that DSLRs and the like are just as good, but they aren't. Digital is all very well, for convenience and sharing and all that kind of thing, but what you gain in the convenience, you lose in the essence.

You need to *feel*.

No matter what the situation, what's going on with your own life, where you've got to be. You need to give your subject your full attention. Nurture them as much as you can. Even if all you're doing is waiting for them to stop something, or start something new. Waiting for them to relax. To forget the camera is there.

Sometimes you don't even know you've got the perfect image until it's developed. When you pull that sheet of paper through the fluid, carefully letting the liquid coat the film. You have to be patient, waiting for the picture to appear. Hanging it up to dry. Waiting.

Always waiting.

It was difficult, at first. But I wasn't going to give up on it. It's like a calling.

I have a job to do.

This one took a lot longer than I expected. I had to wait almost ten minutes, keeping the camera poised and ready, but aware of my surroundings, of the danger. Feeling my heart thumping in my chest, trying not to breathe. Hoping that it would happen soon, and when it did, the fear drifted away, just long enough to allow me to adjust the lens one final time. Zooming in, getting the close-up.

Click and wind.

Then back out, for the entire, perfect scene.

Click and wind.

The centrepiece of this one is red. A dark floral stain against the shocking white of the carpet. The image in the viewfinder is framed by the pale furniture, the delicately painted walls. Just off centre, a figure lies. Half curled, where he has attempted the foetal position. Seeking comfort at the end. Next to him, creeping towards me as if trying to escape its useless host: blood. So much blood.

I feel an ache of sadness, but I push it away. I can't let

it crush me. I can't let it stop me from doing my job. There is a special kind of silence, at the end.

'I'm sorry,' I whisper, as I close the door behind me and step outside into the icy white dark. Cold air against my hot cheeks. Calming.

It took me a long time to perfect my art.

But you know what they say.

Practice makes perfect.

Friday

NINE MORE SLEEPS

1

BECKY

Becky's washing her hands in the sink, glad that it's one of those three-in-one things with no mirror above it so she can avoid seeing the bags under her eyes. She shakes her hands, waits for the dryer to come on, gets a sudden waft of something deeply unpleasant. She side-eyes the woman standing next to her, muttering away to herself, and can't work out if it's the mangy coat that smells like a dead animal or the woman inside it. She holds her breath. She's smelled three-day-old corpses less pungent than this.

She batters through the swing door out of the toilets, escapes into the sanctuary of the restaurant. Blinks at the too-bright lights, inhales the fried egg smell. 'Jingle Bell Rock' is playing on the sound system. The place is packed, as it always is just before ten thirty, when sausage and egg muffins get replaced by burgers and fries. It's a treat, this, she keeps telling herself. Not the surroundings, maybe, but the breakfast. Definitely. After the week she's had.

She's got her tray, head down – looking for a table – has to be at the side, with a seat at the back, facing into the room. Standard copper thing, that. Make sure you can see what's going on. Too busy, though, to notice that she's about to walk slap bang into someone.

A hand stops her.

'Morning.'

She looks up, blinks. Feels her heart slide into her stomach. She'd wanted to enjoy this food on her own. Have a bit of time before work, where it'd be full on as always, even though she was due a day off now, after the mad few days she's had.

'Eddie. You slumming it too?'

'Food of the Gods, this,' he says. He nods at a table where a bunch of schoolkids have departed, leaving an explosion of wrappers and cups and half-eaten hash browns. Last day of term. They don't care if they're late. Before she can say anything, a quiet woman in uniform and a sad little Santa hat appears and sweeps it all carefully away, leaving that damp cloth smell hovering just above the Formica. She can hardly say no. She slides along the plastic seat, and he follows her in. He unwraps his breakfast and starts eating, staring straight ahead. Savouring it. She does the same. Muffin. Hash brown. She uncaps the orange juice and drinks it in one.

'So,' he says. 'Tough week? Saw you were on DS Fyfe's team. The assault on campus. Nasty.'

She wipes her mouth on a napkin. 'Awful. But, you know. We got him. Jack was like a dog with a bone on that one.'

He nods. 'Good. Good. Can't say I've been so lucky. Still working on the Hollis murder. We've got nothing. No one saw anything. Victim had no enemies, no dodgy ex, no psycho neighbour. Nothing. Someone just swooped in, smashed her over the back of the head with a stone vase, and left her there. If it wasn't for the parcel delivery coming that afternoon, noticing that the door wasn't properly shut, we don't even know how long the poor woman might have been left lying on the carpet.'

'Just before Christmas, too,' Becky says. 'Horrible.'

Eddie's face crinkles into a frown. 'To be honest, anything that can distract me from the hell that's Christmas is a good thing. I can't be doing with it all. Never have done. Well, when the kids were small, I suppose. But now? Everyone spends too much money, eats too much, drinks too much, then moans about their credit card bills in January while they try to survive on a diet of avocado and squeezed lemon juice.'

She can't help but laugh. 'Are you finished, Mr Scrooge?'

'Oh come on. Don't tell me you like it, do you? All the crowds, the non-stop jingly music. Drunks wearing antlers throwing up in your garden?'

'I love Christmas, actually. We make quite a big thing of it at home. We don't spend too much money, but we make sure the whole family's there for lunch – turkey, sprouts, sherry – the lot. A small gift each, roaring fire. Christmas CD . . .'

'You're winding me up?'

'Nope. Nine more sleeps, I can't wait—' She's about to say more, when she sees the woman in the fur coat tottering across to a freshly departed table, mine-sweeping the remains. Jamming half a breakfast muffin into her mouth, wrapping up the other bits and shoving them into her pocket. She sighs.

'Lady Margaret,' Eddie says. 'Still going strong, it seems.'

'They'll throw her out in a minute.'

'She'll be gone before they get the chance. She's been doing this for years. You must've seen her before?'

Eddie slides out of the seat, walks up behind the woman, who's walking casually out of the restaurant as if she belongs there, just like everyone else.

'Morning, Ma'am,' he says.

'Oh, hello, Edward,' she says. Becky sees her row of blackened teeth and starts to breathe through her mouth again.

'Not making a nuisance of yourself, are you?' he says.

'Me?' She laughs. 'You know me, Edward.'

Eddie holds open the door for her and she disappears out into the frosty morning, pulling her coat around herself and bustling off up the street with a purpose, as if she has somewhere to go, somewhere to be, that isn't a bus shelter. Or, if she's lucky, a few hours in the community centre with the rest of her cronies.

'Come on,' Eddie says.

She matches his pace as they walk through the town centre, past the stallholders still setting up their wares – the hotdog stands, the towering tree with its twinkling silver lights. Someone has hung some sort of garland around the long-legged spaceship that is almost hidden on a side street until you nearly walk into it. The HG Wells legacy, more noticeable from the name of one of the popular chain pubs than the giant steel alien. War of the Worlds? That's just this town on a Saturday night.

She's momentarily transfixed by a group of solemn Chinese carol singers, and their sandwich board that reads: *John 3:16 For God so loved the world that he gave his one and only Son, that whoever believes in him shall not perish but have eternal life.*

If only it was that simple . . . Besides – is eternal life really such a good thing?

When they arrive at the station building, Eddie disappears, leaving her with a quick nod of his head. As she pauses next to the front desk, taking off her gloves and stuffing them into her pockets, a uniformed constable appears from a door to the side.

'Ah, perfect timing, Detective Constable Greene,' he says. 'You can take the mail up to CID.' He thrusts a pile into her arms. Brown envelopes. A few white ones that could be Christmas cards – or abuse – they quite often received abuse. And a large square envelope, addressed 'To A Detective who knows what to do'.

2

CARLY

Carly slides the last pile of boxes off the trolley, flips up the base-plate and pushes the handle back inside. The little fold-up thing was the best online purchase for under twenty quid she'd ever made. Getting the stuff from front door to car and then car to the venue was virtually impossible before, without someone to help. No one ever offers to help now. Well, that's not true. No one from her family offers to help – the other people at the fairs are generally as useful as they can be, as long as they've got their own stuff sorted first.

The problem with these things, like all craft fairs, markets, expos and whatever else they're calling themselves these days, is that if you don't get a decent pitch, you might as well forget it. She was naïve in the early days, turning up half an hour before the event was due to open, expecting to still get a reasonable spot. She'd had the worst of the worst, many a time – the table next to the gents toilets, the one next to the draughty back door, the one in the back of the back, with the sellers who were there to pass the time, rather than actually sell anything. Half the time they were asleep, or they'd ask if she could just watch their stall for a minute while they popped off for a cuppa, leaving her with her own stall and theirs, catching the occasional pitying glance from someone who'd walked the length and breadth of each aisle, buying nothing, and who couldn't be bothered to squeeze past the stall selling pet toys that had spread its way across the already narrow aisle, blocking access to the back row entirely.

She wondered why she bothered.

But then she realised that getting there an hour and a half before doors open was the key. And having the trolley so she could bring most of the stuff from the car at once was the way to do it. People were wily at these things – leave something on your table and go back for the rest, and you'd return to find someone had spread their stuff all over it, dumping your wares on the floor, nothing but a shrug as if to say, 'Well it wasn't set up. How was I to know you were coming back?'

All that stuff you think about market stallholders and camaraderie? Fantasy. It's a cut-throat business, and it's made even worse when you get the folks turning up with stuff that's not even handmade – well, not by them anyway. Loads of cheap tat bought in bulk off the Internet, dressed up on the stall with some wafts of incense to make it look authentic. They're undercutting the real craftsmen and women of these markets. Like Carly, who's turned her boxroom into a pottery studio and makes everything from bowls and jugs to the most intricately painted ceramic and glass jewellery. People still buy it, of course, and she does enjoy the markets. She just wishes there weren't so few of them throughout the year. Once a month, she can usually find somewhere to go, but it might be two or three hours' drive. From late November until Christmas, though, she's spoilt for choice.

The market at St Mary's Community Centre is an annual attraction in the town. It's the biggest church hall in the county. People travel from all around, even the fringes of London, to come to it. More than a hundred stalls, every day, for two weeks. It might even be the biggest Christmas Fair in the South East – the organisers certainly like to tout it as that.

She's pleased to be here early today, one of the first in. She's even thought to bring a flask of tea with her, and a slice of yesterday's banana cake, to save her having to nip out for breakfast. It's the fifth day of this year's fair, and every day has been getting gradually busier. There is no quiet time left. People take time off work to go Christmas shopping, and with the church community centre right in the centre of the town, there's no shortage of footfall.

She peels tape off the top of a box and starts to carefully lift the items out. This one is full of brightly painted bowls. Always some of her top sellers. She glances up at the clock. 8.45. Still a while before it opens. She's surprised that the woman with the crochet handbags and purses hasn't turned up yet – she's been next to her since the first day, and although they hadn't spent too much time chatting, she'd felt an easy companionship with the other woman. Hilda, her name was. Unusual, Carly thought, having only heard of the name before linked to that old washerwoman from *Coronation Street*. The actress had died not that long ago. Carly couldn't remember her real name. Maybe Hilda's not so unusual in Sweden though. Or was it Norway she was from? Somewhere like that. She pushes the box under her table and opens the next. Vases, only two left. She's placing one at the far end of the table when she becomes aware of someone standing nearby. She's been engrossed in her unpacking, her arranging. Hasn't noticed the young man who wheeled in a set of large, shallow boxes.

'Hi,' he says. 'OK if I take this one?'

She wants to protest, doesn't know why. Hilda is clearly not coming today. Did she mention it yesterday? Maybe she was only doing the weekend.

'Sure,' she finds herself saying. She glances at his trolley, the boxes. 'Maybe not the best space if you're displaying artwork. Wouldn't you be better along one of the sides? Maybe one of the ones in front of the black curtain.' She points, and he follows her gaze, and they both see that all the stalls against the curtain are already taken.

He smiles and shrugs his shoulders. 'It's fine. I've plenty of stands.' He unclips the first of his boxes and starts to slide out his work.

Carly rips tape off another of her own boxes. Tries not to look interested, but it's hard not to, faced with this man. He's a bit younger than her, she thinks. He's shrugged off his fur-lined leather coat to reveal strong arms, a wide chest in a plain black T-shirt. He props a painting of a beach at sunset on a small easel he's placed on the table and stands back. The air shifts, and she can smell him. Something musky, smoky. A whisper of cold air from the crisp morning outside.

'What do you think?' he says. 'It's Dorset, you know. West Bay? Last summer. I sat for hours on the sand, waiting for the light to be just how I wanted.'

'Very nice.' She's not talking about the painting. 'But wouldn't it have been easier just to take a photograph?' Carly says, with what she hopes is a playful smile.

'I don't take photographs any more. Not for pleasure, anyway.'

A flash of something in his eyes, but it disappears as quickly as it erupts. Intriguing. Just how she likes them. She turns away and lets him finish putting his paintings out on display. Hopes he didn't catch sight of the heat in her cheeks.

She opens the final set of boxes. Displays her jewellery at the front of the table. Tries not to catch the newcomer's eye.

She doesn't need this kind of trouble. Not again.

3

BECKY

'To A Detective who knows what to do'.

Becky's not entirely sure what to make of that. It's either a piece of junk, or some sort of promo crap. Someone having a laugh – at their expense? She slides it back to the bottom of the pile of mail and jogs up the two flights of stairs to the grey-carpeted, beige-walled home of Woodham CID. She hadn't really known what to expect of a real police station before she joined. Was it the drab, shaky-partitioned world of *The Bill*, or something a bit more flash – glass and whiteboards and breakout areas, like she'd seen in some of the US cop dramas? It is neither of those things. It is just an office building, with messy open-plan spaces, small private offices for the higher ranks. The ground floor that she just left is a desk, some plastic chairs, a heavy door that leads to the cells. First floor is more offices, interview rooms and the canteen. None of it is anything special, and from the outside it is one of those brutalist seventies concrete blocks that could be anything from a car park to a hospital.

She pauses outside the door to the open-plan office that she shares with the rest of the lower CID ranks, rifles through the pile of mail. It's not her job to hand out the mail, but now that she has it, she might as well see what's there. A couple of things for her boss, DI Nick Keegan. A few things marked 'CID' – usually opened by one of the civvies who sit partitioned off at the far end of the room, running searches on HOLMES and the PNC. Then that last thing. The big envelope. Not really for anyone, but also for everyone. She's a detective. She has to make a decision. She drops the rest of the mail in the in-tray that sits on a filing cabinet just inside the door. Keeps hold of the envelope and walks over to her desk.

'Morning, Greene. Half-day is it?'

She smiles at her colleague. A straight-backed skinny man in a too-tight red jumper. 'Brought you something,' she says, sliding a hand into the back pocket of her jeans, then pulling it out slowly, around the side of her body. She flips him the finger and sits down.

'Witty,' he says. 'Boss was looking for you earlier.'

'Cheers, Joe.' She pulls out her chair and sits. Takes a letter opener shaped like a dagger from the mug on her desk that contains various pens, a couple of nail files and a pencil with a bobbing octopus that Joe brought her back from a trip to the seaside once. She gets on well with DC Joe Dickson. Probably because they are roughly the same age, did their initial training at the same time (although he's been a detective for a few years longer than she has), and mainly because he always has her back when people say things about her that they shouldn't. It might be all political correctness in the media these days – doesn't mean it's like that on the shop floor. *You're too pretty to be a police officer* is one of the usual ones. When she'd started out in uniform, it was fine – because no one looks good in those army-style trousers and the thick body armour they all have to wear now; hair scraped into a bun. Big black boots. But since she's become a detective, it's like people are seeing her in a different way. Her long hair is dark and shiny, with a natural wave that most women are desperate to emulate. She has huge brown eyes, and a wide mouth and perfect white teeth. It's all natural, as is her trim figure – shapely in all the ways you'd want it to be. But now that she's out of uniform it's causing problems. She's the least showy person she knows, she's never been someone to flaunt their looks – and yet people seem to take exception, as if it's her fault and nothing to do with her genes. She has to work extra hard to be taken seriously, and it rankles. Which is why colleagues like Joe are great to have on-side. Her boss, Nick, has been good too – always pushing her further – testing her, maybe. It hasn't been long since she cast her uniform aside, but she is relishing the challenge. She knows it's exactly what she wants.

She runs the dagger – a present from her parents when she graduated from police college – along the back flap of the envelope and opens it up. She peers inside. A thick sheet of cardboard. Pulls it out and a smattering of glitter is scraped off against the edge of the envelope, flutters to her desk like snowflakes.

'Wow. Haven't seen one of these since I was a kid.' She lays it on her desk, pokes around inside the envelope looking for a note, but there's nothing else in there.

'What is it?' Joe wheels himself around on his chair. 'Is that an advent calendar?'

'Yeah. A proper one. No chocolates inside these. I don't think I've had one since I was about five. Once I found out there were ones with chocolates, I wasn't really interested in the little drawings of bells and snowflakes behind the doors.'

'My mum never bought us advent calendars,' Joe says. 'She was so anti-Christmas.'

'Oh you poor thing.' Becky sticks out her lower lip at him and he flicks her nose.

'Go on then, open it,' he says.

'Hang on. I don't even know who it's for. Maybe I should ask the others.' She glances around the room, but people are either plugged into headphones or having conversations at their desks. No one is paying attention to her and Joe.

'No one cares, Becks. They're trying to sort out their paperwork piles so they can relax over Christmas. No one wants a new case now!' He grabs the envelope and looks at the front. '*To A Detective who knows what to do.* That's a rubbish teaser. What does it even mean? Just open it. What's the date today?'

'Sixteenth. So we've got fifteen to open, plus today. Should I start at one and do them in order, or should I open today's first—'

He rolls his eyes and grabs the calendar off her. More glitter puffs into the air.

'Oi!' She takes it back. Puts a fingernail under the edge of door one and prises it open.

'What is it? Snowman? Bauble? The suspense is killing me here . . .'

She frowns, lifts the calendar closer to her face. 'Weird. I think it's a nativity scene. It looks like a tiny photograph of a room, someone lying in the middle. Some stuff around, I don't know what that's meant to be . . .'

'Let's see.' He takes it out of her hands, squints at it. Holds it up to the light. 'Oh—'

'Oh what? What is it?'

'It's not a nativity scene, Becks. Look.'

She leans across, looks at it at the same angle as he is – the light behind, shining through the thin backing. It's a scene all right. But it's not a nativity.

It's a crime scene.

4

EDDIE

DS Eddie Carmine sits down in a chair opposite his boss and sighs. 'Seriously, Nick. This job is starting to do my head in. You'd think with a case like this, local, broad daylight, that someone would've seen something. Heard something. Anything. Jesus. What happened to nosey neighbours? Good old curtain-twitchers?'

'No one pays any attention to people in the real world any more. You know that. It's all social media and WhatsApp and Snapchat, isn't it?' Nick grins, clearly pleased with himself for his deep understanding of the psychology of today.

Eddie wants to lean over the desk and yank his neatly tucked tie out of his neatly buttoned tweed waistcoat. Did Nick think he was some sort of hipster these days, or what? He'd be sporting a man-bun next. Eddie smirks at his own thoughts and feels his anger dissipating. Nick Keegan might be a suburban try-hard with an eco-friendly Prius and a penchant for herbal tea, but it doesn't mean that he's not right. The bastard.

'So you're winding it down. Is that right?'

'It's been two weeks. You've got nothing. There's only so many door-to-doors you can do. No one's talking. I can use you elsewhere.'

'But—'

Nick raises a hand, like he's stopping traffic. 'I'm not shutting it down, Eddie. I'm winding it down. There's a difference, right? Stay on it. But it's not our top priority any more. Find something today, or forget it. Move it to the cold crew. *Capiche?*'

Eddie looks away. Counts to ten in his head. He knows he needs to calm down, but it's just over a week until Christmas and despite the whole of the street where Linda Hollis was found apparently turning blind and deaf to any weird shit happening at the time one of their neighbours was battered to death, Nick isn't the one who has to deal with the family on this. Nick isn't the one who has to listen to the broken voice of the dead woman's son – *not wanting to cause anyone any inconvenience, but do you think you might catch who did this to my mum?*

'OK,' Eddie says. He stands up. 'So what do you want me on, Nick?'

Nick has disappeared under the desk. Eddie waits patiently for the rustling to stop, and eventually it does. His boss reappears, banana in hand. Paper bag on the desk, sitting there next to the blotter. Eddie imagines he can see a face in the contours of the bag. A disapproving face, saying: *You shouldn't have had that cheeky McMuffin for breakfast, you revolting slob.* As if on cue, a burble of stomach acid roils. Then Nick's phone rings and he is waved away before he can find out more.

Fuck it.

Back in the main room, the rest of CID are getting on with their business. It's not a huge department. An

23

offshoot of the main unit a few miles down the road, set up three years ago to deal with the increase in major crime in the area. It's busy, and they're understaffed, just like every other department. But sidelining a murder case after fourteen days is totally out of order.

He sits down at a free desk near the window. He doesn't have his own desk since the move into this building. The four Detective Sergeants in the department are meant to hot desk, as they're supposed to spend more time out on the job. The DCs all have their own desks, as they're apparently the ones doing the donkey work. Never really works out that way though, and the DS hot desks are either full or empty. Stupid bloody set-up. There's a family photo in a frame on this desk. Not his family. He turns it round to face the padded partition board that's covered in pinned notices that no one ever reads.

He's contemplating going back home. The house'll be empty this time of day. He could just shut his eyes for a few hours. Daydream. Pretend he has a normal job and a normal family and watch normal TV for a while. He closes his eyes, almost imagining himself there. Then he senses movement behind his chair. Someone coughs.

He opens his eyes and spins round. 'What?'

'Um, morning, Sarge. Eddie. Got something a bit odd here. Thought you might take a look?'

Eddie's ears prick up. He's not lazy, not at all. He's just bored. The hesitancy in the younger officer's face makes the back of his head tingle.

'Odd?' He sits up straight and slides his chair towards them. Two DCs. The fellow slob from breakfast time,

Becky, and her sidekick Joe. She's wearing latex gloves and gingerly offering him a piece of sparkly cardboard. 'What is it?'

'It's an advent calendar. Becky picked it up with the mail. Weirdest thing . . .' Joe Dickson's voice trails off. Eddie pulls a pair of gloves from a box on the desk and snaps them on. He takes the advent calendar from Becky's hand, holds it up to the light at the window. Takes a good look at the small image behind the open door. The tingle in his head turns spiky, like a blast of cold water from the shower.

'Number one. You haven't opened any others yet?' He can see that they haven't, but he is buying time. Trying to process what he is seeing.

'I've got tweezers,' Becky says. She pulls a seat from an empty desk and sits. She offers him the tweezers. Joe leans on the back of her chair.

'It's a crime scene, isn't it?' she says.

Eddie nods. Mutters something under his breath. Something between a grunt and a curse. He hasn't sworn out loud yet today. He's sworn in his head, but that doesn't count because no one heard him, and he's refusing to add any more money to that swear box, even if it is for fucking charity. He takes the tweezers between his thumb and forefinger and gently prises open the next door. He lets out a breath, unaware that he was holding it in. He opens the next. Then the next. At some point, Joe leans over and switches on the desk lamp. At some other point, a crowd has gathered around the desk. No one says anything. Eventually, with all the doors now open, he holds the advent calendar up to the light again and looks at the tiny images, which are, unmistakably, tiny photographs.

Twenty tiny photographs. Four blanks.

'Negatives,' he says, to no one in particular. '35mm film. Do people still use that stuff? Thought everything was digital these days.'

'My dad's got an old camera,' Becky says. 'He tried to show me how to use it once.'

He's only forty-five, but Eddie suddenly feels old. Ancient. Was it really so long ago that people used to take photographs on film, take a roll into the supermarket and wait several days before getting back the wallet of photos with the overexposed, headless, red-eyed, out-of-focus gems that were your holiday snaps?

'I need these blown up,' he says, holding the cardboard out towards Joe. 'Either find a place that still develops film, or get someone in tech to sort it. You can probably get it done down at Snappy Snaps but this is sensitive stuff. I don't want their geeky little technician getting hard over this.'

'The university, maybe?' Becky again. Keen. Good. He likes keen.

'Good idea. Get it fast, and make sure they keep it quiet. There's a liaison there. Check with Miriam.' He pauses. 'Try tech first though.'

From across the other side of the room, Miriam smiles and catches his eye. Everyone hears everything in this room. Nothing is private, especially not for Miriam who has the body of a porn star and the ears of a bat. One of their civilian support staff, she knows everyone and everything. She also makes excellent cupcakes, although her flapjacks are overly honeyed for Eddie's liking. He's not a huge fan of honey.

'Hang on though.' He pauses. Takes the thing back. 'Let me have another look at that, would you?'

During the last few minutes, the door to Nick's office has opened and Nick has come out, joined the oddly quiet fray, who are finally becoming a bit restless. They were hoping for more drama, probably.

Eddie holds it up to the light again. Focuses on the first door. It's not that easy, peering at a negative, the lines green-tinged and reversed. 'Nick—'

Nick walks across the room and the murmurings and mutterings stop again. Eddie hands the calendar to Nick, and waits, frowning.

'Well?'

Nick gives him a strange half-smile. '*Well*, indeed,' he says. 'Looks like I'm not winding your case down after all, doesn't it? Use Greene. I think she'll be good for this.'

'Can I—'

'Not at the moment, Joe. I need you to stay where you are. This is Eddie's gig now. He'll call you in if he needs another body.'

'Bollocks,' Joe mutters. Delves into his jeans pocket for a 50p piece and drops it into the jar near the door as he stomps out of the room.

'So, can I take this now?' Becky ignores her friend, gestures at the calendar. 'Get your prints for you?'

Eddie hesitates. 'Hang on. Just a minute.' He turns his back on her, takes his phone out of his pocket. He lays the calendar flat on the desk and pushes door four open as far as it will go, using the end of a pen. He fiddles with his phone, switches the flash off. Zooms in. It's as clear as he's going to get it, for now. He slips his phone back into his pocket and turns back round to face her.

'Do you know what you've got there,' Eddie says, handing it towards her. 'Did you happen to recognise the photograph behind door number one?'

She shakes her head.

'It's my unsolved, isn't it? Linda Hollis. Bludgeoned in her living room. This is exactly how she was found. This is a copy of the first photo taken by one of the CSIs.' He pauses. 'Or—'

'Or it's the photo taken by Mrs Hollis's killer, before he left the scene.'

Eddie grins. 'Exactly,' he says.

In his head he says, 'Game fucking on.' He likes this Becky. Their dirty breakfast bonding session was clearly more than a coincidence. As for the other photo, the one behind door four, he'll be keeping that one to himself for a bit longer. Just until they get the pictures enlarged.

5

THE PHOTOGRAPHER

I knew the first time would be hard. It's not like I'm one of those psychopaths who spent their childhoods pulling the wings off flies and stamping on puppies. I'd never as much as killed a spider until that day.

Not intentionally anyway.

But after *IT* happened, it was as if I became a different person overnight. After the phone call, I was numb. Went onto autopilot. Bed at 10 p.m., even though I knew I wasn't working in the morning. I like to be fresh in the mornings. I can't do late nights and early hangovers. I need to be on top of things. I need to watch everything. See everything. I need to get it right. But when I woke that next morning, I knew straight away that everything was going to be different. The light was still shining through that gap in the curtains, the gap that would never go away, no matter how I tried to arrange the fabric, pinning the two pieces together, jamming them in behind the back of the units either side of my bedroom windows. There were still spectres of dust, floating in the laser beam of light that dissected my rumpled duvet. There was still that faint damp smell, from when the radiator had leaked, soaking the carpet and the floorboards and never quite going away.

I drove home in a daze, barely clocking the miles as they flew past along the eerily deserted morning roads. I stopped off at her flat on the way. They took me to see her room. All her things in there. Little pieces of her. Her books – ghost stories, mainly. Her CDs and DVDs – the one we'd loved watching together . . . *Someone's at the door* . . . Silly things from her childhood. The stuffed otter that she got from a school trip to London Zoo. The plastic tombola she'd won in the school Christmas raffle. Her advent calendar, propped up on top of the chest of drawers, one door still closed. No one would ever open it now. No one would ever spin the tombola and decide how many marshmallows to try to squeeze into their mouth. One of those stupid games that she'd come up with. Marshmallows had probably been substituted for shots of vodka, since she moved away. Her life, frozen in time. She would always be the same now.

But *I* wasn't the same. I looked the same, I'm sure. I still had the same body, the same hair that stuck up at the back no matter what I put in to try to tame it. I'm sure I still had the same lines around my eyes, laughter lines I'd liked to call them. Not so much any more. It was inside me that had changed. Something had washed through me, leaching my body of warmth, of feeling. I wasn't cold. I wasn't anything.

I was numb.

I stayed like that for a long time afterwards. Weeks turned to months. Nearly a year. I still did my job, spending most of my time away from home, away from the memories. But nothing was the same. The light had gone out from everything that I touched. And then it hit me.

I'd been back home for a few days after picking up a job nearby. Popped into my old local in the afternoon. A Tuesday. I remember the date. I'd done some work in the morning but it'd been a waste of time. Client hadn't bothered to show, left me waiting in a cold car park for two hours. Not so much as a quick phone call to say they wanted to cancel. It happens, when you're freelance, but this one had pissed me off. I'd taken to the pub to drown my sorrows. Wondered if maybe someone might start something and give me a reason to vent my anger.

But it didn't happen like that.

Someone did start something, but not to get me into a ruck. Someone asked me about *IT*. Said they'd seen my face, after it happened. Asked me what was going on.

Asked me what I was doing about it.

Doing about it? What the fuck can I do about it? I'd said. He'd shrugged. Something, he said. If it was me, I'd be doing something.

He was right.

What the hell was the point of my tedious little life now? The work was drying up. Friends were disappearing, never sure what to say to me. I was like the living dead. A genuine zombie. Stumbling through life, seeing everything in drab tones of grey. Hearing everything muffled, as if listening from underwater. The police had given up. Not even a year, and they'd given up! No evidence, they said. We're sorry, they said. She'll be moved to the cold case team . . .

I knew then what I had to do. I had to make them realise that giving up was the wrong thing to do. I had to *show* them. I had to make them *see*. Clearly once wasn't enough for them. I needed to give them a bit of help. Make it a bit more obvious. Give them something to look for! There was really only one way I could bring it back to their attention. Make them re-think their stupid 'cold case' bullshit. I laughed to myself, getting a worried look from the barman. It was so obvious, when I thought about it. And the timing was perfect. I just needed to think about the hows. I knew the whys. Of course I did. What choice did I have?

I just needed to work out exactly who I was going to kill first, how I was going to do it and, most importantly, how I was going to get away with it.

6

EDDIE

Eddie walks back into Nick's office, doesn't bother to knock. Shuts the door behind him. Nick is nibbling on what looks like a dog biscuit. Does the man ever stop eating? Eddie sits down and his trousers ride up slightly, revealing his choice of socks. Black with an orange stripe on the left foot, grey with snowflakes on the right.

'So,' Nick says, his voice muffled by compacted oats and saliva. 'Interesting development.'

Eddie lets out a long, slow sigh. 'How the fuck can someone have a photograph of the crime scene? The CSIs don't even use film, do they?'

'Nope. Been digital for years. Might be worth going down there to talk to them now. Maybe someone's been experimenting.'

'Even so – how did the negative end up in some home-made advent calendar?'

'Someone's idea of a joke? Abby Glengarry likes to think she's funny. Maybe she's been experimenting with old cameras and thought she'd create this anti-Christmas abomination and send it up to see if we'd bite? They're bound to realise they're the first people we'll be questioning. The only people who were at that crime scene last week were us, the CSIs, the paramedics and the duty pathologist. The only people who'd have time to take that photo were the CSIs. It's a joke, Eddie. Someone with too much time on their hands.'

'Wait, what? But you said outside . . . "Get on the case, use Greene." It's something, right? It could be something?'

'Thought it might perk you up a bit. Are you trying to suggest that the murderer might have sent us that advent calendar? Some sort of Hollywood-style serial killer trying to lure us in to play his sick game? It doesn't work like that, Eddie. You know that.'

Eddie knows that Nick is referring to the FBI classification of serial killers. Their methods. The reality. Most real-life serial killers don't leave clever clues and play cat and mouse with the police. Most real-life serial killers are brutal sexual fantasists who can't stop themselves. Well, mostly. There are always exceptions, and who's to say this isn't one right here? OK, it's Surrey. Not a hugely fertile breeding ground for serial killers. But never say never. Besides, he went on that course too. There are other kinds of serial killers, and they don't all brutalise women. Richard Ramirez killed men too. Others are out for revenge, not kicks.

'Right. I'll go and talk to the CSIs. But if it turns out they don't have a clue about what's going on, do I have permission to take it to the next level? With Greene? I've already sent her to get prints blown up. I think it's worth checking which scenes we've got here.'

Nick shrugs. 'Fine. You can be acting SIO. You know I can't make you the actual SIO until you do the courses, push yourself for a promotion, but with this . . . which looks like a dead-end piss-take . . . feel free to add it to your CV.' He grins. 'Don't waste too much time on it though, OK? We've got real crimes to solve in here.'

Eddie walks back into the open-plan and has to try very hard not to shout 'Prick' at the top of his voice. Nick could be a cheeky bastard at times. This was one of those times. Clearly because he is about to fly off to Lanzagrotty for a week's holiday and doesn't give a toss about what is going on right now.

It's been fourteen days since Linda Hollis was murdered, and they've got nothing. Eddie hates to leave a case unsolved. Not his style. There's only one other murder outstanding in his whole career, and even though he wasn't the lead on that one, it still bothers him. The significance of the photograph behind door four is not lost on him.

He'll go down and talk to the CSIs, see what they have to say. If this is someone's idea of a joke, he's going to haul them over the coals for it. His only two unsolved cases are in that calendar, and if someone's trying to mess with his head, they're going to regret it.

7

BECKY

Becky almost skips down the stairs to the offices on the floor beneath. Now *this* is something interesting. This is a definite antidote to the horrible assault from last week. She realises she is being gruesome, imagining that she might be starting work on a serial killer case, but isn't this the kind of thing detectives dream about? Of course real-life serial killers are nothing like the ones in the movies. It's unlikely that there's a Hannibal Lecter living in the wilds of Surrey. But still. A thought flashes through her mind, only briefly – making her wonder if maybe it's a wind-up. Why would it be though? She could tell from the look on Eddie's face that he thought there was something in it. Of course, they'd have to talk to the CSIs, the photographers. See if they can shed any light on it all. But until she has some real photographs to look at – and to share with Eddie – there's not a lot else that anyone can do. Eddie recognised one of the photographs. Even from the tiny three-by-three centimetre image. In reverse, too. She hopes the techs can get on with it quickly.

She marches along the corridor, past the exhibits office and the library and the break-out room, right to the end. The tech team have the whole back section of the floor, and everything in there is a lot higher spec than the space that houses CID and several other key departments. But it's the way of things now – tech are the busiest people of the lot. Checking phones and computers. iPads and disk drives. They've got top quality staff and no end of gadgetry. It's a geek's wet dream. Becky, although she doesn't like to admit it too freely, is most definitely a closet geek.

Maybe it's because her dad always tried to teach her stuff, like how radios work and those huge cathode-ray TVs with the massive back sections full of who knows what, and old computers and phones with circular dials and, of course, his camera. Her dad's not old. Not even fifty. And he likes to make sure that Becky knows that there was life before camera phones and smart watches. He has those too, though. He's far from a luddite. He works in an electronics shop on the High Street. He's one of the only members of staff who knows what they're doing. People take all sorts in there for him to fix.

She was deliberately vague, back upstairs, when she said her dad had shown her how to use his 35mm camera. Not only does she know how to use one, she knows how to take them apart and put them back together. She knows how to adjust the aperture and the shutter speed to take the best photographs in any light. She knows almost everything to do with those cameras. The only thing she's never done is develop her own film. Only because she doesn't have anywhere to do it, and that it isn't so much photography that interests her, it's how the camera works. But if she gets the chance to find out more about the developing side, she will be more than happy to take it.

Her dad will love it when she tells him. The first thing he'd asked her about when she started her job in the police was the radios they use and she'd had great fun explaining about the Airwave and how it works – the system that's half walkie-talkie and half mobile phone. Her dad has a scanner set up at home, tuned into the emergency services frequencies, and although she's told him not to, she's secretly pleased that he's so interested in her work. She had to make him promise not to listen to it too often – scared that he would hear things he had no business worrying about.

She takes a deep breath and pushes open the door. 'Hi,' she says, addressing the room, 'got something interesting . . . it's a bit urgent.'

A woman of about her age with messy blonde hair turns around from the three computer screens she's monitoring. 'You'll need to log it in. Paul?'

Becky follows her gaze towards a guy wearing a New York Yankees cap and a disgruntled expression. She feels his eyes travel up and down her body and she has an instant feeling of unease. Then he nods, which she interprets as 'come here then and don't take all day.'

'Sorry about Paul,' the blonde woman says. 'PMT.'

'Hilarious as always, Linz,' he says. He attempts a smile and Becky wants to believe that he has kind eyes, wearing lines of stress rather than impatience tinged with a smattering of lust. She hadn't enjoyed his brief appraisal of her, but it's not as if she wasn't used to it.

She pulls a rolling chair from the desk next to him and sits down. Lays the calendar on the desk.

'Why's it not bagged?' he says. He slides his chair alongside and his knee brushes hers.

She moves away, just a fraction, uncomfortable with the sudden intimacy. Holds up her hands, showing her alien-like fingers inside the latex gloves. 'It came in the mail and I opened it upstairs. I put gloves on as soon as I realised it might be something. I thought it was junk at first.'

Paul leans in towards the desk, his knee brushing hers again. Was it deliberate? Or is she being ridiculous and paranoid? He slips on gloves from the box on the corner of his desk and picks up a pair of tweezers. He pokes the calendar, turning it round so he's looking at it straight on. He frowns. Then uses the tweezers to lift up a couple of the doors that have started to re-close themselves. 'An advent calendar? This some sort of joke?'

'Hold it up to the light,' Becky says. 'The paper on the back is quite thin—'

He moves away from her again and Becky lets out a breath of relief.

'Fucking hell! Linz, come and see this.'

The woman he calls Linz says something quietly to the person next to her, who nods, then she comes to join them. She stands behind Paul, lays a hand on his shoulder. He holds the calendar up to the light again and she squints. 'Can you push the doors open a bit more?'

Paul pushes them back with tweezers, bending them further so that they don't spring closed again so quickly. Becky can see the amateurish nature of the thing now. The wrong kind of card. Not folded or perforated on the joins.

'35mm negatives. Interesting,' says Linz. 'Did anyone recognise any of them?'

'Yes,' Becky says. 'DS Carmine reckons the photo behind door one is his crime scene from last week.'

Linz smiles. 'Eddie. Typical. Has he gone to the CSIs yet? Seen if someone's playing silly buggers?'

Becky mentally kicks herself. Why hadn't she suggested that upstairs?

Linz seems to read her mind. 'Don't worry. Everyone processes things they see for the first time in a totally different way. Your first thought was that this is real, and why the hell has someone sent it. I imagine Eddie was immediately trying to work out who was trying to wind him up. Either way, both things need looking into. We need to get these photos blown up, see if there's anything worth investigating. Meanwhile, I reckon Eddie is with the CSIs, giving someone a bollocking. Just in case.' She smiles and Becky realises she's a bit older than she thought at first. Maybe mid-thirties. The paleness of her eyebrows marks her as a natural blonde, and Becky feels a momentary stab of jealousy. She'd always wanted blonde hair, but several ill-judged dye attempts had made her realise that her natural chestnut was the best option for all concerned.

'Listen,' Linz says. 'We can get this sorted for you this afternoon, I reckon. Paul's finishing a few things that need to get sent out by lunchtime, then he's all yours.'

'Great,' Paul says. 'I'm just dying to be stuck in that darkroom with that bloody chemical stink for the rest of the day. Not to mention it's creepy as fuck.'

Becky hesitates. She wants to be involved, but she's not sure about Paul yet. Not one hundred per cent, anyway. She takes a breath. 'Maybe I could help?' she says. 'I've never done processing, but I'm a fast learner . . .'

He shrugs. 'Sure. Why not? Come back at four.' He pushes the calendar to the end of his desk. Is it her imagination, or did he smirk as he turned away from her?

Becky opens her mouth to say something, but Linz beats her to it. 'Let's have a look at this thing first, shall we? I suggest we take it apart and photograph it. We should probably get someone from forensics to look at it first. I'll make a few calls. Then, if you want, you can photograph it and see what you can get from the images before we get the prints done, but you might be better doing something else. Maybe check with Eddie. See if he's been to see the CSIs. I'm Lindsey Newport, by the way. Everyone calls me Linz. I supervise the imaging section in here. I don't think we've met?'

'Sorry, you must think I'm so rude! Becky Greene. DS Carmine has asked me to work on this with him.'

'Carmine and Greene, eh? Very festive.'

It takes Becky a moment to realise what she means. Carmine. The colour, obviously. Red. She never thought of his name as a colour before, and now all she can think about is Christmas and elves and candy canes. And she wonders if this might not be some big joke after all.

8

EDDIE

The office that houses the Crime Scene Investigators is pretty much the same as all the other blandly designed offices on the first floor. Except for the walls. The walls in this room are covered with posters displaying various techniques, things that have been presented at conferences, experiments carried out with different chemicals and methods, most of which seem to be written in another language, as far as Eddie can see. Not literally another language, but the words and phrases are not those that most people would find in their usual daily vocabulary, like 'the ever-widening circle', 'passive data generators' and the so-called 'golden hour', which has nothing to do with the sunset. Eddie doesn't like to get involved with the CSIs too much. He's not one of those officers who thinks they know better than the people trained to do this job. They are methodical, careful and thorough. Eddie is hot-headed and impatient. He would make a shit CSI.

He hesitates outside for a minute or two, stares in at the people going about their jobs. Examining things. He pushes open the door.

'Is Abby here?'

A couple of heads look up from what they are doing.

Their faces suggest he is an interruption rather than a curiosity.

'Down there.' A young man with almost white-blond hair gestures towards the far end of the room, where a high partition separates a strip of the office, the only place with any privacy in the open-plan room.

Eddie nods a thanks and walks down past rows of desks, piles of bagged items, computers, microscopes. Thousands of yellow Post-it notes seemingly scattered around at random, like confetti.

Abby Glengarry is on the phone as he rounds the edge of the partition into her lair. She holds a hand up, letting him know she won't be long. He starts to read one of the posters on the wall at the side of her desk. It's an abstract from a conference called *The Crime Scene Analysis and Victim Identification Forum*: 'The detection and age estimation of blood stains using hyperspectral imaging'. Double Dutch. Abby walks out from behind her desk and starts to pace up and down in the small space. Someone is being torn a new one. Par for the course. He almost changes his mind, goes back up to his office. There's no way she's behind this. She'd hardly have the time to spend making something so intricate just to wind him up, even if she did think he was the biggest arsehole in the force.

She ends the call and gestures to the seat on the other side of her desk. Eddie sits.

'So . . . to what do I owe this pleasure, DS Carmine?' She smirks. Can't help herself.

'Did you send an advent calendar full of crime scene photographs to CID?'

'Straight to the point, as usual. No. I did not. Why?'

Eddie sighs and takes out his phone. Opens the photograph. Slides it across the desk to her. 'Someone sent this earlier today. DC Greene picked it up from the mail room. Addressed to "A Detective who knows what to do", but two of the scenes in there are mine. Figured someone was trying to send me a message. Or wind me up.'

'So you thought of me, how nice. I don't even work on crime scenes any more, Eddie. I'm the go-between for forensics and CSIs and all the new fancy geekery that we've got now. I thought you knew that? Oh no, wait, how could you know? You've been ignoring me for six months.' Abby raises an eyebrow and pushes back a stray lock of dark glossy hair. With her other hand, she enlarges the photo on his screen. 'Interesting. 35mm film, eh? Blast from the past. I was always fascinated at how they turned the negatives from the roll of film into the sheets of photos, but when you see it in action, it's really not all that.' She gives him another one of her looks. 'You ever been in a darkroom, Eddie? There's one next door. I could show you if you like.'

Flirting, like before. Or just another of her wind-ups? Eddie couldn't tell with this woman. She blew hot and cold faster than the heater in a 1985 Ford Escort. Besides, she knew fine that he'd been in the darkroom. Not to develop photographs, mind. One kiss. That's all. He tries not to roll his eyes. The affair that never was. He couldn't go through with it.

She clears her throat. Obviously she's realised that he doesn't have time to fuck around. He'd known it from the minute he saw the photographs. This is not a wind-up.

'Want me to ask around? See if someone else is pissing about? Although how they'd find the time, I don't know. From the picture on your phone, it doesn't look like this was a project that took someone five minutes to knock up. Right?'

'Right. I need to check that first door – number one. It's my unsolved from two weeks back. Linda Hollis. I know we're striving for efficiency with this new update on the PND, but can the Hollis case really be on the system already? If not, well . . . then the only person who could've taken the photo is the killer, right? Unless one of the CSIs took it on his own camera before taking the official one on one of yours . . .' He pauses, unsure if he should say any more. He feels like a roll of film is being unravelled inside his head. Images from the past whirring by, too fast, blurred. Something in there he needs to know. Something pings a warning inside his head. What have you missed, Eddie? Why is your crime scene in there? This is a message . . .

'What our staff take onto a crime scene is strictly regulated, Eddie. No one could have two cameras in there. Not without one of the others seeing and asking what the hell they were doing.' Her tone has changed now. Digs and banter have gone and only worry remains. 'Listen, you know I'll help with whatever you need. Let me ask around—'

He stands up. 'Fine. I mean, thanks. That'd be great. Let me know if you find anything. Call my mobile. You've got the number?'

She smiles at him and he sees a sadness there. Something

he'd chosen to ignore before. Something else he needs to sort out. 'Talk to Ashlie Long,' she says. 'She's working with the IT consultancy on the update to the database. They're adding all digitised crime scenes on there now. You might get lucky.'

9

THE PHOTOGRAPHER

I thought about following someone home. Maybe I'd sit on a bench, just letting people pass me by. I'd close my eyes, and when I opened them, I'd pick the next person who passed me and I'd get up and follow them to wherever they might go before they went home. There was a flaw in that plan though. What if they weren't going home? What if there were too many people in their house? It was too risky, and I might end up trailing them for hours before they finished what they were doing and decided to go home. Besides, that's not the way it was meant to be.

There were a few other issues with my plan. I had to choose who and where and when, but I also had to make sure that no one else was going to get in my way.

Thing was, I didn't know at first how many times I was going to do it. Maybe once would be enough. Maybe I'd get caught. Maybe I wouldn't. Maybe I'd get a taste for it.

Maybe it would be easier just to kill myself?

The rational part of me still kicked in at times, telling me not to be so ridiculous. To pull myself together and move on. But the voice of that nobody in the pub was stuck in my head now, playing over and over on a loop.

If it was me, I'd be doing something.

I *was* doing something.

I chose the first one entirely at random. I decided that during the day was a good time, because most people are at work during the day, and if they aren't, then there's a good chance they're at home by themselves. I was worried about it being a young mum. I wasn't sure I could cope with that. Like I said, I'm not a monster. As it turned out, my first one was like fate. Someone up there had decreed that this was meant to be. I was meant to do this. That's what I told myself.

I walked around several residential streets. If anyone looked at me, I smiled and hurried on. Not a grin, nothing too memorable. Just pleasant, that's all. If people were to be questioned later on, they wouldn't remember someone who'd smiled politely and carried on their way. They'd remember someone who scowled, or looked down. Looked suspicious.

I had to do all that I could to be as forgettable as possible.

Did you know that most of us don't pay any attention to people that pass us in the street? That when questioned as a witness, most people struggle to remember the colour of someone's hair and are likely to get their height wrong by at least three inches in either direction? They barely register what someone is wearing. The only people who get noticed are kids in hoodies, especially if they have an exaggerated swagger. That *gangsta* look has the desired effect. They get all sniffy about the stop-and-search, but really they love it. Pretending to be notorious when all they're doing is going round their gran's for egg and chips.

No one was going to remember me. An average guy wearing average clothes, walking along an average street in an average town. In the middle of the day.

I almost changed my mind after I'd rung the doorbell. It took a few moments before I heard the sound of footsteps shuffling along the carpet. I panicked for a moment, imagining my dad. How would he feel answering the door to a stranger? Most people are far too trusting, despite all the suspicion in the air these days. Most people are decent, and they're naïve enough to think that others are too.

The door opened and I was hit by a fug of cigarette smoke. A scowl.

'What is it?'

Faded T-shirt and joggers. Bit of a paunch, from sitting around all day or too many beers. Probably both. Younger than me, but out of shape. Grey-tinged skin. Someone who was scared of fresh air. Perfect.

'Sorry, mate . . .' I shoved my hands into my pockets to show that I wasn't carrying anything. 'Car's broken down.' I nodded vaguely towards a couple of cars parked a few doors down, assuming that he wouldn't recognise one of them if he found it in his living room one day.

He rolled his eyes. 'You not got a mobile?'

'Battery's dead. Ran out of juice just before the car did. I know, what an arse, eh? I better not tell the missus – she'll have a bloody field day with this.'

He grunted what might have been a laugh, might've been a 'I really couldn't give a fuck' and went inside, leaving the door open. For me.

I followed him in.

The living room was dingy. Brown sofa, brown carpet. Walls that might've been beige or cigarette-stained yellow. It was hard to tell.

He'd disappeared.

A bubble of adrenaline popped in my gut. Leave now, or do what you came for.

I walked down the dimly lit hallway towards the back of the house, following the muffled sound of a radio, cheap and tinny, reception crackling in and out while John Denver apologised through the speakers.

The phone handset was lying on the table. He was facing away from me, washing dishes. Crockery chinked together in the basin. An ashtray with a cigarette burning away sat on the draining board next to a couple of side plates and a faded Chelsea FC mug.

I didn't give myself a chance to think about it any longer.

I took the ends of my scarf, flipped it deftly over my head and over his, round his neck. Crossed it at the back. Pulled.

His hands flew to his throat. The room seemed to grow instantly darker as if a huge black cloud had momentarily blocked out the sun; and for a brief second I caught his panicked face reflected in the window.

Pulled.

He struggled, tried to kick back at me, but I was ready for him and he was already running out of air.

The adrenaline surge hit my chest, surged through my arms, giving me superhuman strength as I pulled, tighter, tighter until eventually he stopped kicking and slid down towards the floor.

I slid with him. Let him fall to the floor, then I straddled his back. Pulled again. Twisted. Pulled. I had to make sure. I was panting with exertion. My muscles screamed.

I used the scarf to pull his head to the side, and I could see half of his face, bulging and purple. One of his eyes had almost popped out of the socket, the burst blood vessels leaving a shiny red orb, like the devil's eye, soaked with tears.

I swallowed back bile. This is what she would have looked like when they found her. I tried to push the image out of my mind. Tried to remember her as she was. Beautiful. Smiling. Alive. I couldn't be sick. Not here. I had to get out of there. Fast. My knees clicked as I shuffled back, got myself standing without using a hand for support. I was very aware that I couldn't touch anything, and I hadn't, so far.

The front door had been left open, I hadn't closed it. The kitchen door was open too. I used my scarf. Didn't lay a finger on a thing. When I turned away, at last, I saw that both doors were still standing wide open. I could see right out onto the street, but there was no one there. If there had been, they would have come in, wouldn't they? Saved this man from his unfortunate fate. Or maybe they wouldn't have. Maybe people just didn't care about each other any more. I took the photo as quickly as I could. Fumbling with the camera, hands shaking. It wasn't my best work, but it was a start. I wasn't sure why I needed the photograph, but something told me that I had to take it. *You* told me, somewhere inside my head. An image flashed up in my mind again: a ruined face, sunken and colourless with dark pits for eyes. Another wave of nausea hit me.

I hurried out, holding my sleeve over my hand to pull the front door shut.

The street was deserted. The dark cloud was drifting slowly away, the last of the day's sun peeking its way through. I lifted my collar and took a deep breath of cold, crisp air.

I'd done it! I sat in the van, heater turned on full, shivering suddenly after the burst of heat from my exertions. My mouth was dry. Adrenaline can do that, you know. I closed my eyes, tried to conjure up that beautiful face that I missed so much, tried to think about all the things you loved.

Someone's at the door . . . someone's at the door . . .

I scrabbled around in the seat door pocket, looking for a packet of mints to soothe my dry mouth. Found a crumpled up lottery ticket. An old one, I knew. I hadn't bought one for months, convinced I was never going to get lucky.

And then everything slotted into place, just like that. I knew what to do next. How I was going to choose them. How I was going to keep a record of what I'd done. I was an artist, and this would be my life's work. I noted down the number of his house on the back of a petrol receipt, tucked it into my pocket.

'You'll like this,' I whispered. 'I'm doing this for *you*.'

You didn't whisper back.

10

BECKY

After sending the photographs from her phone to her computer, Becky spends a non-productive hour staring at the images, trying to see if anything jumps out at her. But even blown up onscreen, she has no way of making the negatives into proper photographs. There's nothing to be found this way, and all she ends up with is the beginnings of a headache from squinting at the screen.

She'd hoped to see Eddie, find out what else he wanted her to do while they were waiting for the prints, but he was nowhere to be seen. She assumed he was with the CSIs. Thought about going there to look for him, but decided not to push her luck. She didn't want to piss him off on her first day of working with him by stepping on his toes.

The rest of her colleagues are getting on with their own things. Coming in and out of the office, appearing with various items of food and drink. After catching a waft of something spicy from a container left on DC Keir Jameson's desk, she gives in and admits that despite the late, greasy breakfast, she is hungry again. It's one thirty. Loads of time to grab something before she goes back down to tech to work on the prints with Paul. She's decided she was being ridiculous. That his appraisal was nothing more than a glance, and that his leg brushing hers was completely accidental. She mentally chides herself for being pathetic, then picks up her bag and locks it in the bottom of her filing cabinet. It's not like anyone in a police station is likely to steal something from a fellow officer, but it's a habit she's developed since she had stuff stolen at college, and it's a hard one to break. Her wariness of certain men comes from college too, but she isn't going to think about that now.

She walks out into the corridor and straight to the vending machine. There's a cheese and onion sandwich in there, calling her name. She takes it, and collects a cup of hot chocolate from the drinks machine next to it and heads along to the break-out area, hoping for an empty sofa.

Joe is there, scrolling through his phone. A rumpled Subway wrapper and a can of Sprite are on the table next to him.

'Ah, there you are. Found anything exciting yet, Little Miss Hotshot?'

She peels the plastic off her sandwich, sniffs it. Takes a bite.

'I'm going back down to tech later. We're developing the prints. Then we'll see.'

Joe sniffs, pulls a face. 'Thought Carmine might've sent you to speak to his girlfriend.'

'Who?' she says, her voice thick with a claggy mix of white bread, cheese, onion and cheap mayonnaise.

'Abby. Ahhahhbeee . . . you probably don't even know that song, do you?'

'That's Angie, you knob. And yes, I do recognise the

Rolling Stones, actually, even if you did manage to make it sound like Mick Jagger was strangling a cat.' She pauses and takes another bite. 'Abby who?'

Joe rolls his eyes. 'Queen of the CSIs. Ask him.' He blows her a theatrical kiss and walks off.

Becky stares at the rest of her sandwich and decides she doesn't really need it after all.

11

He finds her with a half-eaten sandwich and an odd expression on her face. 'Been looking for you,' he says. 'Fancy a trip?'

She stands up, shakes crumbs off her shirt. 'Where we going?'

'Linda Hollis. I want to speak to her son again. See if there's anything we've missed. He's been calling every day, and we've got nothing. I want to go back to the house, see if anything shakes itself loose.'

'He's not a suspect?'

'Nah. Ruled him out early on. He was at work in Currys. CCTV and several staff members confirmed.'

She follows him to the car park. 'Those shops are a nightmare. Why does no one in there have a clue about anything they sell? I don't even know who shops there any more. Do you?'

He shakes his head. 'Everything's online now. Not sure why they haven't folded yet. He's a manager. Been there ten years. I'm guessing he gets a decent employee discount. Got to be some reason for working in there.'

'My dad works in an electronics shop. A proper one though. Where they fix stuff.'

'Not Harry's?'

'Yep. You know it?'

'Christ, I bought my first car stereo in there. About a million years ago. Has he worked there long?'

'Pretty much forever.'

Eddie wipes at the inside of the windscreen with a grubby yellow chamois pad then drops it into the shelf inside the driver's side door. They've stopped at traffic lights in the centre of town, despite there being no other cars at the junction. The car is still cold, the heater pumping out but not enough to stop their breath from fogging up. He winds down his window. 'Come on,' he mutters. He pushes a CD into the player.

Becky glances around the car, says nothing.

'It's the wife's car. Sorry about the cheesy tunes, although I don't actually *hate* Spandau Ballet, if I'm honest. She's got mine this week. More space. Better heater. All my bloody music.'

Becky smiles.

'Not what you expected?'

'I was thinking Nickelback. Coldplay, maybe.'

He laughs. 'Jesus. That's your impression of me? I need to work on that.' He turns the volume up and starts singing.

Linda Hollis's house is no longer cordoned off as a crime scene. The CSIs released it a couple of days ago, after exhausting every search. It's a lower-floor maisonette with a paved front garden, an ornamental wishing well outside the bay window, overflowing with weeds. Or maybe it's some sort of grass. He's never been very good with gardening.

The door opens before they can knock.

A woman with a face that suggests sixties but an outfit more suited to a thirty-something stands in the doorway.

'He's been calling you every day. Busy, were you?'

'Sorry, who are you?' Eddie says. Trying not to sound as irritated as he feels.

'Brenda Motram. I live upstairs. 1A?'

Eddie frowns. 'Isn't this number one?'

She scowls. 'Yes. Ground floor is number one, upstairs is 1A.'

He thinks about this. 'Do you have the same front door?'

'Well, no. Mine is there, isn't it?' She nods her head to the left. 'But I don't use the front now. I did a conversion a few years ago. Stairs leading down the back from my kitchen, so we can both use the back garden. Linda and me came to an agreement, even though the leasehold says it's meant to be hers. We took it in turns to cut the grass.' She looks away, as if contemplating this.

'Can we come in?'

She opens the door wide, and they follow her inside.

'Were you good friends with Linda, Mrs Motram? Only, I don't remember us meeting before . . .'

'I've been away. Only got back yesterday. David's filled me in. Poor lad. I can't believe it.' She ushers them into the lounge. It looks pretty much as he remembers it. Pink two-seater sofa, TV on a mahogany unit in the corner. Square coffee table with a bowl of fake fruit. Display stand full of miniature ceramic dogs. A couple of Christmas decorations. The only thing that's missing is the carpet. They've left the underlay, which is thankfully unstained.

'Did someone come and help with the clean-up? I left a card . . .'

A young man in grey tracksuit bottoms and a rumpled navy T-shirt appears in the doorway that leads through to the small kitchen. 'They did it yesterday. Said they could clean the carpet, but I just wanted it gone, you know? I've been calling you, Detective Carmine. I've left messages.'

Eddie nods. Although David was supposed to call the Family Liaison Officer, he'd given him his card too, after a few days. Once it became clear that it was going to drag on. He wanted the man to be able to get hold of whoever it was he wanted to talk to, just in case he remembered something key. It wasn't strictly protocol, but David was a young man who'd lost his mother, and Eddie knew how that felt. Father was out of the picture too, living abroad. Eddie's was still around. Not that he saw much of him now.

Brenda Motram appears from the kitchen carrying two mugs. 'Brought you both coffee. Sorry, there's no milk.'

'Thanks.' Becky takes hers and lays it on a coaster on the coffee table. 'So, have you been on holiday, Mrs Motram?'

She waves a hand. 'Brenda. Please. And no, not really. Visiting my sister in Manchester. She fell and broke her hip. Bloody pain in the arse. As if she wasn't miserable enough already.'

Becky smiles into her coffee. Eddie takes over. Addresses David again. 'Have you thought of anything else since we last spoke? Anything at all?' He sighs. 'I want to be honest with you here. We've got very little, if anything, to go on. It appears to have been a completely random attack. Someone came to the door, and for some reason, your mother let them in. No one saw anything, no one heard anything . . .'

'Oh, I almost forgot to mention,' Brenda says. She claps her hands together. 'My cleaner told me . . . I thought it was a bit strange. She texted me when I was away but it made no sense. She's Polish and she's only twenty-three, so you can imagine . . .' She rolls her eyes.

Eddie glances at Becky, who takes her notepad out of her pocket. 'What did she say?'

Brenda pulls her phone out of her too-tight jeans, taps away. Scrolls. 'Here.' She hands the phone to Becky.

Man front door. Cdnt c
him. No key.

Becky shows the message to Eddie. 'What does this mean?'

Brenda takes the phone back. 'Told you it made no sense. I phoned her last night when I got back. She says someone came to the front door, but she couldn't open it because there was no key. I told you. I don't use that entrance now, so it's locked . . .'

Butterflies hatch inside Eddie's stomach. Something. Finally. 'When was this?'

Brenda glances across at David, a look of guilt on her face.

'About the same time as someone knocked on Linda's door. Only, she opened hers.'

Back in the car, Becky asks, 'Did no one follow up on the upstairs neighbour?' Eddie drives too fast around a mini-roundabout and she bumps her head on the window. 'Oi. Careful. Don't take it out on me . . .'

'It was supposed to be followed up, yes. I realise now that I don't actually have a report on this, or if I do, I've missed it.' He slams his hands on the steering wheel. Swears under his breath.

Nadia Kowalski smiles nervously as she opens the door, although it doesn't quite meet her eyes. She looks as if she's been expecting them. Clearly Brenda Motram has called ahead.

'I'm sorry,' she says. 'I should have called you before. I wait until Mrs Motram is back. This was wrong of me.'

'Don't worry,' Eddie says. He shows his ID. Becky follows suit. They step inside but they don't sit down. 'Can you tell us what happened?'

'Please. Sit.' She gestures at the immaculate white sofa that he'd been scared to sit on for fear of soiling it with his mere presence. Becky perches on the edge, clearly thinking the same.

'It was just before I left Mrs Motram's house. At 11 a.m., two weeks ago today. I clean nine until eleven, Tuesday and Friday. The doorbell rang as I was putting on my coat. No one ever rang the doorbell before when I have been here. People come around to the back door. That's the only one Mrs Motram uses. I ran down to front door, but there is no key. I spoke through the door, I said, "Sorry, one minute please." And a man says to me, "Can you open the door?" and . . .'

'Did he say who he was? What he wanted?' Becky is scribbling in her notebook.

Nadia shakes her head. 'No. I start to tell him that I have no key, can he go to other door, but then is silent.'

'He left? He didn't come to the other door?'

She shakes her head. 'No. I think he was bored. He decided to leave.'

'And then you left to go back home. Did you see anyone when you came round the front?'

'I left out of back gate. It leads to lane. It is quicker to come back here to my house.'

Eddie sighs. 'Was there anything unusual? Something about his voice? Did he sound young? Old?'

She shakes her head again. 'No. Nothing. I only text Mrs Motram to let her know, in case maybe it was something important to her.'

'Thanks,' Eddie says. 'You've been very helpful.' He hands her a card. 'If you think of anything else, please call me.'

'I'm sorry,' Nadia says. 'I hope you catch this man.'

Back on the front path, he tosses the car keys to Becky and she plucks them out of the air. 'You better drive. I'm too pissed off to concentrate.'

12

BECKY

She leaves Eddie in the office, bollocking one of the other DCs, and goes back upstairs. The darkroom is a bit of a disappointment. She'd expected a high-tech room full of machines and gadgets, and what she got was a walk-in cupboard jammed full of seemingly random bits of crap.

'Let me guess, you thought it'd be bigger?' Paul says. That smirk on his face.

She has that feeling again of being played. Is this actually a darkroom, or is this another part of someone's elaborate wind-up?

'Stand over there,' he says. 'That machine on your left – that's the condenser. That's where we slot the negatives and project them onto the photo paper. The worktop on the other side is where I'll lay out the trays for setting them. We don't have film to develop, as such, as we already have the negatives, so I won't bother showing you that stuff. Unless you want to see it?'

'I do, actually, if it's not too much hassle? I've never really understood how it all works.'

He sighs. 'OK then. You better go and stand in the far corner. I'll need to get the bottles of developing fluid out from under that bench behind you. See that plastic thing over there?' He gestures towards a cylindrical container to her left. 'That's the Patterson Tank. They used to use stainless steel ones, but they were fixed size. These are adjustable for different sizes of film.'

She picks it up, slides the base away from the lid. 'Right. So you wind the film around the centre?'

'Yep. Then you fill it with fluid. See that chamber in the middle? There's a couple of stages to develop and set it, then it's ready. I've got some film there, if you want to see this bit?'

'That'd be great.'

'Only, you won't actually be able to see anything, because that bit has to be done in complete darkness . . . not that sort of green light you might've seen if you've seen darkrooms on TV or anything.'

'Oh right. But how do you see what you're doing?'

'You don't. You just have to feel it. You get used to it. Practice makes perfect, you know?'

'Is it . . . like completely, totally dark?' She feels a trickle of unease. She's no longer sure she wants to be in this confined space with this man. Not in the dark.

'Like this.'

He flicks off the light and they are plunged into an inky blackness.

'Everything's sealed around the edges to make sure not the slightest bit of light can get in. Even the tiniest flicker and you've ruined your film.'

'OK.'

He doesn't say anything else, and for a moment all she can hear is his breathing, a slight whistle through his nose. She can smell him. A light tangy sweat, mixed with the faint chemical smell of their surroundings.

'OK,' she says again. 'I get it. You can turn the light back on.'

'You're closer,' he says, and she whirls round. His voice has come from the other side of the room. How did he get past her without her sensing it?

'Where's the light?' She hears the panic in her own voice, threatening to choke her. Arms outstretched like a mummy in a Scooby Doo cartoon, she lurches and scrambles towards the door, scrabbling for the light switch. 'I can't—' The lights come back on and she blinks, stars flashing across her eyes. 'You—' She can't get her words out.

'Sorry,' he says. That smirk again. 'I forgot there was another switch over here.'

'I . . . I've changed my mind. I'll wait outside. Let me know when the prints are ready, please.' She stumbles out the door and back into the office. No one seems to notice her distress. She sits on a chair nearby, takes deep breaths.

Nothing happened. You're safe here. Nothing happened.

She pushes the thoughts out of her mind. Takes her hands and rubs her face, pushes her hair back. Breathes. Tries to calm down.

The door to the darkroom opens. 'I'll have two sets of prints for you in about half an hour . . . Are you OK? I didn't mean to scare you—'

'I'm fine. I just . . . I just got a little spooked for a minute.'

He sighs. 'Come back in,' he says. 'At least see how it's done, now that you're here.'

She follows him inside.

13

CARLY

She doesn't bother to unpack the car when she gets back home, knowing that she'll only have to re-pack it all in the morning. She doesn't always do more than a couple of days in a row, but the arrival of the new artist who'd set up next to her was more than alluring. She'd felt it straight away. Wondered if he did too. That spark. That thing that you can't describe but just know that it exists. It was dangerous, of course. She'd got herself into trouble before. More than once. But fuck it, she wasn't getting any younger, and she was lonely. She'd never felt more lonely.

Her husband had forgiven her for her dalliances of the past. Even the one where she'd disappeared off to Spain for three weeks, before she'd had an attack of the guilts and come back grovelling, tail between her legs. He'd done his best to look after the kids, but the episode had taken its toll. 'They blame me,' he'd told her. 'They think I'm trying to drive you away.' It had affected his relationship with them, and she can't forgive herself for that. He keeps them at arm's length, scared of hurting them. Scared of being hurt himself. He keeps her as far away as he can get away with, still living under the same roof.

She has a quick shower, soaping herself with ginger-scented gel, trying to cleanse herself. Forget about the artist.

She knows nothing about him. And yet. She runs her hands across her breasts. Shivers, despite the heat. Imagining his touch. It has been too long since someone has touched her there.

Or anywhere.

She turns the shower dial to cold and gives herself a quick blast. Gasping as the air is almost knocked out of her.

It works.

Afterwards, she dresses in comfy loungewear and pads through to the living room in her socked feet. A note is propped up on the coffee table against a pile of magazines.

Gone to Matt's. See you at the weekend. Washing in basket. X

Her eldest daughter is spending more and more time at her boyfriend's lately. Her youngest isn't back from boarding school yet and her son could be in the room that he stays in when it suits him, but she's unlikely to find out until he appears at some point, scratching himself in his boxer shorts, pulling open the fridge and looking disappointed, as usual.

She considers ordering a takeaway, Chinese maybe. Then quickly dismisses the thought. She pours herself a large glass of wine, takes the rest of the bottle and a tub of cashew nuts and gets comfortable on the couch. She switches on a film, but it doesn't really hold her attention. She's thinking about the artist again. The painter. Thinking about his hands. Thinking about his hands on her.

It's been a long time since she's felt like this. That

instant attraction. Desire. He felt it too. She's sure of it. She doesn't even know his name, and yet she is already imagining what they might do together. Where? A hotel was the obvious choice. She can hardly bring him back here, and she'd sensed that he wasn't local. Was he in his hotel room now? Thinking about her? She feels herself getting aroused. A warmth spreading through her body. A tingling, deep inside, teasing her. Taunting her.

Maybe she could wait for . . . no. She pushes the thought away. She could lie naked on the doormat and he would walk over her as if she were invisible.

She finishes the wine, leaves the bottle and the glass on the coffee table. The bowl of nuts lies barely touched. She swallows a sleeping pill and slips into bed, relishing the crisp, clean sheets. She keeps the bedroom deliberately cold, because she knows that's how *he* likes it. Despite the fact that he barely notices her presence any more. If he sleeps in their bed, he does so without alerting her, disappears again like a ghost, leaving nothing but a faint indentation in the pillow and the hint of his musky scent.

When he bothers to sleep beside her at all, that is.

Saturday

EIGHT MORE SLEEPS

14

Becky takes the photographs out of the plain cardboard folder and begins to lay them out on the table. They'd been lucky to find the boardroom empty. It's always the first choice of meeting space, not because the meetings are always large or important, but because it's the brightest, airiest room with the most comfortable chairs and the water-cooler bottle is the least likely one on the floor to be empty. Plus, when you book the boardroom you get the services of Miriam, who brings tea and biscuits on demand. Becky is sure that it isn't actually Miriam's job to do this, but because she can see into the room from where she sits at the far end of the open-plan, she can always see when someone is in there. She uses her never-ending supply of biscuits and her weekly home-baked treats as an excuse to go into the room and find out what's going on. This is why Miriam knows everything about the entire force's comings and goings. It's a special skill, and one utilised often during times when someone wants to know what another team is getting up to. They're like schoolkids, sometimes, with their rivalries. All trying to impress the powers that be. All trying to find ways for overtime allowances and extra staff by showing that they were doing the most important jobs.

Becky hasn't worked out yet if this job is important or not. Eddie is keeping uncharacteristically quiet this morning. Do they have something here or not?

She clears her throat. 'Right. Here's what we've got.'

Eddie stops pacing and looks at her. He drops his phone into his pocket. He walks to the middle of the room, looks down at the photographs on the table.

Becky has spread them out neatly, into four rows of five images. On the bottom corner of each one, she's stuck a miniature Post-it note with a number carefully written in black marker pen.

'You've kept them in the order of the calendar. Good.' Eddie leans over the table, surveys her work. At the end of the table, the calendar sits. The negatives that had been removed for developing have been carefully replaced. All of the doors have been pushed open wide, and although the backing has not been restuck, the front piece has been carefully laid on top, and the calendar wrapped in plastic to keep it free of further contamination and to keep all of the components together. They still have to analyse other parts of it – the paper, the glue – anything that might provide a clue as to where and how it was made. And most importantly, who made it.

Becky is still feeling slightly unnerved from her experience in the darkroom with Paul. His knowledge of his work had impressed her, and she'd enjoyed watching how the negatives had been made into photographs – developed and blown up into A4, in perfect, crisp quality. But she still isn't sure if she'd imagined his hand brushing her breast when they'd been in the full dark stage for the development of the film. She doesn't know if telling Eddie is a good idea or not. Is it relevant? Does she believe that Paul might have something to do with the calendar? She isn't sure. His reaction when he saw it had seemed like someone genuinely shocked at what it contained. But who knows what had been going through the mind of the person who made the calendar. Someone that methodical would be careful to be a good actor too, if they knew that they would be called on to analyse the thing. Wouldn't they?

Eddie sits down at the table and flips open a fresh page of an A4 notepad. He writes the numbers of the photographs down the left-hand side, leaving a gap in between each one. He draws vertical lines down the page, splitting it into columns that he titles with various descriptors: Sex, Age, Characteristics, Setting . . . Then he starts to list what's in the photographs. Male. Female. Young. Old. Blond. Brunette. Carpet. Wooden flooring. Living Room. Kitchen. Blood. No blood. He pulls a pair of latex gloves from his pocket. Slips them on.

'Do you see anything?' he says. 'Patterns?' He starts to shuffle the photographs around. Puts all the males together, all the females. The younger victims, the older ones.

Becky stares down at them. Sees nothing at all. There is no pattern. There is no 'standard' victim and no usual M.O. To all intents and purposes, it looks completely random.

'I, er . . .' She pauses. 'Nothing yet. But I think there's something. He wants us to think this is random, but—'

'*He?*'

She nods. 'Right. I just assumed—'

'Never assume. In my case from a fortnight ago . . .'

he leans across the table and drags forward the image stickered with number one, 'there was no sign of forced entry. Remember? Nothing to suggest that any of this was done with force, is there?'

Becky leans over and pulls across two of the images. Numbers three and fourteen. No blood. In one, the victim's scarf lies bunched up next to their head. In the other, a cushion lies on the floor beside them. 'It looks like they might have used the victim's scarf to strangle them in this one.' She pushes the image across to Eddie. 'It takes strength to strangle someone with a scarf. We did an experiment during training. The dummy was rigged to make a sound when the windpipe was crushed. Not that many people managed it.'

Eddie nods. 'Go on.'

'In the other,' she slides the photograph with the cushion in front of him, 'it looks like they might have smothered the victim with the pillow—'

'A female could do that. They often do—'

'Yes, but how did the victim end up on the floor?'

Eddie is about to say something more, when the door opens and Miriam comes rattling in with a trolley. Pot of coffee and a pot of tea. Cups. Plate of biscuits. 'No Caramel Wafers, I'm afraid. Some little monkey has nicked them out of my bottom drawer. If I find out who, I'll . . .' Her voice trails off. She has obviously clocked Eddie's murderous expression. She flushes red. 'I'll leave you to it then,' she says. Leaves the trolley at the end of the table and backs slowly out of the room, letting the door close behind her.

'We need to get these prints scanned in,' Eddie says. His face is still set into a scowl as he picks up a chocolate digestive and bites into it. 'See if we can get any hits on the new fancy image searcher. If they are genuine crime scene photographs logged by us, it'll pick them up with a certain degree of accuracy, so even if they aren't exactly the ones we've got in there, it should still match any with similarities.'

'Already on it,' Becky says. She pours tea into two cups. 'I got tech to scan them in before they let me take the prints away. Milk? They told me to go and see Ashlie.'

Eddie grins. 'No sugar. I think we're going to make a good team, DC Greene.'

Having exhausted all they can with the photographs, they stop for more drinks at the machine in the corridor and go into the small, yellow-painted office next to CID, where the IT consultancy developing the latest version of the Police National Database spend their days working with senior PNC operators in the hope of creating a bigger and better system for forces countrywide. Woodham successfully pitched to trial the system, and their best operator was given the role of working with the consultancy to help develop it.

The office is small, warm and always full of a certain kinetic energy. Something to do with all the computer screens and the non-stop clicking of the keyboards. Eddie and Becky have brought chairs into the farthest pod, the one with the most privacy and their star computer operator – Ashlie Long. Ashlie is in her mid-thirties, and always looks like she's spent an inordinate amount of time getting ready, with immaculate shiny hair and neat clothing. Eddie is always amazed that she looks like this when she starts work at 7 a.m. Some people are just naturally organised. Although all requests for work come through a central repository, to be assigned according to whoever is free, people always try to prioritise things to go through Ashlie.

Eddie has managed to get her to reschedule the rest of her workload with the promise of a half-day on Christmas Eve. Something he hopes he will actually be able to pull off. Unfortunately, Ashlie's line-manager can be a bit of a dragon. Fortunately, she is currently off sick.

'Right,' Eddie says. He places two cups of something with steam billowing out next to the computer and sits down.

'You not having one?' Becky says. She picks up the cup and sniffs it. Wrinkles her nose. 'What *is* this?'

'Coffee's off. That, apparently, is tea.'

The tea is made from granules and UHT milk and Eddie knows better than to let it pass his lips.

Ashlie ignores him, and the tea. She's focused on her screen. 'OK. I've got ten straight matches. The others aren't coming up so easily, so I'll probably need to run them in sections—'

'Whoa there, Ada Lovelace, back up a bit for the technological dinosaurs. What are you doing?'

Ashlie rolls her eyes. 'I've run your photographs through the reverse image-search on our system. It's picking up each one and comparing it against every crime scene image logged on the database since it was beta launched in the summer. Obviously, I'm relying on other forces to have kept up to date with digitising their images, which as you can imagine is an onerous task. The CPS demands that all crime scene photographs are digitised now, but it doesn't mean that everyone is through the backlog. Sussex and Thames Valley are well on-board. I think they're trying to show us they're as efficient as us. The cold case teams as far as the Midlands are up to speed, or so I'm told. It's most critical for them, if this new part of the system is going to be of any use.' She pauses, takes a breath. 'We should have everything from within a 150-mile radius, updated to the end of November, all being well. That's what we set as the first target for the beta testing . . .'

'Brilliant.' He pulls his chair in closer to the screen. 'We need to start a log.'

Ashlie presses a couple of keys simultaneously, and a new screen appears. It's a spreadsheet version of the lines and columns he started in his notepad when he looked at the photos in the boardroom with Becky. He feels a fizz of excitement. Abby left a message on his voicemail just as he was getting the teas: none of the CSIs have made the calendar as a *joke* or for any other reason that she's been able to find out. None have admitted it, anyway, Eddie thought, on hearing the message. Abby suggested following up with some of the photographers who used to work in the department, or those who were freelance. He scribbled a note on his pad, with plans to follow up after this meeting.

'Nice one,' he says. Feeling slightly redundant at her efficiency, but secretly pleased that she is one step ahead.

'Anything jumping out at you?' Becky says.

All three of them are staring at the list of names on the screen. Next to each name is the contact officer's name, location and a link to the case report. Ashlie has been thorough. He leans forward and runs a finger down the screen, hovering over the locations. Basingstoke. Milton Keynes. Bracknell. Weybridge. He blows out a breath of frustration.

'These towns are all over the place. It doesn't make any sense.' He leans back in his seat and crosses his arms.

Ashlie clicks something and a map appears onscreen, a red dot in the centre, blue dots elsewhere. Lines connecting them, with numbers written in a font that is just too small to read comfortably. 'I triangulated them from here, assuming that this is our core. It might not be, of course. I was just basing this on the fact that the calendar was delivered here, and your latest murder happened here. I can change the central point to anywhere you like—'

'Can you blow this up and print it out?'

'Of course. Biggest it lets me do is A3, but I can print in four sections and you can stick them together.'

'You're a genius,' Becky says.

Ashlie is beaming. 'It's just my job.' She clicks a couple of keys and the printer starts to whirr.

'What were you saying about these partials?' Eddie says.

Ashlie taps at the keyboard again. Back to business. 'These are the nine images that haven't matched yet. I can try them in sections, and if that doesn't work, I can blow them up, see if there's anything specific that might be a distinctive object to match with.' She moves her mouse around the image onscreen. Clicks. The image splits into pieces. 'It might be that the real crime scene photographs – the ones on the system – are not taken at exactly the same angle as the ones in the calendar. So, that's why I was thinking to look in sections—'

'How long do you think it'll take to match the other nine images?'

Ashlie frowns. The first hint that things might not be

as simple as Eddie was starting to hope. 'I've no idea right now. I haven't tried any of the partials yet.'

'Can we do one now, do you think? Or are we distracting you?' Becky pushes the cup of vile tea towards the back of the desk.

Ashlie clicks at her keyboard again. The four pieces of the image disappear, and a box appears in the centre showing a ticker with a rapidly scrolling number of images and a flickering bar with red at one end, green at the other. Eddie looks away, the movement making him feel slightly sick. Not a job for anyone who suffers from migraines, this one.

After a moment, the movement stops. He turns back to the screen. At the bottom of the box it says 0.8 seconds. The bar is glowing green. Two of the image segments are on the left-hand side, and in the centre is a full photograph marked with the case ID and exhibit number.

'Well,' Ashlie says. 'That was easy. Assuming the others run like this, I should have the rest of the images matched, the log updated and your map printed by, say . . .' she glances up at the clock, 'about the time it takes you to nip out to Costa and get me a decent cup of coffee?' Her face is deadpan, but Eddie thinks he can see the hint of a smirk at the edge of her lip.

Becky stands, opens her mouth as if she is about to put in her own coffee order, but changes her mind. 'I'll come with you,' she says, instead.

Eddie nods. 'See you in twenty.' He slaps an approving hand on the back of Ashlie's chair. 'Good job. Very good job.' She doesn't even flinch.

He glances over his shoulder as they leave the room

and watches as the green and red bar starts flickering again. The numbers below whirring by like a spin on the fruit machine. It stops, and the image is right there onscreen. He's going to have to tell Greene about Judy Dorringer, before someone else does. He pushes the door open. Becky walks out in front of him.

'Oh wait, Eddie . . .'

He turns back round.

'I meant to say at the start. Linda Hollis isn't on the database yet—'

'Well she wouldn't be,' Eddie says. 'It's only been two weeks. We haven't uploaded the photographs.'

'Right. So I checked the calendar photograph against the one in the case file – which I uploaded onto the database for you, by the way – hope that was OK. It's not identical, but it's close.'

He walks back towards her computer, where she has pulled up the two photographs. The image from the calendar is angled fractionally to the left, showing a bit of the door frame, casting a shard of light from the window in the stairwell.

Eddie frowns. 'OK, so it's definitely two different photographs, and only one of them is in our file. From what Abby told me, there's no way this could've been taken at the same time as the crime scene photography.' He grins. 'I think we can rule out the calendar photo coming from the CSIs then. I was right. This is real. You'd better give me that list now. The coffee will have to wait.'

16

BECKY

She waits for him outside the office. 'So I guess we're having a briefing now?'

Eddie nods. 'Yep. Can you round up the troops? I know we've not been assigned anyone officially yet, but once we update Keegan on what we've got, he's going to have to give us a team.'

'Right, boss,' she says. She heads towards Keegan's office.

'Oh hang on, Becky. Come back a sec.'

He hasn't moved. She can't read the expression on his face.

He beckons her to the other side of the corridor. Lowers his voice. 'I need to tell you now, and then we can discuss it later, but . . . Linda Hollis isn't my only unsolved in that calendar.'

'Oh?'

He frowns. 'The one I took a snap of yesterday. Door number four . . .'

She feels a wave of impatience. Is he trying to hide something? 'Go on?'

'Judy Dorringer. Ealing, West London. 2006. I was there. Seconded. I'll tell you the rest later. Just wanted you to be aware. You know . . . in case it's not a coincidence that two of my cases are in this calendar.'

'Right,' she says. Thinks, it *can't* be a coincidence, can it? 'Can't you tell me now? Might make it easier when you bring it up with the rest of the team. If there's something we need to be thinking about—'

He sighs. 'I'm sorry, Becky. I don't mean to be vague. But what with Linda and Judy and the calendar being sent here, to this station—'

'It wasn't addressed to you though, was it?'

'No, but I can't help feeling it was meant for me. I just need a bit of head space to work it out a bit. I want to make sure I'm not missing something important before I share it all with the team. You know what it's like . . .'

His voice tails off and it's clear he's not going to say any more about it right now. She nods at him, and he returns it. It's his problem, not hers. She shakes her head. Focuses.

'Oh, one other thing,' he says. Smiling now. 'The door numbers on the advent calendar? They match the door numbers of the victims' addresses.'

She's grinning when she knocks on Keegan's door. Lets it slide off as she walks into his office. She has to remind herself that these are real people, not just pieces in a puzzle. But the door thing . . . Eddie spotted that fast. She's excited to be working with him. Even if he does like to play his cards a bit too close to his chest.

'OK,' Eddie says. He has pinned the A3 sheets on one of the partition boards in the far corner of the room. Cleared the whiteboard. Keegan told her to get Joe involved, plus a couple of others. Probably not enough yet, but it was a start.

He's written the list on the whiteboard. He clears his throat. 'Right. Here's what we have so far: eleven victims, including Linda Hollis, spanning eighteen years . . . I've sorted them here by the order they occurred.'

1. Dave Connolly. 22. Strangled. 5 Romsey Road, St Albans. 10/12/1998

2. Sally McGee. 40. Smothered. 14 Oakridge Road, Basingstoke. 09/12/2001

3. Kate Steele. 41. Strangled. 9 Cheviot Road, Worthing. 06/12/2002

4. Brian Cowley. 67. Suffocated. 13 Penryn Avenue, Milton Keynes. 20/12/2005

5. Clare Jones. 35. Strangled. 3 Stoke Road, Aylesbury. 17/12/2008

6. Laura Davis. 22. Strangled. 19 Iffley Road, Oxford. 04/12/2010

7. Lydia Simms. 67. Blunt force trauma. 8 Fletcher Way, Hemel Hempstead. 03/12/2011

8. Jason Smythe. 39. Blunt force trauma. 11 Rectory Lane, Bracknell. 18/12/2012

9. Victoria Moon. 65. Suffocated. 24 Oatlands Close, Weybridge. 22/12/2013

10. Sam Brown. 44. Strangled. 2 Grange Road, Lewes. 08/12/2015

11. Linda Hollis. 56. Blunt force trauma. 1 Stanley Road, Woodham. 02/12/2016

'Victoria Moon is Surrey. Kate Steele and Sam Brown are Sussex. The others are Thames Valley. Thankfully, that's only three cold case teams to contact initially, but we're still trying to identify the other victims and we might end up with more. Surrey is DS Wendy Lawson. Linda Hollis is mine, as you know. Sussex – it's DS Mark Bradford. I know Mark, should be easy enough to get what we need there. And Thames Valley, that's—'

'DI Stevie Swift,' says Keegan. 'He's a right sort. Typical that the bulk of the victims are on his patch. I'll give him a call, soften him up. Then one of you lot can take over.'

'Thanks, Nick,' Eddie says. 'Joe – I'd like you to follow up with the cold case teams. Let me know if there are any problems.'

'Sure,' Joe says. He grins at Becky, excited to be involved.

'Hang on.' Becky walks over to the board. 'Just to give everyone a bit more information based on what we've already been looking at . . .' She glances at Eddie, and he nods. 'The house numbers are important here. They correspond to the number of the door on the advent calendar that the photograph was behind—'

'Anything else you've uncovered so far?' Keegan cuts in. 'Time is of the essence, and all that . . . Linda Hollis was murdered a fortnight ago. We might want to consider the fact that he might be planning another one this year—'

'It's been one a year as far as we can tell,' says Eddie, 'but yes. We're aware of that. Assuming we've got the first one, we're missing years 1999, 2000, 2003, 2004 . . .' he hesitates, glances quickly at Becky before continuing, '2006 . . . 2007, 2009 and 2014. That means there's a year missing, so either he did two in the same year, or Dave Connolly in 1998 isn't the first victim.'

'Also,' Becky cuts in, 'there are four doors with no

photo behind them. Six, twelve, eighteen and twenty-two, so . . .'

'So potentially we're looking at him targeting houses with those numbers, in Surrey, Sussex and Thames Valley? Over the next four years?' Keegan says. He shakes his head. 'We're going to have our work cut out . . .'

'Don't worry,' Eddie says. 'If there is a pattern, we will find it. Have I let you down before? I said the Linda Hollis case wasn't ready to disappear, didn't I?'

Keegan sighs. 'You've nothing on that though, have you?'

Eddie glances at Becky again. 'Maybe. Maybe not. We spoke to her upstairs neighbour yesterday. She was away at the time of the murder. Only just got back. Her cleaner reckons someone came to the door at around the time that Linda was murdered.'

'And she didn't think to tell us before now?'

'She's young. She didn't see anything. She didn't think . . .'

'Right then,' Keegan says. 'You better be getting on with it. Let us know when you've identified the remaining victims. Another ten, is it?'

'Nine,' Eddie says. 'Nine more to ID. Then we need to see what we can do to stop these four empty doors being filled . . .'

Ashlie appears, red-faced, eyes shining. 'I've printed it all out for you, Eddie,' she says. She has brought in the map, the four sections already taped together. He helps her to stick it up on the wall, next to his own sheets of notes.

'I'll get back to it. I'd like to get the remaining scenes for you ASAP.'

'Thanks, Ashlie. Let us know what you need from us. I can assign someone to help you if required.' He waits for her to scuttle back out of the room before carrying on.

'OK,' Eddie says, addressing his cobbled-together team of DCs and uniforms. There is no other DS available right now, so he's going to be landed with the bulk of that work until something else happens to raise the profile. Nick is overseeing, but it's Eddie's show. 'First up – the dates. As you can see from the list, the cases span an eighteen-year period. This, of course, is going to be a frustrating, logistical nightmare. In my experience, gleaning information across forces is a right royal pain in the . . .' he pauses, roots about in his pocket and realises he has no small change for the swear box, 'backside.'

'We need a list of swearword alternatives, Guv.' DC Keir Jameson smirks at him. He knows how much Eddie hates having to tone down his language, and he knows how much he hates being called Guv. They're not in a seventies TV cop show.

'Thanks, Keir,' Eddie says, flatly refusing to allow this man to wind him up. 'The other thing that should jump right out at you, is the timings. The actual dates—'

'They're all in December,' PC Leo Roberts says. One of the newest uniforms to be seconded to them during busy periods. Like now.

'Yes. More specifically, they've all occurred in the pre-Christmas period. So it looks like our advent calendar is spot on.'

'The doors don't match with the dates though, right?'

Becky says. 'They match with the addresses of the victims.'

'Correct,' Eddie says. He walks across to the sheet that has been tacked to the wall. 'The doors on the calendar match the doors of the victims. Not the dates. What's this telling us?'

Becky clears her throat. 'That we don't know when he's going to strike next. But we know which house numbers he's going to target?'

Eddie can't help but grin. 'Yep. Only, that's all we have . . . house numbers. Six, twelve, eighteen, twenty-two. No streets. No towns. Let's look at the map. We are still missing the locations and details of nine of the crimes, but what we have now is quite interesting. Assuming we are taking our location here as the central point—'

'Every location is within a couple of hours of here.' Constable Roberts again. Good for him.

Eddie takes a pointer and clicks it on. He shines the pinprick light against the map. 'Look what we've got – Basingstoke. Milton Keynes. Bracknell. Weybridge. As Leo pointed out, all within a two-hour drive. Traffic permitting. What's this telling us?'

'Someone who drives around a lot? A travelling salesman?' Roberts says.

There is a ripple of laughter.

'Is there such a thing any more?' Jameson says.

Eddie bristles. This man is a wind-up. He can't help himself. 'Of course there is, smarty-pants.' He uses the juvenile, non-sweary term to further humiliate him. 'Sales reps still travel, don't they? I don't think Leo meant someone who goes round doors selling dishcloths from a suitcase, although saying that, it's an option.' He drops the pointer into his pocket and picks up a Sharpie from the desk nearby. Flips over to a fresh page on the giant easel pad. Writes:

Sales rep – all sorts of industries – look into industries in these towns

Traveller – sells cloths etc. and/or offers to do your drive/collect metal etc.

'What about a taxi driver? I mean, like the luxury car service rather than normal taxis. Most people don't take normal taxis for two-hour journeys, but there must be businesspeople who use a car service?' says Becky.

Eddie writes:

Chauffeur/luxury car service – businessmen/women? Again, industries/companies in these towns.

Then he writes:

Van/lorry driver – check all the private parcel companies, haulage etc.

'What about those consultants that go into different companies to do different bits of work here and there?' Leo again. 'My brother works in IT. He has to go all over the place.'

'Yes, good one.' Eddie writes:

Consultant/contractor – companies/industries (again).

Then:

Freelancers.

He pauses. Waits for more to come to him. Waits for more suggestions.

'Like reporters, photographers, that sort of thing?' Becky says.

Next to Freelancers, Eddie writes: *reporters/photographers*.

He underlines *photographers*.

This one makes the most sense. A freelance photographer can choose to go anywhere for work. They could work with the police, for the press, doing private shoots . . . Private shoots!

'It'd be fairly usual for a freelance photographer to go to people's houses, wouldn't it? If they were doing portrait stuff, maybe? Or discussing weddings? That sort of thing?'

Murmurs from the team. 'I had mine come round so we could discuss what they were going to do on the day, and they took some test shots to make sure we were happy with the style. But most people meet their photographer at the venue, don't they?' Jay Osborne says.

'It's a possibility though. We need to find out if any of the victims had booked a photographer to come round to their house.'

'Christ, Eddie,' Jameson says. 'These cases go back nearly twenty years. You said yourself it's going to be difficult to work across jurisdictions, and twenty years ago the Internet barely even existed – this is going to be nigh on impossible.'

'In that case, you can start looking into it, Keir. A man of your knowledge will be able to figure this one out.'

Keir sighs. 'I don't think this is it. I don't think that many people book photographers to come to their house—'

'Have you got any better ideas?'

'Not at the moment, no, but—'

'Right then. It's all yours. Joe can help you. He's good

at this sort of thing. Go and speak to Ashlie too. See what she needs from us. She won't ask for help but she can't do this all on her own. Becky, I want you to think outside the box a bit – see what other links you can find. See if you can think up any other possible reasons that our man is getting into people's houses without force.'

'I thought you said we weren't to assume it was a man?' A slight smirk.

Eddie smiles. 'You're right. I did say that. In fact, I don't think we should assume that we're looking for a freelance photographer either. We need to explore all avenues. Jay – I need you to look at companies that might have offices in more than one of these places – reasons for someone to be travelling to each one. Then look into some of those IT agencies. See if you can find a link with any of their consultants or contractors or whatever they call themselves.'

He waits until they've all gone before he walks in closer to the map. The Ealing case isn't on there yet, but it's only a matter of time before Ashlie identifies that one and all of the others.

17

THE PHOTOGRAPHER

I took the box from your bedroom, didn't I? I knew that everything was going to stay exactly how it was the last time you'd been there. No one was going to pack your things away, shove them in the loft. Give them to charity. I knew that after the police took your stuff back home, that box would just sit there in the middle of your bed forever and ever, gathering dust. Leaving the sad cloud of your memory right there on the duvet. Your most treasured things – the things you took to university because you couldn't bear to be without them – brought back to your bedroom at home, and left there on your bed.

To rot.

I took them because I wanted something of you. I took them because I didn't know what else to do. But there must've been some higher power at work that day. Something that invaded my subconscious and set things in motion.

After the first time, when I sat there in the van, pleased with myself for going through with it – I worked it all out. I drove to the usual place and parked. Took the box out of the little space in the van where I keep it wedged tight. Safe.

Took out the things I needed.

Your advent calendar (the last door still closed, because you never got to open it – I always wondered what was behind it, but I didn't open it, I would never do that to you).

Your tombola (I took out all the numbers past twenty-four. I put them in a bag and took it back to your room and put it under the pillow so they'd be safe, and I know no one will touch the bag because no one will ever take the sheets and pillows off your bed again, will they?).

Your figurines (I remember watching you make them . . . all that care and attention you put into it. Such small hands, tiny fingers. I was too clumsy, although you did let me stick the polystyrene heads on).

I think you would've liked how I planned it all. It was quite clever of me, I think. To use your things this way, and yet no one knew that I had. No one knows that I am still using your things. I almost gave it all up ten years ago. I had the chance to confess. That girl – she reminded me of you. It woke me up. Made me start to doubt my mission. I'd given the police plenty of cases, and they'd done nothing – just like with you. No one cared, not like me. Not like I cared about you.

But I came to my senses again, just in time. I kept going. I will keep going, until it's done. Until the police finally notice. Why can't they see? Why haven't they worked it out yet? How many more Christmases do I have to ruin for them to open their eyes to what's been staring them right in the face?

I will run out of numbers eventually.

I sit on the mattress in the back of the van, and I spin the tombola. It's not as much fun now, with so few balls left in there.

Six . . . twelve . . . eighteen . . . twenty-two.

What am I going to do with you?

(I'm a poet and I don't even know it.)

A ball falls down the chute and lands on my lap. I turn it over in my hands, pondering another rhyme. Number six. Easy.

Number six, number six; strangle, smother or hit you with bricks?

My laughter echoes inside the metal walls of the van. Laughter sounds so hollow when you've no one to share it with.

18

BECKY

For some reason, the heater next to Becky's desk, which only has one temperature – scalding – has decided to pack in just as the weather has taken a turn for the worse. According to the radio in the canteen, Storm Hannah is on her way, ready to wreak havoc on them all, after attempting to turn most of the East Coast of America into Narnia.

Odds of a white Christmas have dramatically shortened to 3:1. Which is all very well if you're wrapped up warm at home with your family and your two litres of Baileys and your forty-eight-pack of mince pies, but it's no use at all if you're in the middle of a murder investigation that's starting to look like it's going to involve travelling around the country.

Becky pulls the sleeves of her cardigan over her hands and attempts to type with her thumbs. She hopes the heater is a temporary glitch. She silently prays for it to return to its usual sweat-patch-inducing heat, vowing never to complain about it ever again, even when it's twenty-eight degrees outside and the sun is bouncing off the windows. She also silently prays that Jay will find out enough about companies in the area with offices elsewhere to avoid her having to go anywhere in the car that's not going to get her home in time for tea. She knows her thoughts are selfish, but it's nearly Christmas and she prays desperately for the third time in minutes that all of this will be resolved before then. There is still time. Seven days before it's one more sleep till the fat man tries to squeeze down the chimney. They're going to nail this one fast, aren't they? *Please God*. Her fourth prayer and she hasn't set foot inside a church since she was at school.

Shortly after the briefing, Ashlie brought in an updated list, with all but two photographs identified. She's good, that one. Becky wanted to ask her to help with what she's doing now, but she knows Ashlie is busy enough as it is. Becky is playing around with a piece of software that looks for patterns in data. Cluster analysis. Trends. Venn diagrams. Likelihood ratios. She's not entirely sure how it all works. Despite doing a statistics module at college, she's not particularly good with the theoretical aspects, but she knows how to work the software. She is trying to make sense of what they have so far: eighteen murders – seven men and eleven women. All approximately within two hours' drive from where they are right now. Ages range from twenty-one to sixty-seven, the average is forty-two but that seems meaningless. Just because the statistic can be calculated doesn't mean it's relevant – that much she does remember from the course. Correlation doesn't mean causation. Chances are, the victims are entirely random – which is a nightmare for them, of course. How do you find links when there aren't any? How are they supposed to know where he is going to strike next . . . and when? There's a good chance it will be before Christmas, but who says he's going to do it before Christmas this year? Maybe it's all part of his big plan. He's sent the calendar, let them know he exists. He's killed Linda Hollis. If he's been doing one a year, he might've disappeared again already. He's been doing this for nearly eighteen years. Who says he's planning to stop now?

Becky is in the process of looking up each address on Google maps to see what kind of house each person lived in, when Ashlie appears at her desk. Her face is flushed with excitement and she's holding out a printout.

'I found another one.' She offers the piece of paper to Becky. 'Chrissie Thacker. Age nineteen. 24th December 1997.'

''97? That's the earliest one so far.' Becky takes the paper and looks down the brief report. She feels a flurry of hope. They'd thought the first one was Dave Connolly, 10th December 1998. In St Albans. Which had seemingly no link to the current cases and was proving to be a bit of a head-scratcher. But Chrissie Thacker lived in Guildford, less than ten miles away. Another one on their patch. This is a big deal. 'So there's only one left to identify now? Any luck with that yet?'

Ashlie frowns. 'No. Sorry. If it helps though, I don't think it's older than 1997. The décor in the house would suggest it's more modern. For some reason I'm just not getting any hits on it. The photo is a bit blurry . . . I'll keep trying.'

'Thanks, Ash. I still owe you that coffee. A decent one.'

'Don't worry, I'm high as a kite on all this anyway.

Another shot of caffeine and you might have to peel me off the ceiling.'

Ashlie leaves her to it, and Becky immediately keys in the case ID from the printout into the computer, bringing up the whole file.

Chrissie Thacker. Killed one week before her twentieth birthday. Studying Art History at Guildford University, lived on Bray Road close to the main campus. Home address was Hazel Avenue, on the other side of town, closer to where they are now. Becky wonders why she chose to live in a flat when she could've driven from home, but she knows that not everyone is happy enough to stay with their family when they're crossing that boundary from teen to adulthood. That new life that university brings. There was the money thing too, but maybe it wasn't so hard twenty years ago. It's lucky that Becky is close to her family and more than happy to live with them, because she certainly can't afford to move out and live on her own. Not right now. Then again, she spends half the time at Gary's anyway. It's only a matter of time before he asks her to move in, but the truth is, she kind of likes things the way they are. She picks up a pen and starts to roll it between her fingers. Carries on reading.

Chrissie lived with two other girls. Tabitha Smart and Erin Mockley. Something else that doesn't really appeal to Becky. It's all very well dealing with your siblings and your parents, but she's not sure she can imagine living with what are essentially strangers, unless, of course, they were girls she'd known from school and they'd all decided to move in together. There will be a full report on all of this, hopefully. If the lead investigator on the case was doing their job, those girls would have been questioned thoroughly.

They may still have to be contacted again, of course.

She wonders how they'll feel to have the past dredged up again now, assuming they can track them down. They're hardly likely to be living in the same house.

Tabitha Smart. The name sounds familiar. She's sure there's a newsreader or something like that, with the same name? Ah no, that weather girl. The one who wears the inappropriately tight dresses. Can't be her, can it? Although the ages would fit.

Becky flicks the pen across the desk and leans back in her chair. She stretches her arms back, trying to move some life back into her stiff muscles. She's been sitting here for so long, so engrossed, that's she's barely moved for hours. She's only been vaguely aware of people coming and going in the office. Has a dim memory of Joe coming in and leaving her a sandwich, but there's nothing on her desk. Maybe she dreamed it. Maybe she has screen-staring psychosis.

She needs a break.

Becky stands up, shakes life into her legs. Hears bones clicking. Not good when you're only twenty-eight. She used to be good at staying in shape, swimming on Mondays, Pilates on Wednesdays, circuits at the church hall on Saturday mornings, but that's not on at the moment because of all the Christmas stuff happening in there. She remembers Lady Margaret muttering something about it the other morning in McDonald's.

Christmas market.

She walks across the room, windmilling her arms. Something is trying to force its way from somewhere deep inside her head, but her brain is overworked and sticky from staring at that screen for so long. She writes up Chrissie Thacker's details at the top of Eddie's list. She licks her lips. Realises that she is desperately thirsty. When did she last have anything to drink, never mind eat?

There is a large cardboard box on Miriam's desk. Gold and red tinsel poking out of the top. She glances around, but Miriam is nowhere to be seen. She pulls apart the top flaps of the box and peers inside. Shiny garlands. A miniature plastic tree. A Perspex box filled with multi-coloured baubles. A one-armed elf. She hates elves. Too creepy. Especially those ones that were all the craze last year – Elf on the Shelf – people taking photos of them doing ridiculous things – making it look like they'd arranged things themselves. Probably had. These were the kind of things from those old horror films her dad sometimes watched. Ancient stuff from the seventies, with dolls with blinking eyes. She shudders. In the corner of the box is an angel. Gold lace dress, blonde hair. Sparkly halo. She smiles, lifts it out of the box.

'Having fun?' Miriam's voice comes from behind another plastic tree – this one a lot bigger, and a lot more . . . pink.

'I've got to hand it to you, Miriam. I'm pretty sure we're the only CID in the country that is home to a pink, glittery Christmas tree and a one-armed horror elf.'

Miriam laughs and almost drops the tree on the floor.

'That's Alf. Don't be rude!' She doesn't make any apologies for the tree. Becky is secretly impressed by Miriam's attitude. Why not, eh? What's wrong with a bit of pink glitter . . . Eddie is going to love it. She can't wait to see his face.

She's pulling other random decorations out of the box, laying them on the desk. Trying not to let herself join in with Miriam's infectious but tuneless humming of 'Mary's Boy Child'. She used to love making decorations when she was a kid. Angels made of toilet rolls and cotton wool and glitter. Ping-pong balls for heads. That's when it comes to her. Works itself out of her brain. Unsticks itself from the depths.

Christmas markets. They sell arts and crafts, don't they? People travel all over the place to sell their stuff at them. There's a large proportion of utter tat at most of them, but there's often some decent stuff too. Paintings. Photographic prints. The kind of things that would be easily transportable and reasonably inconspicuous, if you were to travel from town to town.

Every single Christmas. Someone needs to look into that.

Eddie walks in just as she is placing Alf on top of the computer monitor on the desk he's taken ownership of this week. He gives her a look that suggests that Alf will have no arms if she doesn't remove him straight away.

'Ashlie's found our first victim,' she says.

Alf is saved. For now.

19

EDDIE

He walks over to the board where they have listed all of the identified victims. Becky has added the latest one right at the top.

1. Chrissie Thacker. 19. Strangled. 10 Bray Road, Guildford. 24/12/1997

2. Dave Connolly. 22. Strangled. 5 Romsey Road, St Albans. 10/12/1998

3. Rhian Cummings. 46. Suffocated. 16 Greenhill Road, Winchester. 05/12/1999

4. Kevin Tumnell. 42. Stabbed. 20 Crows Road, Epping. 14/12/2000

5. Sally McGee. 40. Smothered. 14 Oakridge Road, Basingstoke. 09/12/2001

6. Kate Steele. 41. Strangled. 9 Cheviot Road, Worthing. 06/12/2002

7. Jack Thomson. 55. Blunt force trauma. 21 Randolph Road, Portsmouth. 15/12/2003

8. 2004???

9. Brian Cowley. 67. Suffocated. 13 Penryn Avenue, Milton Keynes. 20/12/2005

10. Judy Dorringer. 21. Suffocated. 4 Eaton Rise, Ealing. 16/12/2006

11. Stephen Jackson. 37. Stabbed. 7 Queens Road, Richmond. 19/12/2007

12. Clare Jones. 35. Strangled. 3 Stoke Road, Aylesbury. 17/12/2008

13. Fran Davies. 32. Strangled. 15 Coombe Road, Kingston. 11/12/2009

14. Laura Davis. 22. Strangled. 19 Iffley Road, Oxford. 04/12/2010

15. Lydia Simms. 67. Blunt force trauma. 8 Fletcher Way, Hemel Hempstead. 03/12/2011

16. Jason Smythe. 39. Blunt force trauma. 11 Rectory Lane, Bracknell. 18/12/2012

17. Victoria Moon. 65. Suffocated. 24 Oatlands Close, Weybridge. 22/12/2013

18. Lewis Kane. 34. Stabbed. 23 Rye Hill Road, Harlow. 12/12/2014

19. Sam Brown. 44. Strangled. 2 Grange Road, Lewes. 08/12/2015

20. Linda Hollis. 56. Blunt force trauma. 1 Stanley Road, Woodham. 02/12/2016

'So,' he says. 'Nineteen years accounted for. Just 2004 left to find?'

'Ashlie is still working on it,' Becky says. 'That last one is proving to be difficult to match.'

'Any significance to that?'

'Photo is a bit blurred. Other than that—'

He runs his eye down the list, sees Judy Dorringer's name in there from 2006. Tries to push the case back into the little box in his mind where he keeps it. He can't focus on that one now. It's not the key. Can't be.

'So what've we got now . . . seven for Swift in Thames Valley. Two for DS Mark Bradford in Sussex. Three in Surrey . . . Three for the Met, two for Emma Burns in Hampshire, and two for DS Jim Leonard in Essex.' He sighs. '2004 is still unaccounted for, and we've got doors six, twelve, eighteen and twenty-two left blank. Right?'

'Right . . . I was thinking we should look into Chrissie Thacker. Let the others continue with the rest of the cold cases.'

'Because she's the first, and she's on our patch? That what you're thinking, Becks?'

'Yep.'

'Good. Me too. Let's get the file—'

She hands him a beige folder, bulging at the seams, held together with a thick elastic band. 'One step ahead of you, Guv.' She smiles.

He rolls his eyes, takes the file. 'Don't call me Guv.'

They sit down at her desk, and she taps the keyboard, bringing the file up electronically too, so they can search it more easily.

'Killed on the morning of Christmas Eve,' Eddie says. 'Hmm.' He leans over and scrolls up and down through the screens, hoping that something is going to pop out at him. It doesn't. From the details here, and what he's been updated on so far by Joe and the others, it's another random, senseless killing. No obvious motive, and more importantly, no obvious suspects. He sighs, sits back in the chair.

Becky takes control of her computer again. 'I know it's

under the cold case team now, but there's an address here for the lead detective who worked the case . . . DI Allan Inglis. It's an address in Woodham . . .'

'If it's up to date,' Eddie says. 'He could be in an old folks home by now.'

'Hang on.' Becky types into the search box. Pulls up the details of the DI. 'Well,' she says. 'He only just retired last year. He's sixty-four. There's a phone number here . . .'

Eddie nods. 'Ring him. Tell him we'll pop round. Assuming he's not on a golf course somewhere. Isn't that what retired detectives do?'

Becky rolls her eyes and picks up the phone.

He's about to go down and see Ashlie about the missing 2004 case, when Joe Dickson walks in. He drops a box of Krispy Kreme on the desk next to Eddie.

'Boss,' he says. 'Good timing.'

'I don't like doughnuts.'

Joe shakes his head. 'There really is something wrong with you, Sir. No offence.'

Eddie can't be bothered with the banter right now. 'Have you got an update for me?'

Joe pushes the second half of an original glazed into his mouth and nods. 'That DI Swift that you and DI Keegan were moaning about? Nice as pie. Maybe it was just me . . .' He winks. When Eddie only frowns in return, he carries on. 'Couldn't have been more helpful. Sent through all the reports, even though we have them online, just in case there was anything in there that might've been missed. He also went through them all with me on the phone, and I'm sorry to say there's not a lot of interest

. . .' He wipes his hands on his jeans, leaving trails of sugar and grease. Takes out his notepad. 'Three married, two single, a girlfriend and a divorcée. Three strangled, two suffocated, two blunt force. Four women, three men. A range of ages and jobs . . . there are just no obvious patterns. I've spoken to the others too. Our Sussex and Surrey cases don't add any additional insight. It's almost as if no one actually wants these cases to be linked. They don't want the headache of a serial killer on their patch, the week before Christmas.'

Eddie sighs. He kicks the metal bin under the desk and sends it skittering into the corner. A brief flash of fear passes over Joe's face. He opens his mouth to speak but Eddie silences him with a raised palm.

'Sorry,' he says. 'Thanks, Joe. You might need to give them a bit more of a push. This thing isn't going away.' He takes a deep breath. Lets it out fast. 'You know what, maybe I need to try one of these . . .' He lifts the lid off the doughnut box just as Becky hangs up the phone.

'You'll be pleased to know that our retired detective is not on the golf course. He's on his way down to see us. Said he's glad for an excuse to get out of the decorating.'

Eddie bites into something powdery that oozes bright red jam and feels instantly better.

20

THE PHOTOGRAPHER

They must've received it. What are they playing at? Maybe I was getting ideas above my station, expecting them to take it seriously straight away. Maybe I didn't realise how long it was going to take them to decide that it was real. A thought did occur to me, after I posted it. What if they thought it was a prank? One of the crime scene photographers trying to wind up the detectives.

Maybe it's still at the bottom of someone's in-tray.

Idiots.

I'd thought addressing it ambiguously was the right thing to do. I'd hoped that the right person would see it – someone sufficiently interested to open it and see what was inside. Someone who'd be intrigued by the whole thing.

Maybe I was wrong. Maybe I should've addressed it to the person who already had a clue. Obviously I was too subtle. But I wanted to give him a chance.

It might seem weird, but I'd actually been hoping that I wouldn't have to kill anyone else.

Yes, I know. I left four empty doors. They'd assume that meant I had four more kills planned. Four more years of this torture.

But I don't want that. I really don't.

I'm so tired of it.

I never meant for it to go like this. I swear I didn't. But I've set things in motion now. I can't back down now, can I? Or else what's the point?

I need to get them back. They shouldn't have stopped your investigation so soon. I thought I'd given them enough links. Same crime scenes, same time of year. But it didn't work! No one came and told us they were going to re-open your case. No one really cares, do they? So what choice did I have but to carry on. Give the bastards more work to do at a time when they're already stretched to the limits. Ruin Christmas for all those other families. Does that sound callous? Well, I'm sorry. But why should everyone else get to be happy when I'm stuck in this perpetual misery?

Luckily, I've got the things I need. Enough for four more, if it comes to that. I hope it won't. I hope that one more might do it . . . that, along with the photos, should be enough.

It's strange to be back in my home town again. I try to avoid it as much as I can. One trip a year, and never at this time of year. I've been busy elsewhere.

I don't want the memories. I don't want to have to talk about it.

I don't want the grief.

I've decided to go with one of the new estates on the far side of town, where there's still building work going on. I'm sure these weren't even here last time I was home. These beige, boxy houses with their perfect patches of grass and their scalloped-edge porch trims. Nice, neat cars parked on the perfectly laid driveways. Christmas tree lights twinkling from the slatted wooden blinds, left open just enough for the people outside to catch a glimpse of the idyllic Christmassy scenes inside.

The streets are dimly lit. The streetlights on sensors after eight o'clock. Ecological and money-saving. Besides, no one needs to be out in the dark, do they? Not without their cars. No one walks around these American-esque estates.

Maybe it's too risky.

Are these the kind of people to open their doors to a stranger at night?

Depends . . . Depends what the stranger wants, doesn't it?

I see a man walking towards me, throwing my theory into turmoil. I flip up my collar and keep walking. I look straight ahead. These houses don't interest me. I'm on my way home on a frosty night, just like him. I'm prepared for a hello. A 'Cold one tonight', if necessary. But the man turns off the street up a pathway ahead of me and I am saved the trouble. He barely glanced at me. It's all still OK.

I know I can't go to one of the houses on this street. Not now. They're family homes, and as much as I can, I try to avoid those. Like I said before . . . I'm not a monster.

Around the corner, past the larger end houses with the twinkling lights around their windows, is a section of different shaped dwellings. Maisonettes. Flats. Places where I'm more likely to find someone on their own.

I pause next to a wooden-slatted bin store that's been built at the end of the block of smaller housing. I breathe in. Out. Watch puffs of breath in the icy air.

A rush of blood. Adrenaline.

I walk up the path. Before I can change my mind, I knock on the door.

A man answers. He looks bored, but most importantly, he looks utterly unthreatening.

Opening my bag, I smile at him and tell him my story.

He smiles back, before disappearing back inside his house, leaving the door wide open. I can see straight into his living room. I can see an open pizza box on a small coffee table. I can see the glow of the TV.

I step inside.

21

EDDIE

Retired DI Allan Inglis is dressed in neat-fitting jeans and a dark green jumper and, despite his lack of hair, looks at least ten years younger than his sixty-four years. Eddie can only hope that he looks as fresh when he gets to retirement age, assuming stress hasn't driven him mad by then. When they shake hands, Eddie notices that the other man's hands are flecked with white paint.

'DS Carmine,' he says, smiling. 'I've heard good things.' There is a hint of a Scottish accent in his voice, despite him having lived in Surrey for forty years. There is something about his handshake and his voice that makes Eddie trust him immediately. 'You wanted to talk about Chrissie Thacker?'

Becky opens the door to the boardroom and they follow her inside. 'I've asked Miriam to bring us tea.'

'Becky's read the file in detail. I've only had a chance to skim. But I'm hoping you might have some insight. Something that might help . . .'

'I remember it well,' Allan says. 'I was about your age when it happened. It's one of those that swims back into my dreams now and then. We all hate unsolveds.' He smiles at them both. 'I never expected it to come up again. Not like this.'

'As part of a wider enquiry, you mean?'

'Aye. I always hoped something would happen. The cold case team would find something I missed, open it up again . . . young girl. It's never nice.'

'Boyfriend?'

'Ruled out. Flatmates too. One of them is dead now. Erin Mockley. Car crash a week before graduation. Drunk driver. I remember because of the link to the Thacker girl, and also the name – quite distinctive.'

'What about the other flatmate? Tabitha Smart . . .' Becky looks stunned, suddenly, as if a bright light has just flashed in front of her eyes. 'Not *the* Tabitha Smart? I wondered earlier, but I dismissed it . . .'

Eddie frowns. 'The BBC weather girl?' The name hadn't registered with him when he'd skimmed through the file.

Allan chuckles. 'That's her. Bit of a colourful personal life, that one. She moans about her privacy but she can't do such stupid things and not expect the press to latch onto it.' He shakes his head. 'Can never understand why people want to be celebrities.'

Becky scribbles something into her notebook. 'The boyfriend,' she says. 'Sebastien Black.'

Allan visibly shudders. 'Slimy character. But there was nothing on him. He was in London the night before the attack. Chrissie was found early in the morning. His alibi stacked up – he was out for dinner with his parents. They were over visiting from the States. Well-to-do couple. Didn't seem any hint of uncertainty that you get when someone is covering up. Waiters at the restaurant backed up his alibi too. He was definitely there. My theory was he'd come back down here late, let himself into the girls' flat in the wee small hours. While they were asleep . . . but it was a hunch, nothing more. No evidence. I had to let him walk.'

Eddie drums his fingers on the table. 'Maybe we'll have another word—'

'Good luck with that,' Allan says, crossing his arms. 'He moved back home right after Chrissie died. Didn't even go to the funeral.'

'And what about Chrissie's family? Her dad . . . her brother? Ruled out fully, I assume?'

Allan uncrosses his arms and leans back in his chair. 'Rob was at home. Alone. But he'd recently been having some issues with his eyesight. Doctor and optician both confirmed that he'd been advised not to drive at night, and it was confirmed that he hadn't taken his car anywhere for a while because we checked it for signs of recent use and found the battery flat as a pancake. As well as that, friends and neighbours confirmed how much he'd loved his daughter. He was never really in the frame. Not for me.'

Eddie frowns. 'What about the son – Colin? What was his story?'

Allan shakes his head. 'Colin was devastated. He'd been doing some freelance work in Edinburgh at the time. Finished a job the day before Christmas Eve, due to drive · back down to spend Christmas with his dad and Chrissie. It tore him up. They'd always been close, by all accounts. Rob was devastated too. One child dead and the other one pushing himself away. It was awful. Just terrible. You know when you just want to go home and hug your family tight and never let them go?'

Becky tries to catch Eddie's eye, but he purposefully looks away.

Eddie stays in the office as late as he possibly can. His mind is whirring, details of his current case mixing in with the photos from the calendar and his curiosity about who might have sent it. He'd sent Becky home at 7 p.m. She'd wanted to stay longer, work with him on the photographs, but he needed space. He needed to try to work out if this was connected to him, or if it was just a strange coincidence. If it was connected to him, then why now? The murder in West London had been ten years ago. His eyes flick up to the large-type calendar hanging on the wall next to the oversized clock – no excuse for not knowing the time or date in this office. 17th December. Does that mean something? Is that the date of his unsolved, from ten years before? He's concerned that he's missed something. Two of his cases. This bloody advent calendar. Was it meant for him? He's done well since he joined CID. He is terrified now, thinking that something he's done or not done might have led to all this. He needs to pull up the case file, but something is holding him back. He remembers most of it anyway.

Judy Dorringer. Aged twenty-one. Barmaid in the North Star, not far from Ealing Broadway train station. He knows which street she lived on. Can picture it clearly in his mind. It wasn't far from where he was living at the time, on his own. Happy with the secondment and in no rush to return home. They'd found her face-down on her sofa, head twisted sharply to one side, glassy eyes staring at them as they walked into the small living room. *EastEnders* blaring out on the TV. Cause of death was asphyxiation. The medical examiner said she'd been suffocated face-down on her newly purchased beige Ikea *Extorp*, bruises on her back from where the perpetrator had knelt on her, finger marks on the back of her neck from where he'd pushed her face into the black and white cushion adorned with the smiling face of Marilyn Monroe.

She had a boyfriend. Working night shift in a call centre, air-tight alibi. The alarm had been raised when she'd failed to turn up for her late shift on Thursday night. She'd been spotted earlier on the store camera in Morrisons, left the shop at 5.57 carrying two carrier bags, a baguette sticking out of one and a bottle of white wine out of the other. The shopping had been on the table when the first officer on the scene had tried the front door and found it unlocked. The wine was warm. A tub of Ben & Jerry's chocolate fudge brownie melted and leaking into the bottom of the bag. Had someone followed her home? Maybe. There weren't as many CCTV cameras back then. None on her street. No one had seen anything. Broad daylight? Someone who blended in. Someone who she'd felt safe enough to open her door to. Someone who had snuffed her out and walked away.

Why?

That was what bothered him the most. The sheer sense-lessness of it. Nothing had been taken from her flat. Nothing obvious anyway. It had hit Eddie hard.

Because Judy Dorringer looked uncannily like his eldest daughter.

At home, he takes a plate of cheese and crackers and a giant mug of coffee, and shuts himself in his attic office. He spends most of his time here, these days. Even when there's no one else in the house. As well as his desk, he has a sofa bed, his CD player and collection of beloved CDs. He's toyed with the idea of adding in a bathroom and kitchenette so he doesn't have to leave the room at all, except to go to work, but for now he's happy enough as it is. On a clear night, or a warm summer's day, he opens the skylight and sticks his head outside, taking in the view of the rooftops, observing the town as if from the crow's nest of a ship. It's all still going on down there. The drunks, the bullies, the sad little lives. But up here, he's away from it all. Away from the rest of his house, away from the rest of the town.

He spreads the photographs out on the floor. Judy Dorringer right in the middle. It can't be about her. It can't be about him. Can it?

He lays a piece of cheese on a cracker, eats it whole.

Someone has been careful to stay under the radar. But now they want to be seen. And they want him to be the one to see them. Judy Dorringer is a clue. He leans back against the sofa bed. Doesn't realise he's fallen asleep until the vibration of his phone wakes him up.

Sunday

SEVEN MORE SLEEPS

22

BECKY

'No McDonald's this morning, Greene. I'll pick you up in twenty minutes.'

Becky rubs sleep out of her eyes and stumbles through to the bathroom, where she walks in on her dad. Thankfully he's fully clothed and is hanging his towel over the rail, and not naked and climbing out of the bath. She did that once before and she still isn't sure which one of them had been the most embarrassed.

'Pee the bed, did you?' he says. He ruffles her hair and she swats at him.

'Gerroff! Got to go in early today. Just had a call from my new partner.'

'At seven o'clock? Must be important. I don't think I've seen you up before eight since you left school.'

'Funny,' she says. 'Anyway, what are you doing still here? Don't you usually leave at quarter to? Not going to be *late*, are you?'

Her dad has worked at Harry's Audio for longer than she's been alive. Some people think he actually *is* Harry, but the original owner is long gone. He is one of those people who is never off sick, never late, never the slightest smudge against their name. She'd tried to follow in his footsteps, but sometimes the tiredness grabbed her and

119

she'd do anything other than get out of bed. Usually it meant rushing around like a headless chicken and going without breakfast. Hence yesterday's late start and greasy breakfast. She'd kill for one now though. Maybe she can persuade Eddie to go to the drive-thru on the way to wherever it is he's taking her. His voice hadn't given anything away, and he'd cut her off before she could ask any questions.

'You OK, Becks?'

She blinks and realises that her dad is still in the bathroom. The mirror still has pockets of steam misted at the edges. She can smell fruity shower gel and toothpaste.

'Sorry, I was out of it there for a second. I don't think I'm awake yet.'

'Better get on with it then, eh? I doubt they'd be coming to pick you up at this hour to deal with double-parking.'

She rolls her eyes. 'I told you, Dad, I don't work in traffic any more. I'm with the Major Crimes Unit.' She swallows, taking it in herself. She's still new to the department. Sometimes she felt like she was on a film set, and the victims were actors. Sometimes it didn't feel real. That assault at the weekend had been real though. That could've been her or any of her friends at the college. It was only a couple of years ago when she'd been spilling out of the Union late at night, looking for the next party. Look at her now.

'Get yourself sorted, Becks. Do a good job.' He kisses her on the cheek and she hears the creak of every stair as he thumps down the staircase. Someone's going to fall right through one of those stairs, one of these days. The house that her parents bought when they got married in 1986 seems to have been made entirely from plasterboard and plywood. She's surprised the thing hasn't blown away. But it's like all of these estate houses built back then, with their identical layouts and shoebox-sized bedrooms. Worn but still standing.

Which is exactly how she feels, right now.

She turns the shower on, turns it up to the hottest it'll go, even though she knows that means that the last person in line will have to deal with a lukewarm trickle, drops her T-shirt and knickers on the floor and steps into the steam.

He says nothing when she gets into the car. He drums his fingers on the steering wheel as they sit at the lights. She waits, until she can't wait any more. 'So, is it a good morning, or a shit morning, or a—'

'If you've eaten, I hope it's fully digested.'

She's starting to get used to his moods, even after less than twenty-four hours of working with him. Ignore, don't provoke. 'Are you going to tell me where we're going?'

The lights change, at last, and he revs the engine too hard and they shoot across the roundabout towards the edge of town. Past the 'All Routes' sign that people need to follow to find their way out of the one-way system and back onto a road that actually goes somewhere.

'We're going to the Appleford Estate. You know it?'

'I don't think so.'

'Edmonton Avenue. Number six.'

He lets it hang, but she's already there. One of the

empty doors on the advent calendar. 'Number six. Right. What's happened?'

'UPS driver found a body. At home. No sign of a break-in. Chris Hardy. Works in IT. Thirty-five. Girlfriend, but he hasn't been with her long.'

They shoot through two mini roundabouts and turn left into an estate not unlike her own. Lots of beige, boxy houses. Perfectly straight lawns, roll-up garages. They look newer than her house, but the feeling is the same. Outside, on the driveways, frosted cars sit waiting. Some already have exhaust fumes belching out into the cold morning air, people trying to defrost their cars so they can take the kids to school or get to work, unaware that one of their neighbours will never have to defrost his car ever again. They drive along a street where the houses are bigger, given a bit of flourish. They look newer. Fresher. Around the corner, back to the same little boxes.

It's obvious which one is number six.

They pull up across the road and Eddie winds down his window again to stop the car fogging up. Frosty air fills their space, and she wishes she'd worn a thicker jumper. Several cars are parked outside, partly blocking the street. Crime scene tape has been hung a bit too loose, like a Christmas garland. The delivery van is parked behind the other cars. She can see the face of the man sitting inside, staring out unhappily. Wondering if he can get on with his job today, or is he going to end up working over-time? He doesn't look excited by the prospect of what lies within number six. He just wants it sorted so he can leave.

'So how come you've got all the info?'

'One of the delivery men is the victim's best mate. He noticed this morning that the front door was open, so he went in. Found him lying flat on the living room floor. Out cold, after a heavy night, or so he thought. Until he gave him a gentle kick and a trickle of blood came out of his mouth. He called 999 straight away. Operator said he was near hysterical on the phone.'

'Not a suspect, then?'

A car door slams and a uniformed officer climbs out. Jogs towards them, puffing out clouds of icy breath. He appears at Eddie's side, pops his head inside.

'Morning, Ed,' he says. The familiarity indicates that he knows Eddie well enough not to have to ask him for his ID, but Eddie pulls it out of his pocket anyway, then taps the edge of Becky's seat, suggesting that she should do the same. A formality, but one best dealt with. They don't want any gaps in procedure to trip them up later on.

'Shane,' Eddie says. 'How is he?' The uniform glances back towards the car he's just left, and Becky notices another man in the back seat. They've been chatting to the friend. The usual set-up. Comfort them, but find out what they know.

'He's a mess. The victim is his best friend. They've known each other since primary school. The vic— Chris Hardy, he works from home. Runs his own IT business. Taught himself online, after messing up at school. His friend – Malcolm Matthews – he sounded so proud of him. Held him in high esteem. Says he always knocked on the door when he came round this way. Pretty much every day, especially at this time of year. Hardy always gave him a sausage roll to take away with him. A ritual they'd had since Hardy started his company. This morning, when he went to knock on the door, he found it already open. He suspected his friend had had a late night – he'd texted him around eight, saying he was planning a few beers – but he said as soon as he saw him lying there, he knew something was off.'

'Christ. Poor guy. Did he see anything that looked out of the ordinary? Out of place?'

'He says no, but obviously you'll want to talk to him yourself. Duty pathologist is in there now.'

'Preliminary findings?'

'Blunt force trauma . . . he's not finished yet. But he suggested maybe a house brick? There's a lot of building work going on nearby.'

Eddie opens the car door and the uniform takes a step back to let him out. 'Any bricks lying around looking guilty?'

The uniform shakes his head. 'Nope, 'fraid not. I'm guessing whatever it was, the perp took it with them.' He bends down, removing his paper booties.

'Right. Cheers, Shane. Come on, Becky.'

She's already out of the car. Slams the door shut and heads over towards the house. Glances at the other houses nearby. Chris Hardy's house is the end of terrace maisonette, separated from another identical block by the wooden bin store. To the left, the window, which Becky assumes is the kitchen, from the size of it and her knowledge of these types of properties, is in darkness. Clearly no one in, or they'd be in there by now, peering out at the commotion. The next couple of houses along the row have their lights on. Figures in dressing gowns illuminated by the harsh strip-lights. They'll need to start the door-to-door. First though, she wants to see the scene.

'Slow down, Linford.' Eddie's footsteps behind her.

She stops at the front door. A sudden wave of fear hits her stomach. This is a crime scene, remember. A man is dead. 'My dad says that,' she says. Her voice feels small. She remembers her dad's words. 'Do a good job.' He hates her doing this. She knows he does.

Eddie senses her discomfort. Tosses her a folded Tyvek suit. Squeezes her shoulder. 'You haven't eaten, have you?'

She shakes her head.

'Good.'

23

CARLY

It's often quiet before lunchtime. You get the odd few stragglers coming in. People who've got nothing better to do and no intentions to buy. This is why Carly used to think it was OK to set up late. But it doesn't work like that. You set up early, then you wait. Sometimes you wait all day. You can never really predict when people will start coming in, and even when they do, you can't predict those who might buy anything. Usually it's the people that you least expect to do something, that do it. That's just people all over.

The weather can be helpful. If it's dry early on, people will leave their houses, head to town, do a bit of shopping or wandering or drinking coffee – whatever it is that they do – and if the weather changes, say, a bit of drizzle, a bit of wind – if they happen to be nearby, and they happen to see the sign . . . 'Craft Fair Today 9–5', then they might just come wandering in. It's those unintentional visitors that often end up buying the most.

Especially at Christmas.

'It's nice to pick up something different,' they say. 'We're trying to do small, thoughtful gifts instead of the big spend this year.'

These are the people that make it worthwhile.

He's set up next to her again today. She knew that he

would. She picks up a pile of promotional postcards and taps them down on the table, lining up the edges.

'Fancy a coffee?' he says now, standing casually at the end of her display table, arms crossed. Watching her. 'Before the post-church rush comes in?'

She laughs at that. 'Ah yes. God-Botherers Day. That lot are notoriously bad for haggling, you know. All that butter-wouldn't-melt stuff is a great cover.' She winks. 'Listen to me, trying to teach my grandmother to suck eggs . . . you've been doing this for years, haven't you.' It's a statement, not a question. He looks amused.

'How do you know how long I've been doing this?'

'I don't. I just assumed. Well – you seem to know what you're doing—'

'You think I'm experienced?'

A tiny tingle starts on the back of her neck. She looks away. Shrugs. 'Maybe. I could be wrong, of course. I have been wrong before.' She turns back to him and their eyes lock together. Just for a moment. Just long enough.

He looks down at the floor and she sees the beginnings of a smirk on his face. It disappears, and he looks serious for a moment. She doesn't want him to change his mind.

'Come on then,' she says. 'There's a place right next door.'

She picks up her cash tin and puts it in her bag. Calls over to the woman selling knitted baby toys further down the aisle. She's knitting now. Handy to have a portable skill. 'Just popping out for a tick . . .'

The woman looks up. 'Both of you?' She tries for an innocent expression but it becomes a bit of a sneer.

Carly ignores her look. 'Thanks, Trish. Get you anything?'

Trish shakes her head, carries on with her knitting. *Clack Clack. Clack Clack.*

'Someone didn't look too happy,' he says. As they walk through the door, a couple of the town's fragrant tramps make an appearance. He guides her out by the elbow. She feels the warmth of his hand and wonders if it was deliberate or instinctive. She doesn't pull away.

'You still bloody in here?' the old woman says. 'Where we supposed to go during the day then, eh? Bloody outrage this.' Lady Margaret, they call her. No one is quite sure if she's a real 'Lady' or not. Hard to tell if those jewels she wears are real or fake, if her stinking coat is faux fur or a couple of dozen tragic minks. No one asks. Carly has a feeling it is real, and despite the value of the jewels, she won't sell them for her own pride. She doesn't even know if the woman is really homeless, or just as mad as a box of frogs and a stranger to a bar of soap. Lady Margaret is just Lady Margaret, and she has been for as long as Carly can remember.

'We're here until next week. Trish told you that when you came in yesterday.'

The man that she's with – another one that has existed in the town since the dawn of time – mutters something and disappears back outside. He walks with a strange lolloping gait, as if he has one leg longer than the other. Lady Margaret just sighs and shakes her head. Carly holds her breath to avoid the fetid cloud of air that has invaded their space.

He's not so lucky.

'Jesus,' he says. Carly laughs.

'You know, I don't think you even told me your name?'

'I didn't. And you didn't tell me yours. Do you think we should exchange them now, or retain that air of mystery?'

'I'm CeeCee,' Carly says.

'Of course,' he says. 'The logo on your postcards. I'm Caleb.'

'All the Cs . . .' She lets her sentence trail off. She doesn't even know what she was going to say next.

He nods. A look passes across his face that she can't read, and Carly finds herself lost for words. They walk to the coffee shop in silence. She's doubting herself now, just a bit. Is he interested or not? Hard to tell. Maybe he's one of those who doesn't like to share things about himself. Maybe he's got something shit going on in his life and he's trying to get through it. It would explain the silences. The expressions. Like he's got something on his mind. But she doesn't know him, and she can't push it.

She decides that she needs to do all the talking.

In the café, she directs him to a table at the back while she goes to get them their drinks. His order is simple – black coffee. Nothing else. She goes for her usual skinny latte and one of the small chocolates that they keep in a jar on the counter. She comes in here a lot, whether she's doing a fair or not. She has to do something to break up the monotony of her days. Thankfully, the owner, Eliza, who knows everything and misses nothing, is on holiday right now. Three weeks in the States, visiting family. Lucky cow. She's left a variety of people in charge. She doesn't trust one person enough to leave them alone for the whole time. She's one of those deeply suspicious people who envision disasters that never happen. But she's in Florida, and Carly is stuck here with all the usual shit of her life, so what does it matter if she's a paranoid conspiracy theorist? She's glad Eliza isn't here right now, that's the main thing. She doesn't want any questions about Caleb until she knows exactly what she's dealing with. In fact, she's not even convinced it's his real name. But then, she did tell him she was called CeeCee – although it's not technically a lie: it is the name of her little business. But he'd already noticed that.

'You OK, Caleb?' she says. She pushes the mug of coffee towards him but he's still staring out of the window.

'Is this where you usually come, is it? Is this where all the local gossip gets discussed?'

Carly blows on her coffee and takes a sip. 'Technically, yes, but the Gossiper-in-Chief is on holiday at the moment, so it's a bit quieter on that front.' She scans the small room, sees people engrossed in newspapers or their phones. A couple of people have their eyes closed. Resting or sleeping, she can't tell.

'You look a bit tired, that's all,' she says. Takes another sip.

He rips the tops off three packets of white sugar and tips them into his mug. 'Didn't sleep that well, actually.'

She nods. Takes another sip.

Right.

'It's nice to have coffee with someone, you know. I usually come in here on my own. Yes, it's good to talk to Eliza, find out the latest happenings. But it's not real, you know? We don't really have proper conversations. I don't really tell her stuff. Stuff about me, I mean. I don't really have anyone to tell that to.'

He frowns. 'Surely you have family? Friends? Woman like you . . . I don't quite buy it.'

He doesn't mean it unkindly. At least she assumes he doesn't. But she feels a tear start to itch in the corner of her eye. She sniffs it away.

'My kids are grown up now. They've got their own lives. The youngest is seventeen . . . and, well, my husband isn't around much. I swear he's going to leave me the minute she turns eighteen. It's only a few weeks away. 31st of December. She was a mistake. They all were, actually. He barely speaks to me any more.'

If he's uncomfortable with her launching straight into personal stuff, he hides it well.

'Why would he stay with you if he wasn't happy? Why would you stay with him? I've never really understood that myself—'

'Are you married, Caleb?'

The heavy cloud passes across his face again.

'No,' he says. He drains his coffee. Grimaces.

Carly knows the coffee is bitter. That's why she drinks it as a latte.

'We best get back,' he says. Pats her hand. Gentle. Enough to make her shiver.

24

THE PHOTOGRAPHER

I know this is a dangerous game, but I can't help it. I've never had to do it before, and yet it seems to come so naturally. She is so naïve. So trusting. Why does she trust me? A man that she's just met. Just because I've turned up to a fair with a load of artwork – how does she even know that it's mine?

I don't really understand women, but that's only to be expected, I suppose. I haven't had time for a relationship since I started my quest.

It would only complicate things.

Besides, I don't think that this woman wants a relationship. I might not be the best judge of what women want, but I can see that she is lonely. She's on her own in an empty space, and she wants someone like me to fill it.

I feel sorry for using her this way. But then I remember what it is that I'm doing, and I have to carry on. She senses something though. I need to be more careful.

But I am tired. Not just because I don't have a proper place to sleep, but that's part of it, I know. It takes it out of me, the killing. If you haven't done it before, you can't possibly imagine the intense rush of adrenaline that murdering someone releases. Then when it leaves the bloodstream, there's that bone-weary tiredness that hits you. Knocks you right out. But you don't wake up refreshed. You don't forget what you've done. Even if you truly believe that you've done it for the right reasons.

You can see them. Their faces burned into your retinas, there to haunt you every time you close your eyes. You don't even need a photograph to remember them by. But you take them anyway. And you develop the film. Because you need to remember.

You can never forget.

I zone her out, as she witters away about the owner of the café. Then she starts to talk about her family, and I have to show an interest. It's a real interest though, so it's not hard. I actually do need to know what I'm dealing with here.

Sometimes I catch a glimpse of her looking at me when she thinks I won't notice. She thinks I am gazing out of the window, but I can see her reflection. Her sad expression, despite the smiles.

I wonder if I can bring myself to sleep with her, or if it would just complicate things even further. I've never had to do it like this before. Get to know them. But she's different. She's not like the others.

She wasn't picked at random.

Maybe I *should* do it, just for the fact that it's probably the last ever time I might get the opportunity to be with a woman.

'You look tired,' she says.

I smile and pat her hand. If only she knew why.

25

BECKY

She's glad to be away from the crime scene. The pizza box on the table, the games console still switched on. A small artificial tree in one corner, lopsided and sparsely decorated with cheap baubles and a couple of home-made figurines, like the kind of thing that the Scouts and the Girl Guides used to hawk around the doors when she was a kid. A man with his life snuffed out, meaningless detritus surrounding him. She'd tried not to look at the body, but it was hard to avoid it in the small living room.

Attending these things is not a part of her work that she enjoys. She feels detached, like she is watching a play, that none of it is real. It's the way she's dealt with things ever since she joined, because she knows that if she starts to think too much about it all, she won't be able to do the job at all.

It's always been the puzzle element that has attracted her to this line of work.

Who. What. Where. When. Why.

Mainly the why. She used to think she wanted to be a criminologist. Focus on the why. But she knew it wouldn't be enough. She wanted the who, too. She wanted justice. It was probably a bit of youthful naïvety, but she felt like with every person that was caught and convicted, justice was served for everyone who had ever been a victim. Even the ones whose assailants had never been caught.

Especially for them.

She understood why people got themselves involved in their own methods of justice. Revenge. Vigilantism. Maybe it was the only way to get closure, for some people.

She decided to take the legal route. It's working out fine, so far.

'So,' Eddie says. On one board, next to the list of victims from the advent calendar, he's pinned up all the crime scene photographs. On the board next to that, smiling images of the most recent victims, Chris Hardy and Linda Hollis. Next to them, he's pinned *their* crime scene photographs, a map showing where they both lived and a list of names of people they've already spoken to. 'This is where we are. As you can see, we've spoken to a lot of people about Linda, and we've come up with absolutely zilch. Door-to-door is ongoing for Chris, but so far nothing more than we already knew – that his mate is a delivery man, that he works at home, that he's got a fairly new girlfriend . . .' he pauses, points to her name and underlines it with a green marker pen, 'Ange Goldsmith. She's thirty-one. Teacher at St Jude's. Night out with the girls last night. Had planned a quiet day today. She was about to go to Hardy's when PC Roberts and Sergeant Davidson arrived at her house to deliver the bad news. Someone will need to follow up. Get an interview arranged.'

'Is she a suspect, Sir?' Jay Osborne interrupts. 'The significant other is always suspicious, aren't they? Should we speak to her friends, make sure she was with them last night—'

'Yes, thank you, Jay,' Eddie cuts off the young DC before she can babble any more. 'Obviously everyone is a potential suspect until we've ruled them out. But in this case, I'm confident that she's not had anything to do with it. Mainly because Hardy had the kind of neighbours who watched every coming and going, and they said they hadn't seen her arrive the night before. However, there *is* a gap, which might turn out to be something, might be nothing. The neighbour across the road, Mr Marland, says he was in his shed from about six to eight last night, so he couldn't be sure that someone hadn't arrived during that time.' He pushes a hand through his hair. Shakes his head. 'It would drive me mental to have neighbours spying on me like that.'

'It's like that at ours,' Becky says. 'It makes me feel safe.'

'Safe? Don't you get fed up with everyone knowing your business?'

She shrugs. 'Rather that than feel like I was alone.'

She feels the collective weight of the stares of everyone in the team and wishes she hadn't opened her mouth. She was about to tell them all that was why she liked staying at home, but luckily she managed to stop before she made an arse of herself. TMI, as they say. Too Much Information.

Eddie looks like he is about to say something else, when he is interrupted by another DC, Deborah Bell, looking as small and pale as usual. Becky hadn't noticed her coming in. *The Ghost*, they called her, as she always seemed to appear somewhere without making a sound, which was ironic, given her name. 'Sorry, Eddie,' she says, 'Malcolm Matthews is here. I've put him in the Sunshine Suite.'

That had made her laugh when she'd first started. The names of the interview rooms. They'd named them after weather forms, thinking it might make them sound less tedious, or less menacing or maybe they were just having a laugh to break up the boredom of it all, but Becky liked it.

'OK,' Eddie says. 'Jay and Leo, carry on with neighbour follow-ups. Davidson and Bell, you're to work with forensics, see what they've got. Greene?'

'Yes, Eddie?'

'You're with me.'

The Sunshine Suite is the nicest of the bank of interview rooms, usually reserved for witnesses rather than out-and-out suspects. Or, as Becky had realised, for anyone that didn't disgust the custody sergeant. Malcolm Matthews is sitting in the chair, a plastic cup of coffee cooling in front of him. His eyes are red-rimmed, and despite his obvious size, he appears shrunken.

Becky switches on the recorder and they introduce themselves.

'I just can't believe it,' Malcolm says. His voice breaks. Becky hands him a tissue. She wants to walk around to his chair and envelop him in a hug. She can feel the emotion radiating from him across the table. Either he is a very accomplished actor, or he is a man feeling intense, raw grief at the death of his best friend. Becky is going with the latter.

'Can you tell us what happened, Malcolm,' Eddie says. 'I know you told another officer when they arrived at the house, but we'd like you to tell us, please. If that's OK? Can we get you anything?' Eddie nods at the coffee cup. 'Another drink? Something to eat?'

Malcolm shakes his head. 'Thing is, I was going round last night. He'd just downloaded the latest version of *Call of Duty* and he said it was the dog's, know what I mean? Only, I've got a little kiddie now, Alice. The wife likes me to stay in at the moment. She's only six months old. The kid, I mean.' He manages a half-smile. 'She's been knackered. The wife. Patsy. Asked me to stay in with her. I'm not going to argue, am I? I've had plenty of years of going out whenever I please. She fell asleep on my shoulder and I ended up watching *Casualty* by myself. I hate that programme, too. Couldn't seem to turn it off.'

Eddie shuffles in his seat. 'So your wife—'

'Patsy.'

'Patsy. She was asleep from, what, seven? Is that right?'

Malcolm nods. 'That's right. She was asleep on me. Lying on the couch, head on my lap. I had the baby monitor next to me. Baby didn't stir. I think I must've fallen asleep too, because the next thing I know it's *Mrs Brown's Boys* and I'd never have switched that crap on myself.'

Becky tries to work out what Eddie is thinking. Is he trying to verify this alibi? Surely he can't think that Malcolm would've gone out and left his sleeping wife and child, popped round to his best mate's house, got over-excited at a bit of on-screen combat, cracked him over the head and got back in time to watch *Mrs Brown's Boys*? There was no way Malcolm had done anything. Sometimes instinct told you all you needed to know. Plus, Malcolm had a home-security cam at his front door. It showed the whole driveway. No one had entered or left the house after six o'clock. They already knew this. They'd had it checked when Malcolm had been driven home that morning and Sergeant Shane Walsh had spotted it.

'Tell us what happened when you got to Chris's house,' Eddie says.

Malcolm looks down at the table. At his hands. The knuckles white, gripping on as if he fears he's going to fall. Fall into a dark place that he might never get out of. Becky has seen this reaction before.

'The door was open. It's never open. I knew . . . I just knew something bad had happened. You see it on the telly, don't you? *Crimewatch*, that sort of thing. The door left ajar . . . he was my best mate.' He lets go of the table, balls his hands into fists. 'He was my best mate.'

Eddie leans across the table and places his hands over the man's fists.

'I know,' he says. 'I know.'

26

CARLY

It doesn't matter how many things she carries on the stall, there will always be someone who wants something she doesn't have. Usually she just tells them that there are none left, but when someone practically begged for one more of the glazed green salad bowls because it would look nicer her long table, Carly decided to use the opportunity to get away for a bit. She'd overshared to Caleb when they'd had their coffee, and his fleeting but intense stares were making her feel a bit wobbly.

Luckily Hilda had agreed to keep an eye on her stall. Again.

Carly told the customer that she'd be back in half an hour, but the landline rings just as she's about to head out the front door. She considers ignoring it, but she knows it will either be someone ringing about PPI or a car crash she's never had, or more likely, her mother. She'd prefer a PPI spammer at this point, or maybe one of those call centres in India where they tell you your computer's got a virus and they need your details so they can fix it for you. Her instinct says it's her mother, and she hasn't got it in her to ignore the call and deal with the barrage. She slumps down on the chair next to the phone and lifts the receiver. She likes the look of the old Bakelite phone, but having to sit right next to it to take a call makes her feel more trapped than she could ever have imagined.

'Hello?' She can hear the harassed, dejected tone of her own voice in that single word.

'Darling! So glad I caught you. Have you got a minute?'

'Mum . . . sorry, I'm just about to—'

Her mother continues to launch full into the conversation, oblivious to anything Carly might have been going to say. It is always like this. The only way to cut this short is to hang up and pretend there's a problem with the phone line, but she'll only phone straight back, and she'll keep phoning until she gets hold of her. Then she will talk until she has said everything she wants to say, and right at the end of the conversation, Carly will attempt to say something and her mother will say she is busy and hang up.

This is the way it has always been, and this is the way it will always be.

Carly listens with half an ear, already running late and starting to worry about leaving the stall for so long. The other stallholders notice this kind of thing, and they don't like it. Who knew there was so much politics involved in arts and crafts?

'. . . so I was thinking beef wellington, with that nice mushroom pâté that your dad makes with the *Shiitake* from his cellar . . . you know how he loves to feel like he's involved! Plus, Noelle loves mushrooms, doesn't she? Or has she gone off them again? You know what teenagers are like. You were a nightmare back then, chopping and changing your likes and dislikes willy-nilly . . . I was thinking about making a passion fruit pavlova for afters,

I've been practising meringues at my WI classes. Did I tell you I was in the WI now? I know you probably think it's for old ladies, but . . .'

Carly covers the mouthpiece with her hand and lets out a long slow sigh. Then she smiles. Sits up straight. A trick she'd learned when she'd worked as a PA for a while, before Simon was born. It was a mundane, tedious job, but she'd discovered that if you smile and make yourself sound interested, the caller can sense it and the whole phone call is a much more pleasant experience for both parties.

'That all sounds perfect, Mum—'

Maybe she didn't say that out loud, because her mother has either not heard it, or completely ignored it.

'. . . Marion and Keith are coming round in the evening, so I'll have some nibbles prepped for that. Veronica and Kristof are both overseas this year, leaving their poor parents all alone – can you imagine that? We're so lucky to have you near us, aren't we, darling? I suppose that man of yours will be working on Boxing Day, will he? I'm assuming you're staying over at least? Darling? Are you still there?'

Carly's active listening method isn't working. She switched off at the mention of the awful Keith and Marion. No wonder their children were spending Christmas elsewhere this year. If Carly could've managed that, she would. Things were a mess right now and they weren't getting any better. She wasn't going to tell her mother any of that though.

'We'll all be staying, yes. Probably until the twenty-eighth, if that's OK with you? Fiona and Simon are going away for New Year. Noelle will be at home with us. She's not really into the New Year celebrations, and we're happy

enough to spend it with her and watch it on the TV . . .'
She stops talking, sensing that her mother isn't listening.
The irony.

'Got to go, darling. See you all next week. I'll phone
you again if I need you to bring anything, but I think it's
all under control.'

Click.

She hangs up before Carly can say anything else.

There's no doubt that Christmas at her parents' is all
under control. She's not even sure what the point of the
call was, other than something that her mother does so
that she can add it to her list of daily tasks, in order to
tell people how busy she is. Carly's surprised there's time
for the WI, what with the volunteering in the Cancer
Research and helping with Meals on Wheels, dealing with
the household accounts (because her father, who spent
thirty-five years running his grandfather's company, is
apparently 'no good with that sort of thing').

She feels exhausted all of a sudden. She can't face going
back to the market now. Can't face Caleb. She was the
one who'd offered the apple, but now that he seems to
have bitten, she's starting to get cold feet. All the family
talk from her mother drilling it home to her. The call has
deflated her.

She takes her mobile out of her handbag. He's at the
top of her recent calls list, followed by her children, in
reverse chronological order. The youngest does still like
speaking to her, thankfully. The others seem to tolerate
her. Just like he does. He answers straight away, but he
sounds distracted.

'I'm right in the middle of something. Can I call you back?'

She hangs up and shouts, 'Fuck,' into the walls of the empty house. 'Screw this,' she says. Kicks off her shoes and wanders through to the kitchen. She flicks on the radio just as Kirsty MacColl is calling Shane McGowan a cheap lousy faggot. That line always makes her smile. She remembers Simon's earnest little face asking her when he was about five years old, covered in flour from helping her bake gingerbread men, 'Mummy, what's a *flaggot*?' It was a family joke now, that word. Not that there was much in the way of joking these days.

She opens the cupboard next to the dishwasher. Two shelves, full of bottles, cans and giant packs of crisps and nuts. It's just after ten thirty. Even in the run-up to Christmas, there is no justification for drinking wine, alone, at this time of day. She rummages. Spots a bottle of Baileys at the back.

Just a splash. To relax her. It's not like it's *gin* or something. It's barely alcoholic. It's just a nice little Christmassy drink.

That's all it is.

She takes a sip. Texts Hilda:

> *Something's come up.
> Please can you put my
> stuff in your lock-up with
> yours? I'll make it up to
> you. Hugs, CCx*

She fills up the glass.

27

THE PHOTOGRAPHER

It has not made any of the news website homepages. I've scrolled and clicked through all the crap in the *Sun*, the *Mirror*, the *Express*, the *Mail*. I didn't bother with *The Times*. I'm not paying unless it's going to be there and I can tell that it isn't. The *Sun* and the *Mirror* both have a small section about it on the bottom of the sidebar, jumbled in with celebrity nonsense and clickbait adverts. *Man found dead at home by bin men*. Police investigating. It's all very vague and there is no mention of it being linked to another suspicious death that happened just over a fortnight ago in the same town. Are they really so stupid that they haven't linked it yet? Or are they deliberately downplaying it to avoid upsetting the public? I wonder if they'll get me in the Christmas edition of the local paper? At this rate they'll miss the deadline.

I feel like marching into the police station with the murder weapon in my hand, telling them to go on the bloody Internet and read the stupid little article. Shouting at them. Telling them: IT'S ME, IT'S ME! But knowing my luck they'll dismiss me as a crank and throw me out on the street.

This is not how it was supposed to be. *Oh Merlyn . . . why don't you talk to me? Why can't you help me? I have*

*these spinning, jumbling thoughts and I wonder if I am
doing the right thing after all.*

They were supposed to open that calendar and fall into
an instant state of panic and terror. I'd expected a press
conference by now, the Chief Super in full regalia, 'We
are taking this very seriously. The public are in danger.'
Eyes imploring the camera. 'We urge people not to open
their doors to anyone that they don't know. Even if you
think it might be someone completely innocent, a charity
collector, for example. We do not yet know how this
person is gaining access to homes, but we urge the public
to be vigilant.' Flashing cameras. Questions from eager
reporters. 'No further questions at this point. We will let
you know when we know more.' Oz the Great and
Powerful disappearing back behind the velvet curtain, his
grim-faced munchkins following close behind.

I've been dreaming of this moment for so long, and
they've let me down. I thought that my plan would spur
them into action. That they'd see that there was something
to be investigated. Not just another load of cold cases,
chucked in the back of a filing cabinet and left there to
disintegrate. I'm sick of it. Tired of it all. I want them
to re-open your investigation, but the more I do to get
their attention, the more frustrated with it all I become.

Are they even investigating the calendar at all?

I take the house brick from the plastic bag and lay it
on the table. It's one of those creamy-beige ones that are
currently in vogue. I prod it with my finger, swivelling it
around. One of the ends has been stained dark with blood.
A few hairs are present. It looks like someone has dabbed

them on with glue. A gruesome Christmas decoration. Needs a bit of glitter to liven it up a bit. I unleash a strange giggle that makes me feel instantly sad.

I take the brick over to the sink, drop it into the basin of hot water and bleach that I prepared earlier. The chemicals sting my eyes. I put on a pair of Marigolds and take a fresh scourer. Rub and rub until bits of sandy residue are floating in the water. But no matter how long I scrub it for, the dark stain remains.

At least the hair is gone, and, presumably, any trace of my fingerprints.

I'd thought about burying the brick, but where? This is not my house. Plus, the garden will be rock solid. No one digs their garden in December, especially the type of people who live in a house like this.

I drink the dregs of my coffee and throw the mug into the filthy sink. The brick is drying on the drainer. The black stain mocking me. I stare out at the frosty back garden. At the piles of long-discarded building supplies down the bottom, propped against the dilapidated shed. It's so obvious now.

I must leave them another clue.

I take a black marker pen from my bag and write the number 6 on the side of the brick. Perfect. I walk to the Appleford Estate, coming in at a different direction than before so that when I arrive, I am forced to pass 6 Edmonton Avenue. Crime scene tape flutters in the breeze. A police car is parked outside, but the house is in darkness. No sign of life behind the windows. I keep my collar up, walk past quickly, taking in as much as I can of the

scene without drawing attention to myself. Around the
corner, at the section where they are still building, piles
of creamy-beige bricks sit, wrapped in clear tarpaulin,
ripped and flapping in the breeze. The ground is covered
with a thin layer of frost. Bending down as if to tie my
shoelace, should anyone happen to notice, I tip the brick
out of the plastic bag and kick it gently until it is as close
to the others as I can manage without walking onto the
site. There are men around, high-vis jackets and hard
hats, pushing wheelbarrows, shouting at each other across
the site. No one notices me. I walk away.

I am invisible.

28

EDDIE

Eddie had hoped they might've made more progress on the cold cases, found something to help them prevent another murder, but it hasn't worked out like that. While the forensics team continue to work on the Chris Hardy murder, he needs to find out what else has turned up over the last twenty-four hours. He assembles the team for another quick briefing, noticing that any previous reticence has left the building.

Nick has taken notice now. Given Eddie access to a larger team. They can hardly keep denying that there is something big going on. Two murders in just over two weeks. No suspects. Both with house numbers that fit with the missing numbers on the advent calendar. It's too much of a coincidence. He's assigned officers to follow up with Ange Goldsmith, Chris Hardy's girlfriend. The cold case teams are fully engaged.

There can't be any doubt now. It's all connected.

'Right,' Eddie says. He claps his hands and the assembled team falls silent. 'What've we got?'

Keir Jameson speaks first. 'Nothing on the photographers-going-round-houses angle, unless you actually had me and Joe down for visiting every house

149

within a two-hundred-mile radius . . . *but*, I did have another idea. I ran it past Becks, earlier—'

'I think we're on to something here,' Becky cuts in. She nods at Jameson and he gestures for her to go ahead. 'The photography idea is significant.' She walks to the front and turns to face the team. 'The scenes in the calendar are very close, if not identical to the crime scenes that Ashlie has matched them with. Most of them were an easy hit. They're clear, good quality images. Some of them are a spot-on match. It seems like not only does this person know how to take a professional photograph, they know how to take a professional photograph of a crime scene—'

'Almost as if they've been trained,' Eddie says.

'Exactly,' Keir says. 'We're looking into a list of freelance photographers who've been registered as crime scene photographers. Problem, as usual, is anything that happened ten years ago or more isn't necessarily easy to find.'

'Good work,' Eddie says. 'What else?'

'I think the Christmas thing is really important,' Becky says.

'No shit,' someone mutters from the back of the room. Eddie scowls in the general direction but doesn't let it stop Becky's train of thought. 'Go on . . .'

'Obviously we've got the calendar, and the time of year – all the murders happening in the run-up to Christmas. But there's something more. I don't know what yet. I keep seeing weird decorations. Home-made ones. Maybe I'm just hyper aware, I don't know. But I was thinking too . . . Christmas markets. Loads of towns have them on, don't they? Someone could travel from place to place, doing markets here, there and everywhere. It wouldn't be unusual. A photographer selling prints is a pretty common sight in those places. They could pop up in any town at any of the markets and no one would think anything of it.'

Eddie scribbles on the whiteboard. 'Good. Excellent work. Deborah – can you look into this? Let's stick with the two-hour drive radius for now. Let's see if we can match market dates to the dates of the murders. If we can put our man in these towns, we've got a solid link between them. Well, maybe not quite solid. More like a packed snowball than an icicle – but it's definitely a start. Keep us updated.

'OK. Me and Becky are going to follow up with the Thackers. We've spoken to the DI from the case, verified the case file. The plan is to talk to Chrissie's dad and brother again, see if we can shake a few pine needles off the tree.'

Becky laughs. 'You're starting to enjoy the festive analogies, Sir.'

He gives her a half-smile.

'Tasks are on the board. If anyone finds themselves without much to do, give yourself a kick up the backside and let's get on with this.'

29

EDDIE

Eddie picks up his car keys from the tray on the desk he's been using. He gestures to Becky with a nod of his head. She fumbles about in the bottom drawer of her desk, unlocking it, pulling out her bag, locking it. He's clicking his fingers. Doesn't even realise he's doing it. Miriam shoots him a look from behind the ridiculous pink tree that she has plonked on the end of her desk. He stops clicking. Just one of those things he does when he's anxious or, in this case, excited.

Becky stands up. Her face is slightly flushed from being upside down. 'Don't you want to take a pool car?'

'I promise I'll find some better music.'

As they walk out of the room, he throws the keys at her and she plucks them out of the air.

'Impressive.'

'I was St Jude's senior rounders champion for four consecutive years. Am I driving?'

'Is that true?'

She unlocks the car. Answers him with a smirk. She hands him the printout from Ashlie with the address of Chrissie Thacker's father. Her mother, she found out from the report, died when Chrissie was seven. 'You know where this is?'

Eddie nods.

While she's adjusting her seat, checking the mirrors, he switches on the radio to his usual channel and the unmistakable sound of The Smiths starts up. 'I Started Something I Couldn't Finish'. He recognises it from three bars.

They pull out of the car park. 'This is better?'

'Are you kidding? This is a classic.' He turns it up. *Typical me*, Morrissey laments. Yep. 'So Ashlie came up with the goods then?' He's reading the printout. Glances up. 'Head for the War Memorial. It's not far from there.'

'She's great, isn't she? One left and she's already dated it without a match. So we can be pretty sure that Chrissie is our first victim. Do you think we should've phoned first? Made sure someone was in?'

'Probably. But we don't really have the time to muck around here, do we? We don't know if our man is about to strike again or not. I suspect he probably is. I can't see why he would decide to send us that calendar and then not carry on. Classic escalation. He's coming to the end of it. He wants us to catch him. He's enjoyed staying undetected for all these years. Getting away with it. But he's had enough. It's nineteen years since the first one. In fact . . .' He pauses, looks out of the window, as if he's forgotten where they are. 'Turn right at Homebase. Chrissie Thacker was killed on Christmas Eve. I'm sure there's something significant about that. That's the trigger. Find out what went on there, and we're on track.'

'Ah, I know where we are now,' Becky says. She turns right, then left. Past a grim-looking pre-fab school and a small parade of run-down shops. 'I had a friend from school who lived over this way. I know it sounds bad, but I hated going to her house. Not that there was anything wrong with it, but the streets round here, I don't know. There's something nasty about them.'

'They weren't this bad twenty years ago. Believe it or not, this estate was fairly new then. It was actually quite nice.' He realises that he's not been here for years. Nothing has brought him here. The houses used to be white, but now they're grey. The postcard-sized lawns have been concreted over and turned into driveways, but even that's not enough. The streets are littered with cars. It's just gone 5 p.m. People get back from work early round here. If they work at all. Everyone seems to have a car though, whether they need it or can afford it, it seems.

There is little sign of Christmas cheer on this joyless estate, until they turn the corner. The house at the far end of the cul-de-sac is more than enough Christmasness for anyone. Neon Santa and his sleigh are on the roof, along with reindeers, a snowman and a tree. Lights are strung around every window, and all through the branches of the bare silver birches that separate their garden from next door's.

'Bloody hell,' Eddie says. 'The electric bill . . .'

They pull up next to number forty-seven. Outside, the air is tingling with a frosty wind. The storm is on its way.

'There's a house like that on our road. People drive round from all over the place to see it. Take photos. The family collect donations for charity,' Becky says. She's zipped up her coat and pulled up the fur-lined hood, even though they are only walking about ten feet to the front door. She has her hands deep in her pockets.

'You look a bit like that elf.'

'I'd slap you for that, but I'm too cold.'

Eddie knocks on the door.

'I could've looked into the Christmas markets you know,' Becky says. 'After this. I love stuff like that. Could've done some last-minute shopping too . . .'

Eddie groans. 'My wife loves those things too. I can't bear them myself. All that shite that they sell . . .' He hears the sound of a chain being removed. Several locks being turned. Good man, he thinks. People need to take their home security more seriously. It's a pity that the door could probably be opened with one swift kick though, if it had to be.

'Yes?'

The man has one of those faces that could put him at anything from fifty to eighty. He's got an old-man salt-n-pepper clippered haircut and he's wearing a faded Nike sweatshirt that might have been black, once. His eyes are questioning. Someone who doesn't get many visitors? Or someone with something to hide?

'Mr Thacker?' Becky has removed her hood and taken her hands out of her pockets. 'We're with the police. Wondered if we could have a quick word?'

'Got any ID?'

'Of course.' They both take their cards out of their pockets. He takes slightly longer than necessary to examine them, and Eddie is now regretting not putting his coat on. The temperature seems to have dipped since they've been standing here, and it's only been a couple of minutes, if that. 'Do you mind if we come in, Mr Thacker? It's a bit nippy out here—'

He disappears back inside. Eddie glances at Becky and she shrugs. He hasn't shut the door in their face, so presumably this is an invitation.

Inside, the sound of the TV, slightly muffled. Chinks and clatters. Cupboard doors opening, mugs being removed. It's a familiar sound. They walk through the small hallway, follow the sound of the TV. Everything is very clean and neat. Beige, brown and clutterless. Pictures on one wall. Family snaps from a time past. Behind the worn, comfortable looking sofa, a large print of a beach scene with a row of small huts on stilts looks out of place. On the other wall, above the TV stand, a set of three smaller prints. A man in bright-coloured clothes standing next to an elephant. Craggy mountains shrouded in a purple mist. A giant Buddha. Exotic places. A million miles from here.

'I made you tea, hope that's what you wanted. Your lot always want tea.' He appears from the kitchen carrying a tray with mugs and an unopened packet of Cherry Bakewells.

Eddie's stomach does an appreciative flip. 'Spot on, Mr Thacker, thank y—'

'It's Rob. Please . . .' He gestures at the sofa. Becky sits and Eddie follows. He was right about the sofa being comfortable. He sinks into it, can imagine leaning back, drifting off. Pretends for a tiny moment that they've come round to visit an old friend, and that they don't have to ruin the moment by dredging up painful memories from a man who has to live with them every single Christmas.

Rob Thacker seems to read his mind. 'It's OK, son. I'm happy to talk to you about Chrissie. I'm assuming that's why you're here. I thought I'd done all my talking back then, but it never ends, does it? I've had people in and out of here over the years. Fresh faces, new notepads. Every one of them hoping they might find something that'll help us find out who killed her. Not likely though, is it?' He picks up his mug and pours in milk from a little jug. 'Another one of those cold case teams, are you? Go on, help yourself, son . . .' He offers the packet of cakes to Eddie.

Becky shuffles forward and starts dispensing milk and sugar.

Eddie opens the box of cakes and slides one out. 'I'm Detective Sergeant Carmine, and this is Detective Constable Greene. Eddie and Becky. And no, we're not a cold case team, as it happens.' He peels away the edge of the foil and bites off half of the little tart in one.

'Oh?' There is hope in Rob's voice now, and Eddie feels bad for putting it there. They don't have any good news for this man. Not yet. Soon though.

Hope. It's an emotion that you want to keep hold of, but one that can destroy you the most.

'Maybe you can tell us what happened. To Chrissie, I mean. Bring us up to speed.'

'Don't you have all this in the file?' Rob looks suspicious again.

Becky slides out a Bakewell tart from the box and starts

to peel away the foil. 'We do, Rob, but to be honest, it's better for us if you can tell us. We don't want to be influenced by things that others have said . . . it might help us get a fresh perspective on things if you can take us through it. When you're ready. We're not in any rush.'

30

BECKY

Back at her desk, Becky types her password into the computer and opens up Chrissie Thacker's file again. In her absence, someone (presumably Miriam) has sellotaped tinsel around her monitor and hung two small gold bell tree decorations off the top corners. They tinkle as she swivels the monitor back into its correct position and a trailing piece of tinsel slips forward onto the screen. She pushes it away. She's not really in the mood for this now, after talking to Rob Thacker. It takes a lot to rattle her, but seeing the old man's eyes was enough. He's not even that old. Only in his mid-sixties. But the stress of losing first his wife, then his daughter – not to mention his son abandoning him – has taken its toll.

She'd asked him about the photographs in the living room.

'My son took them,' Rob had said. 'He used to enjoy travelling. Not sure where he is now.'

Becky had glanced over at Eddie, wondered if he'd also been curious about the son. Eddie had looked preoccupied, but they'd discussed it in the car. They'd made a note of his name. Colin. Planned to look into him, once they'd dealt with things on the current investigation of

Chris Hardy and Linda Hollis. Nothing that Rob Thacker had said had jumped out as a concern. The murder was nineteen years ago. It had destroyed him, and devastated Colin.

She takes a chocolate ball from the jar that has found its way onto her desk – also Miriam, she presumes – and unwraps the foil. Pops it in her mouth. She scrolls through the pages of the report. Hoping that something might jump out at her and help her find a link to the other murders. Chrissie was found in the kitchen of her shared flat by her flatmate, Tabitha, who had tried to revive her and then called an ambulance. Post-mortem confirmed that she was already dead by the time she was found. There was nothing Tabitha could have done. Becky scribbles on a Post-it pad beside her keyboard: *Call Tabitha Smart.*

Colin, Chrissie's brother, had been working in Scotland at the time of the murder. He'd arrived back the next day, after getting the call from his dad. He'd been very close to his sister. According to Rob, he fell into a deep depression, barely speaking or leaving his room for months afterwards. Then one day, he just upped and left, and Rob had barely seen him since.

Becky remembers the look in Rob's eyes when he had told them that. He'd looked away. Made a show of looking at the photographs, telling them where they were taken.

'This is a beach in Bali. Mountains in China. A Buddha in Thailand. He used to love taking photos, our Colin. Not sure if he still does.'

A fleeting thought crosses her mind, but she pushes it

away. Colin is obviously a talented photographer. Just a coincidence. Lots of people take good holiday photographs. Besides, he wasn't even in the area. His alibi was sound. He'd been interviewed at the time, and there'd been no red flags.

The thing that was bothering her, since she'd gone to the Chris Hardy crime scene, was how the perpetrator was getting into the houses. It appeared that in both cases, Chris Hardy and Linda Hollis, there was no sign of forced entry. They'd willingly allowed the murderer into their homes. Did they know him? Assuming, now, it was a him. The report from the medical examiner had suggested that the injuries sustained were consistent with someone showing extreme power and strength. The vase, in Linda's case, weighed five kilos, and to swing that at the woman's head suggested someone bigger and taller – and the victim was 5'8" and weighed 13st. A strong woman herself, and according to her family, fit and healthy. It was unlikely that another woman could have overpowered her, they said.

'Still hard at it, I see.' Joe plonks himself on a chair and wheels himself over to her. He takes a handful of chocolate balls and starts unwrapping them. 'I've been phoning up the family contacts of the victims and asking if their dead relatives had arranged any photo shoots before they died.' He rolls his eyes. 'Absolutely nothing, obviously. Some of them sounded downright hostile. I think they thought I was a crank caller. Anyway, I can safely say that line's a dead end. How you getting on? Is Eddie going ballistic yet?'

Becky feels like she's missed something. 'Ballistic? No. Why?'

Joe unwraps another chocolate. 'He gets annoyed when there're no leads. Makes him a bit punchy . . . took a swing at Keegan once, you know—'

She raises an eyebrow, and Joe flushes slightly. 'Or so I've heard.'

Becky sighs. 'Don't you get bored spreading mindless gossip? Anyway, seeing as you're here, you could actually help me. I'm still trying to work out how this guy gets into their houses.'

'Jay is doing another door-to-door. Asking if people in the neighbouring streets have been visited by any randoms lately. People selling stuff. Jehovahs. Whatever. Has to be something like that, I reckon.' He squashes all the individual foils into a ball and flicks it across the room. 'What've you got?'

'Nothing. We went to see Rob Thacker. The dad of the first victim, Chrissie. Apart from dredging up the past for the poor bloke again, all we got was a Bakewell tart and a suffocating atmosphere of ennui.' She shakes her head sadly. 'I'm starting to think this job is too dark for me. Maybe I need to join the department that visits school-children and encourages them to lock their bikes.'

Joe laughs. 'Oh, you just reminded me of something . . . there was a Christmas film on Channel 4 last night. I'm not sure if it was meant for kids or not. Kind of sinister, but then I liked that kind of shit when I was little. *Krampus*. Have you seen it? Basically it's about this scary Christmas monster thing who tries to stop this miserable family being so miserable. Or something. One of those weird Christmas traditions. This Krampus fella. We don't have anything like that here, do we? Have you heard about that little log thing they have in Spain that basically shits out presents?'

'Caga Tió. Yes. Christmas folklore. Nice one, Joe.' She stands up and pushes the bowl of chocolate balls across the desk towards him. 'You can have these if you like . . . oh, you've already eaten forty-seven of them.' She rolls her eyes at him. 'If anyone asks, I've gone home to do some research.' She's almost out of the door when she remembers the swear box. 'Oi,' she calls across the room. Joe is busy eating the last of the chocolate. 'Two quid you owe this thing.'

He gives her the finger. 'You can have that one for free.'

As she drives past the church hall, she notices that the door is still open and the lights are still on. Deborah Bell might be looking into the cold cases being linked to markets, but would she think to look at this one? Either way, Becky is curious enough to take a look for herself. Spotting a parking space nearby and taking it as a sign, she pulls in and zips up her coat before getting out of the car.

Storm Hannah is in full rage now. What had started as a flurry of snow has turned into a biting cold wind and a shower of hailstones as big as the chocolate balls that Joe had demolished from her desk. She pulls up her hood, just about losing her car door as she pushes against the wind. She hurries into the church hall, almost colliding with people on their way out, wrapped up in scarves and hats, hoods all but obscuring their faces. The instant heat of the hall turns her from ice to fire in a second, and she feels her cheeks burn in that cosy way that instantly reminds her of coming in from school after playing in the snow on the way home. She understands now, why the hall is so popular with Lady Margaret and her cronies. She drops her hood, walks up the central aisle.

Stops suddenly, glances around. A strange feeling that someone is watching her. She scans the rows of stalls, but everyone is going about their business. She's just a bit jumpy. She's like that sometimes. She walks to the end of the aisle, turns back.

Stallholders are already packing up. The market is almost done for the day. She's not sure what's she's looking for. Joe's mention of Christmas folklore had sparked something in her head, and she planned to go home, make a huge mug of hot chocolate, get under the duvet and start searching for things online, looking for something that might trigger something else. There has to be some connection to Christmas here. The advent calendar . . . and something else. This market isn't inspiring her though, so she might as well come back another day, when she's worked out what it is that she's looking for.

Monday

SIX MORE SLEEPS

31

CARLY

A shaft of light pierces the gap between the curtains and shines straight into her eyes. She squints, turns over and tries to pull one of her thick pillows over her head, but she's not lying on one of those. It's a furry cushion. She opens her eyes. She's not sure if she put the blanket over herself or not. It usually hangs over the back of the couch, so it's not that much of a stretch to imagine that she got cold and pulled it over herself.

Problem is, she can't remember doing it.

Shit.

If the sunlight is this bright, it must be late. Past eight, anyway. She squints at the red digits on the DVD player, but she can't see properly. At least she remembered to take out her contact lenses. She pulls herself up too quickly. The room spins. Something slides about inside her head as if it has come loose. She is scared to move again in case she dislodges it further, another clump of brain cells snapped off and dying. Killed, by their host's own stupidity.

Trying not to move her head, she leans forwards slightly, eyes seeking carnage on the carpet. But there is nothing there, except for a plastic bottle of water, cap still on. The options are: she somehow managed to take the bottles through to the kitchen and hide any evidence of her 'day off', or, and this is more likely, as she is not getting any flashback bursts to suggest otherwise, someone else did it for her.

Shit. Shit. And more fucking shit.

She drags herself through to the kitchen. There is a cereal bowl and a spoon, rinsed and resting on the drainer. She pulls out the recycling bin, crouches down to see what's in there. Empty bottle of Baileys, check. Two empty bottles of Chilean red. Christ. No wonder her head feels like it's been split with an axe.

'Right, Carly,' she says, out loud. She often talks to herself when she's hungover. Which is quite often, these days. She realises that. She's not an idiot.

She's not an alcoholic.

It's just . . . sometimes it's easier just to switch off. Blot it out. Her mother. Christmas. Her family. This year especially. Two weeks left until D-Day. She closes her eyes.

'Don't think about that now,' she says. 'You need to focus. Never mind who cleaned up for you this time. It won't happen again. OK?' She slams the recycling bin back under the sink. 'OK.'

The turns the shower too hot and it stings like burning needles. But it helps. She turns the dial round to cold and gives herself an icy blast. She gasps. Her breath coming out in small, shocked bursts. By the time she's wrapped herself in her towelling robe, she feels better. She rough-dries her hair. Moisturises. As she applies her make-up, slowly, carefully – pausing occasionally when her hand shakes too much – she glances out of the window and watches as the willow in the back garden sways violently. A spatter of hail hits the window like a car churning up gravel, and she flinches. Catches her gaze in the mirror. Tries not to frown at her pale, scared face with the dark-rimmed eyes.

She's arrived early, and her preferred table at the back of the hall is still available. Hilda has left her plastic boxes of stock next to it in a neat pile. The table on the other side is empty.

He is not there.

She feels the irrational need to cry. Blinks hard to stop tears from escaping. He is not here, and so what? She barely knows him. He doesn't owe her anything. They had a brief moment, or maybe it wasn't even that. She is prone to building things up in her head. Obsessing. Building castles when there are nothing but a handful of bricks and nothing to hold them together.

This, she knows, has been her problem all along.

She had vowed to stop it. To live in the moment and be happy with what she has. But it is not enough. It has never been enough.

She lifts the first box onto the table, flips off the lid. But her heart isn't in it. She should've popped in to get a coffee before coming in here, but she was desperate to get here. After going AWOL yesterday afternoon, she already feels out of the loop. She had hoped he would be here, to tell her what she had missed. She would've invited him out for a proper drink, and this time she wouldn't have rambled on about her crappy life; she'd have asked him about himself, made him reveal more. She would've got under his skin. She always managed it. Eventually.

She lifts a glazed bowl out of the box. Someone in the hall is playing a radio, just too quietly for her to hear properly, but she can tell that it's a Christmas song. The one about snow falling all around. Was it Shakin' Stevens? Or David Essex? She always got those two mixed up. Who knows why. She leans into the box for another stack of bowls.

'Hey, there you are . . . I was beginning to think you weren't coming in today either.' She turns at the familiar sound. A few days ago, she'd have been delighted to hear Hilda's sing-song tones. She'd missed her. Liked having her around. But since Caleb had appeared on the scene, she'd barely given the woman a thought. She feels a stab of guilt for putting on her the day before.

'Hi—'

'Your mysterious friend left this for you yesterday afternoon.' Hilda waggles an envelope in front of Carly's face. 'Obviously I have been desperate to open it up and see what he has said to you, but I couldn't work out how to do this without you noticing. I am not very good at espionage.'

Carly can't help but smile. 'Thanks. I wasn't feeling too well yesterday afternoon. I'm fine now. I really appreciate you packing my stuff away for me.'

Hilda dismisses her with a wave of a hand. 'Well you still look a little *peaky*? Is that the correct word? Maybe you need some camomile tea . . . In Sweden, this is always the best drink for when you are not feeling good. Would you like me to get you some?'

Carly barely hears her. She's sliced open the envelope with her nail, taken out the folded note from inside.

I heard on the grapevine that Godalming Market was the place to be this week. I'm heading there in the morning. There'll be a table there with your name on it, if you fancy? Not sure how long I can make them hold it. See you there? C

She smiles. Godalming is nice. Not too far, but might be just what she needs. She starts to re-pack the bowls.

'Everything is OK?' Hilda says. Her voice is one of curiosity, mixed with just a hint of amusement. Carly could tell when she first met her that they were of similar minds.

'Everything is perfect.' She grins, and Hilda grins back.

32

THE PHOTOGRAPHER

It was all starting to go to plan, I'd thought. Until yesterday, when she didn't come back to the market. I worried if she'd been spooked, somehow. That I'd pushed her away.

Also, I was starting to worry that no one was going to find the brick.

I wasn't even sure if one of the workers would notice anything strange about it, but I'd hoped by leaving it next to the neatly stacked pile that it would look out of place. That, and the bloodstained edge. I knew the bleach wouldn't get it out, but I wanted to create something for them to play with. The Scenes of Crime officers, or the Crime Scene Investigators. Whatever they were calling themselves now. They'd be pleased to find the murder weapon, and they'd be perplexed as to why I had cleaned it and taken it back. But there you go. It's about time I had some fun with all this.

I realise that makes me sound crazy, but you know what? Even I've realised now that I probably am. The old me died the day that she did. My beautiful Merlyn.

I'd always hoped that when one of us died, we would never leave the other. That was how it was supposed to be. That was what we had told each other.

But then where is she?

I've got several things belonging to her. No one else knows that I've got them. They had to be small things, due to the fact that I don't stay in the same place too long and I don't want to have anything permanent set up, like one of those horrible corrugated-metal storage units. I could never leave Merlyn's things in there.

My beautiful, beautiful Merlyn.

I wish I could talk about her properly with someone. But who? It's too dangerous now, with everything that's happened since. It would be too easy to slip up. That's why I have to be careful with CeeCee.

Especially with her.

Anyway, I'd been looking forward to seeing her again. I'd planned to take her out for a proper drink. I was going to tell her a few things about myself. Nothing incriminating, of course. Just enough to keep her intrigued. Enough to make it look like I was interested. I would make sure my hand accidentally brushed against hers again, when reaching for a cup across the table. She'd liked that when I'd done it before. I'd seen the lust in her eyes.

I'd made my mind up to push things to the next level. It's a game now, right? But then she didn't come back. I'd wondered if I should pack up her stock. Find a way to take it to her. But then that fucking annoying Scandinavian woman had insisted on taking over. Smiling at me. Telling me that CeeCee had asked her to look after it for her. She'd tried to engage me in conversation, in that precise way that non-native English speakers have, and to be honest it made my blood boil. I tried to avoid her as much as I could, which was difficult when she was standing behind her table, less than six feet away from me.

I had to grin and bear it. The market stayed busy all afternoon. Sometimes there were so many people, so much chatter, echoing around the old walls, the peeling ceiling, that I wanted to run outside and scream at the sky. Let the wind batter me and take me away. Let myself be soaked through from the whipping wet snow. Hoped that I might dissolve.

I pulled myself together eventually. Sold quite a few pieces, actually. Decent ones too. The more expensive ones. I let them haggle as I knew they were overpriced anyway, and to be honest I didn't really care. I always get by somehow.

It was by chance that I overheard someone talking about the market at Godalming. They'd moved to a new venue. First year they'd tried it. Might've bitten off more than they could chew, unless word got round. Punters in Godalming had money. It was worth checking it out. I hadn't been there for years. Last time was at a small market on the main street, as part of some bigger thing about Aldous Huxley – he'd grown up locally and they had some sort of appreciation society. The craft market attached to this was ill-placed, on my view. The Huxley fans weren't interested in my paintings, or the artisan cheese and meat platters that were set up on the stall next to mine. They were interested in old books that smelled of damp, and talking about conspiracy theories and the fall of civilisation over a half-pint of Hogsback Bitter in the Star Inn. I'd decided that Godalming wasn't my kind of place, after that. Perhaps unfairly. It was several years ago, and there was no mention of Huxley fans now. It was a Christmas market. Like this one, but bigger. Besides, I was getting bored being back here. A change of scene would do me good.

I was chatting to someone who'd just bought my last painting of Dorset's West Bay, when I spotted her. The young detective that DS Carmine had taken under his wing. DC Becky Greene.

What? You think I don't know who's looking for me? You don't think I'm one step ahead?

I have always been one step ahead.

I'd had high hopes for Carmine, but so far he'd been a massive let down. At least his sidekick had made it into my vicinity, not that she knew it.

I watched her walk up and down the aisles. Her mind whirring, but she didn't know what she was looking for. Not yet.

She was getting colder.

I stared at her, but she didn't see me. She didn't walk down my aisle. She stopped, glanced around. She had her hands in her pockets. She looked irritated. I wanted to shout, 'You're in the wrong aisle,' and then duck down behind my table. I had to look away so that the Scandinavian couldn't see the smirk on my face and ask me what I was looking at.

Becky Greene picked up a few leaflets from the table at the end of the central aisle that had all the information about markets in the area.

She was getting warmer.

Good work, detective. It's a shame I won't be around tomorrow, I'd thought. Once you've worked out why you're here.

I take out the small wooden box. I keep it with me at all times. Just opening it reminds me of her, and as I open the lid, the sounds all around me seem to disappear. I have to take out the figurines to get to the paper and envelopes beneath. I wonder if CeeCee will realise what a treat she is getting? A handwritten note from me on one of the few remaining sheets of Merlyn's special paper. She bought them at a craft supplies shop and kept them in this box, filled it with rose petals to scent the paper. I lift it up, inhaling the faint scent. There aren't many sheets left. The figurines are almost gone too. I remember her making them, using the old wooden clothes pegs that she'd found in the shed. Cleaned them, bleached them. Polystyrene balls for the heads and fabric offcuts to make their tiny little clothes. All in sets of two: Jesus and the Virgin Mary. Each set with its own unique faces.

Sometimes I let the customers choose them themselves. I thought that was a nice touch.

Not that they got to enjoy them.

33

BECKY

It's only 7 a.m., but Becky is already in the thick of it. A large latte (extra hot) from the coffee shop next door, and an almond croissant. She can't decide if this is better or worse than a sausage and egg McMuffin. She's already vowed that January will bring healthy breakfasts and at least some form of exercise. She's let things slip recently, since Gary has been on the scene. He's being neglected this week though, that's for sure. He's keeping her going with jokey WhatsApp messages and pictures of him in bed. Fully covered, of course. He doesn't send *those* types of photos. She messages him now, telling him she will visit him tonight, no matter what. She's waiting for him to bring up their arrangement again. Ask her why she keeps refusing to move in with him. He loves her family, he says, but he can't understand why she'd choose to stay in that poky house with them all when he's offering her half of his flat. What he doesn't understand is that he's only been around for eight months. Her family have seen her through twenty-eight years. Not all of it plain sailing.

She has ten browser windows open, each one of them with a different list of weird, quirky and in some cases, disturbing, Christmas folklore things from around the world. In Iceland, there are the creepy little trolls called the Yule Lads who like to terrorise people in the run-up to Christmas, and their terrifying mother, Grýla, a giantess who steals children. Not to mention Jólakötturinn, the demonic Christmas cat. In Germany and Austria, they have Frau Perchta, a witch who likes to rip out the internal organs of the sinful and replace them with rubbish. In France, there is Père Fouettard, who along with his wife, likes to kill, chop and salt children before eating them. She shudders at the last one. Such gruesome stories – fairytales based on legends, where no doubt there were real men who committed such crimes, and they'd been turned into fiction to allow the people to deal with what they had done. In the search history on her browser, the phrase: *Are Christmas monsters real?* comes up. Yes, she thinks. Yes, they are.

Maybe it's not such a shame after all that all they have here are department store Santas and an over-reliance on commercialism. Jeez, she's starting to sound like Eddie. She's just a little disappointed that the UK doesn't have any shitting logs or devilish elves. There used to be more, back in Victorian times, it seems. There was something she'd found last night, but it had been late, and she hadn't saved the link. She'd been coerced into baking an angel cake with her sister and hadn't got to bed until midnight. Her search then had brought up some different results to the ones she has now. She's sure she'd found something interesting and had just assumed it would pop up again, but it hasn't, so far. She would have to check her search history at home.

She wants to have something to show Eddie when he gets in. She's aware the progress on this case is frustratingly slow, but so far they haven't found any links between the victims.

They're assuming that the killer is someone who travels around for work, and that he has a simple way to get the victims to let him into their houses. But there's nothing strong jumping out at them. The photography angle is a good one though. She's hoping for an update from Keir soon.

The other thing is that she can't find any information about Colin Thacker. Something about the way his dad had said he wasn't in touch with him had niggled at her. Why? It was understandable that he would be as devastated by the death of his sister as his dad was, but why shut himself off from his only remaining relative? People deal with grief in different ways, but this had seemed strange. So she'd looked him up on all the databases they had access to, including the electoral roll, and found nothing. His last permanent address is listed as his dad's address, but he's not been registered to vote since 1998. Not being on the electoral roll makes it difficult to do the most basic things, such as get credit-checked for a bank account, or a rental agreement. She's sent a request up to tech, asking them to follow up with the agencies they use for checking, asking them to find out what they can. Because as far as she can see – no bank account, credit cards, driving licence or passport – Colin Thacker no longer exists. Has he changed his name? She'd need a warrant to find out any info on name changes from Births, Deaths and Marriages.

The office is quiet this morning. Only a couple of others have come in. The others, she assumes, are out in the field. Investigating. Or maybe they're in the canteen eating bacon rolls and drinking tea, laughing at her for being at her computer so early. Her mum and dad were always intrigued by what she did at work all day, expecting her to be haring around in an unmarked car, solving crimes like Columbo. She's tried to tell them that the majority of her work involves searching things on the computer and filling in forms, but she knows they don't believe her.

It's almost eleven before Eddie appears.

'Hey . . .' He's panting slightly. He holds up a hand to prevent her question. 'Just ran up from the basement. I've been up and down those stairs six times today. Abby in forensics, Ashlie in the analysts room, coffee, evidence room, in here, looking for Nick . . . have you seen him?'

She shakes her head. 'I've barely seen a soul in here today. Not even Miriam. I was starting to think I'd missed the apocalypse.'

'Miriam's on a training course at Hendon. Effective Office Communications. I think she's only doing it so she can get the tube into London and spend a few hours on Oxford Street under the guise of being away for work. Rather her than me. Can you imagine the crowds?'

'Oh God, you just reminded me. We're meant to bring in the things for Secret Santa tomorrow, aren't we?' She turns back to her computer and opens up her email. 'Yep. 11 a.m. in the canteen. Mince pies and alcohol-free mulled wine.'

Eddie lets out a stream of obscenities, then digs around in his pocket for change. He tips a handful into the swear box, before muttering a final 'fuck' under his breath. 'I can't wait until this is over.'

'Christmas?'

'Christmas. This case. All the . . . oh never mind. Listen,' he pulls up a chair and sits down next to her, 'Abby's given me a name at the university. Guy in the photography department. She says she's spoken to as many of the current lot as she can, but some of them are working elsewhere right now – she mentioned a big case at Thames Valley. The uni guy has been teaching there for years. He's probably met every crime scene photographer that's passed through these doors—'

'Hold up. We're looking at crime scene photographers now, specifically? Not just freelancers?'

'Your mate Joe followed up on the freelance angle. Like trying to find a needle in a haystack. I think it makes more sense to target it like this. It was Abby's idea, actually.' He pauses and she notices a faint flush on his cheeks. 'She's been pretty helpful, actually. I don't know if you know, but things were a bit tricky with her for a while. It's all sorted now. Anyway, between her and Ashlie, I think we've got something a bit more concrete to go on. The missing crime scene has been ID'd. If you go into the file . . .'

Becky clicks open the reporting screen and calls up the case file. Their operation, which has been seasonally named Operation Turtle Dove, now lists twenty-one murders (including Linda Hollis and Chris Hardy), spanning nineteen years. 'Which—'

'Door number seventeen.'

'Thanks. Oh. It was in a nursing home? That's weird. How did he manage that?'

'Not a nursing home as such, sheltered housing. There's a warden on site, but no one in the property apart from the victim, Albert Hemming. The reason it took so long to match this one is down to a couple of things, one – the photo is a bit blurred, out of focus. Which leads to two, they were already in motion when they took it.'

'They were interrupted?'

'He didn't spot the emergency cord next to the couch. Albert managed to pull it as they lay struggling on the couch. This one fought back. Ex-army man. He wasn't going down without a fight.'

'Is any of this relevant to the recent two? I mean, it's great that he fought back, but then what? Did anyone come? Did anyone see our man?'

'The warden who appeared two minutes later described an overweight man with long dark hair, tied back in a ponytail. He was wearing a blue baseball cap and a non-descript outfit of blue jeans and a grey sweatshirt. There was a composite made up at the time. It was shared on *Crimewatch*, but no one came forward.'

Becky clicks through to find the image. It doesn't look familiar. To Becky, the face is bland. Generic. Suggesting that the witness didn't get a very good look at him. They have no idea from this of his age, or in fact how overweight he might have been.

'He probably looks completely different now,' she says.

'Right.' Eddie frowns. Peers closer at the image onscreen. 'It was twelve years ago. Plus, if he saw this on TV, he'll have made sure to alter his appearance anyway. Let's print it out and take it with us, just in case.'

Becky looks up. He is already standing. 'Where are we going?'

'I'm taking you for lunch. There's something I need to talk to you about.'

'Oh?' A prickle of excitement runs through her.

'Come on,' he says. 'Not here.'

34

EDDIE

They're in an Italian restaurant called Luigi's. He's chosen it because no one else from the station is likely to come in, as it's too expensive and they're on expenses lockdown until the new year, but also because it does the best calzone in the British Isles, if not the world, and he has a feeling that Becky appreciates good food as much as he does. That McDonald's thing is a red herring. People think if you want fast food then you have no taste, but what they don't realise is that McD's breakfast is something else entirely. It's the sign of a discerning palate, not the other way around.

The other thing is, he wants to have this conversation out of the station and off-record, as much as it can be, for now. He knows Becky will want to take it straight to Nick, but he needs to get the whole story off his chest first. He's hoping he might get some reassurance that maybe it's not his fault. That he couldn't have stopped all this from happening. He wants her to tell him that he's overthinking it all. But he knows that's not what she'll say.

OK, he admits to himself. He's scared. He actually loves this job, despite his moaning to Keegan the other day. He wants to catch this guy. He wants to make a difference. It's not like he's managed to cause much of a ripple in any other part of his life. Sure, he has three healthy children. That's an achievement, of course. But an achievement like that loses its shine when you know the background to it all. Poor kids. He just hopes they aren't as fucked up as their mother.

They order quickly. The house calzone for him and spaghetti carbonara for Becky. A small bottle of Peroni each. Sparkling water to share. It feels almost like a lunch date. Something that Eddie hasn't experienced with any joy for a very long time.

Becky takes the printout of the photofit out of her pocket and lays it on the table. 'Well?' she says. 'You looked interested in this, when I had it onscreen.' She takes a breadstick from the metal container and unwraps it. Takes a bite. She has nice teeth, Eddie notices. Perfectly white, slightly crooked at the front, but that just makes her more real. He can't say he didn't notice the looks they got as they entered the restaurant. She'd taken her hair out of the clip that was holding it back from her face and shaken it out. He'd caught a whiff of coconut shampoo. Wondered if she realised how sexy it was when women shook out their hair. Wondered if everyone thought she was his daughter. *Technically*, he was old enough to be her dad, if he'd been a teenage terror, and he felt protective towards her. The sexy hair thing had been unexpected.

He gives himself a mental shake. 'OK. So what I was saying earlier, about me being seconded to the Met a few years back. Ten, actually. I was based in Ealing for thirteen months. I lived in Brentford. Near the Thames. It's a bit different over there now.'

She nods. Takes another bite of the breadstick. 'Right. So tell me about door number four.' She rolls up the breadstick wrapper into a ball and drops it into the metal container. She pokes about at the other sticks, as if trying to decide if she wants another.

The food arrives.

Eddie's calzone is covered with a large dollop of fresh tomato sauce and sprinkled with basil leaves. The combination of the herbs and the tomatoes in the steam makes his stomach flip in anticipation.

'*Buon appetito*,' Becky says, sticking a fork into her carbonara and spinning it around expertly without the use of a spoon.

Eddie swallows the first bite. Washes it down with beer. Bit naughty of them having this, but it's only a small bottle and it'll be soaked up by the food. He hadn't realised how much he needed a proper sit-down meal. 'Official line was that it was a career development placement, with a view to bringing back some of the practices to train others. The real story was that I was ready to leave the force altogether. I wanted to up sticks. Emigrate. Get as far away from my life as possible,' he takes another bite, waves his fork as he speaks again, 'and when I say life, I mean wife. She had an affair. It tipped me over the edge.'

'Oh shit, I'm sorry. Are things better between you both now? I mean . . . you came back, didn't you? You're still together?'

He nods. 'Yes, but I don't know for how much longer. Anyway, forget it. I need to tell you about what happened in Ealing.' He smoothes the photofit flat on the table.

'Go on.' She takes a bite of garlic bread. He wants to wipe away a bit of parsley from her cheek, but he stops himself.

'Judy Dorringer. Door number four. I was a DC back then. I was working with a DI, which was unusual, but it was all about the resources, just like now. Steve Burwash. He was great. Really did his job as a mentor. Didn't ask me why I was really there, although I'm sure he knew. I attended the Judy Dorringer crime scene. It was one of my first murders, and it hit me for six. She was a pretty girl. Only twenty-one. Her whole life to look forward to. My eldest daughter was well into her teens and already starting to look like the young woman she was going to be, and it just got me thinking. Put things into perspective a bit. Afterwards, I mean. At the time I just felt sickened.

'Anyway, the night after, I'd gone out for a drink with Steve. He'd told me I needed some time to get over it. Your first murder is a tough one to deal with, especially if you're right there in the thick of it. We went to the North Star – the place that Judy worked. It seemed fitting, but also it was so we could keep an eye on things. See if anyone a bit shifty turned up.'

'And did they?'

He takes a drink of water. 'Steve left early, said he had to get back home. I was on my own, right? I had nowhere I needed to be. I decided I'd have one more before walking back to my digs. It was three miles away. The walk would sober me up. Not that I was drunk, not at all . . . but I knew I had to be in work early the next day. You know what I mean . . .'

She nods. Twirls more pasta on her fork.

'This guy comes over to me. Tells me his name is Caleb. Says he's the crime scene photographer. I'd never seen him before, but why would I? I was new to the area. Anyway, he asks if I know someone called Lucas Buck. I tried to dismiss him. I wasn't really in the mood for chitchat. But he pulled out a stool and sat there in front of me. He looked like he was carrying the weight of the world on his shoulders. Anyway, we start chatting. He tells me stuff. Something about his sister dying, but I can't remember the details. I don't know if he told me them. I realised that I needed someone to talk to. Not about the murder, about everything else that I'd been bottling up. He's got this way of asking just the right questions. He caught me off guard.

'I tell him stuff . . . too much stuff. About my wife, about everything.'

'Christ, Eddie,' Becky says. 'I'm a bit worried about where this is going—'

'He said to me . . . but you wouldn't want anything to happen to your wife, would you? You wouldn't want to be the one to attend her crime scene.' He pauses, takes another drink of beer.

Becky raises her eyebrows at him. 'And you didn't think this was a bit strange?'

'I'd had three more pints by then, Becks. I know. You don't have to say anything. At the time, I waved it away. Told him I'd had enough and I needed to get home. I got a cab home, passed out as soon as I got in. Thing is . . .' he picks up the photofit, 'I think this might be him.'

'Might be?'

'He was pretty normal-looking. Nondescript. It was dark in the pub, and I was three sheets to the wind. But there's something about the eyes. The more I look, the more I think that this is him. This Caleb. I'm wondering now if I might've had a drink with our killer . . .'

She sighs, puts down her fork. She takes her phone out of her bag and starts texting.

'What're you doing?' Eddie says.

'I'm asking Joe to look up that name you mentioned. Lucas Buck. It's pretty unusual. It has to lead us somewhere, right? I'll get him to find out about this Caleb too. If he was the crime scene photographer on Judy's case, it'll be in the records. Somewhere. Won't it?'

'Maybe,' he says. 'It might have nothing to do with any of this. We don't even know if those are real names. I don't even know if he was at the crime scene. I didn't see him there—'

'Do you remember everyone who was working there that day?'

'No, but—'

'Right, so I think we need to call Abby. Find out who the crime scene photographer on Judy's case was. This Caleb had a murdered sister, right? Could it be Colin? Could he have given you a fake name to throw you off? Was he trying to play you – see if he could rattle you? Was Colin a crime scene photographer? I think we might have something here, Ed . . .'

'Can he have been under our nose this whole time? I don't buy it—'

'Maybe not. His dad said he worked freelance. Maybe

he did this for a bit then moved on to other things. Or the other way round. Freelance photographers can take on all sorts of jobs, can't they? That's the whole point. If he was moving around for work it gives him legitimate access to all of the towns we've got on our list. Plus – it makes sense, doesn't it? – the first victim was his sister. All that stuff about an alibi? I'm sure that could've been faked. He could say he was anywhere, there doesn't have to be a record of it . . . and the fake name – alarm bells are ringing loud right now, Ed. We need to go to Nick. Now.'

He swallows down the fact that his junior is now telling him how to do his job. After all, it's his own fault that this hasn't been followed up before. 'Please. Don't go to Nick yet. We don't know any of this for sure. Let's follow up on Colin ourselves first. See what else we can find out. I could get into the shit over this, Becks. How could I have missed something like this?' He waves his hand, gestures for the bill.

'Don't panic, Eddie. You couldn't have known. Back then, you thought you were dealing with a one-off case. There was no way of knowing that a drunken conversation held any significance.'

He slams a pile of notes onto the table. 'He's played me for a fool, Becks. We need to find Colin Thacker and find out what the hell he has to say.'

Back in the office, Becky feels torn. She knows that Eddie should be telling Nick about what happened in Ealing. But they don't know yet that it's Colin. Not for sure. If it was Colin, what was he doing? Did he kill Judy Dorringer? Did he kill the others? Was he playing a game with Eddie? Maybe it was a spur of the moment thing – he saw Eddie there, knew he was on the case. A little game. Still high on adrenaline.

But is this all linked to Eddie now? Is he trying to get his attention?

She has a sudden flash, an image. A man at one of the stalls in the market. She'd only been in there for a few minutes, had barely looked around, but she remembers now. She'd felt someone's eyes on her. Looked across, but the man had looked away. She'd dismissed it as nothing. But now . . . now she isn't so sure.

Is this what 'Caleb' is doing? Touring around Christmas markets, selling photographs . . . killing people on the way.

It sounds crazy, but then the whole thing is crazy. The advent calendar. The seemingly random choice of victims.

But how does it link to Chrissie? Was that an accident? Was Colin involved? Could he have lied about being in Scotland?

She needs to find out exactly where he was.

She's going to call Rob Thacker again. Try to squeeze some more information out of him. It's still a bit of a leap – accidentally killing his sister – if it was accidental – then carrying on to kill twenty more? Why? She's heard of people doing stupid things to cover up one mistake, but this would be extreme in anyone's book.

'Having a break, are we?' She blinks. Comes back into the room. It's Joe. She'd been gazing out of the window, her mind whirring with thoughts. Her concentration now broken, she's aware that there is Christmas music playing quietly in the background. There's a hint of cinnamon and ginger in the air. She remembers seeing the tin full of gingerbread men on the desk. Had meant to pick one up. Got distracted. She glances back at the window, sees the sparkly decals of Santa and his reindeer. How had she not noticed them before? Miriam has really gone to town.

'I can't actually imagine ever having a break again,' she says. She swivels her chair around and finds herself face to face with Joe's Christmas jumper. It's bright red, with a snowman that seems to be made from pompoms, giving it a startling 3D effect. And is that glittery wool for the snowman's scarf? She blinks hard, trying to dislodge the image from her retinas. 'Jesus Christ, where did you get that monstrosity? I hope you aren't interviewing anyone today.'

Joe grins. Delighted with her reaction. 'Primarni, hun. There's loads. Was going to get you one but I didn't know if you'd be more of a fairy or an elf. You can go after work. Better get one for Carmine too, so the pair of you don't feel left out.' He wiggles his torso and she realises that the eyes are little gold bells. She snorts out a laugh.

'There's more chance of Eddie juggling snowballs on *Britain's Got Talent* than me getting him to wear a Christmas jumper.' She laughs at her own fantasy image of him on stage in front of Simon Cowell, telling him he's a detective from Surrey, but that he really, *really* wants to be an entertainer. *It's all I've ever wanted . . .*

'Anyway,' Joe says. Trying to look serious is difficult in that get-up. 'Count your lucky stars that HMV are on the ball.' He drops a DVD onto her desk.

'What's this?' She looks at the image on the front. A young, menacing Gary Cole. A boy stands in front of him. '*American Gothic*? Is this the thing that's on Netflix just now?'

'Nope. But there is another show, with the same name. This one's from the nineties. I found it online, when you asked me to look into those names . . . Lucas Buck. Caleb. Just so happens, HMV are cashing in on the confusion of anyone who vaguely remembers this series from before. It only lasted one season. Can't say I remember it.'

'I think we were both a bit young for something like this, don't you think?' She turns the DVD over in her hands. It's set in South Carolina. She has an urge to watch it straight away.

'I did a bit of digging into it. It's about this kid, Caleb Temple, who's the son of the local sheriff, who's actually the devil. Lucas Buck . . .'

Becky draws in a breath. *Caleb . . . Lucas Buck . . .*

'. . . and, there's a dead sister in there. Merlyn. She's a ghost.' He raises his eyebrows.

'When was this on TV?' Becky says. She peers at the small lettering at the bottom of the back of the box. '1995? Is that right?'

'It ended in '96. Only one series. Don't know why, 'cause it sounds brilliant.'

'Chrissie was murdered in December 1997. She was almost twenty. Colin was twenty-two. They were both old enough to have watched this.'

'Interesting. Does it help us, though?'

'I don't know yet, but it's starting to make some sense.' She picks up a pen and starts absentmindedly chewing the end. A man calling himself Caleb tells Eddie that he's a crime scene photographer, and he just happens to have a dead sister . . . Eddie reckons it *could* be him from the photofit. They know that Colin Thacker is a photographer, and that *he* has a dead sister. The first case in the calendar. The trigger for all this . . .

Joe clicks his fingers in front of her face. 'Earth to Becky?'

She takes the pen out of her mouth. 'Sorry. Thinking.' She smiles. 'The name thing is interesting. What if Colin Thacker was calling himself Caleb Temple? His dead sister Chrissie was his Merlyn. The dad was a bad guy though, right? In this TV show . . .'

'Well, no . . . the biological dad, yes – but the man that Caleb thought was his dad was good. The sheriff got rid of him.'

'Cheers, Joe. I might be trying to read too much into it . . .' She has to stop herself, realising she was about to tell Joe about Eddie's meeting with this mysterious 'Caleb' ten years ago.

'Yeah, well I suppose you can ask him, if you ever find him. Any luck with anything else?'

She shakes her head. 'Not yet. I've got a couple of things I need to follow up on. Can you do me another favour?'

'You want me to go and get you a coffee from next door?'

'Spot on. You know the score.' She grins. 'No cinnamon though, right?'

He salutes her, making the snowman's eyes jangle.

She picks up her desk phone. There's another thing she needs to clarify. Dials the number on the Post-it she's stuck on the side.

'Mr Thacker? Rob? It's Becky Greene. We came round the other day—'

'Yes, love. What is it you want now?' His voice is not unkind, but he is clearly bothered by another interruption.

'Do you know if Colin ever sold any of his photography at craft fairs . . . Christmas markets. That sort of thing?'

'I don't know, to be honest. Not sure it sounds like his thing, but then, it's been a long time since I knew much about what my son was up to.'

'So he didn't sell anything like the ones you've got in your living room?'

'Like I said, I don't know. The photography thing was a new thing. He used to paint a bit when he was younger. No idea if he still does.' The line goes silent.

Painting now, too? He hadn't mentioned that before. Was he trying to throw her off, now that she'd mentioned the photography again? Could he have any idea about what his son was up to?

'Are you still there, Rob?'

'Yes . . . sorry. I was just thinking. Chrissie was more of the crafty one. Her and her mother were always saving bits and bobs, making them into things. I'm sure there was a box of that stuff somewhere, but I imagine Chrissie took it when she moved into the flat.' He sighs. 'I still don't know why she moved into that flat. She could've stayed here. If she'd stayed here, she might still—'

'Please, Rob, don't upset yourself. I'm sorry for dredging it all up again. You have to remember, none of this was your fault. What happened to Chrissie – it could've happened to anyone. And just because she was away from home didn't make her more vulnerable. She was twenty. She was in a shared flat. She wasn't alone.'

His voice becomes small. Tinny, as if he has taken the phone far away from his mouth. 'She was alone when they found her. My poor baby . . .'

The sound of sobbing. Then rustling, like he's trying to balance the handset.

'Can I come back round to see you, Rob? I think it would help . . . I can bring you something, to say thanks for the Cherry Bakewells. What do you fancy?'

She hears him blowing his nose. Crackling again. 'You choose.' He hangs up.

She thinks about the three empty doors in the calendar. Twelve . . . eighteen . . . twenty-two. Wonders if they can track down Colin before he can ruin anyone else's Christmas.

36

THE PHOTOGRAPHER

I see her long before she sees me. Probably because I've been unable to stop watching the door all morning. She's taken longer than I expected. I turn, glance up at the clock that hangs on the back wall behind me. Nearly twelve thirty. Where has she been? I feel a stab of annoyance as I wrap a painting in brown paper. Realise too late that the customer has been talking to me. Watch as his face falls.

'I'm so sorry, what did you say?'

The man shrugs. His shoulders stoop. I recognise it as the look of dejection, when your excitement has been quashed by someone else's indifference. I hate myself for causing this. The last thing I want to impart to another human being is indifference.

'I was just saying, that's me finished my shopping now. I'd no idea what to get my mum until I popped in here on the off-chance. I don't usually come to these sorts of things. Anyway, you're busy. I'll let you get on.' A cluster of people are hovering around the table, trying to politely push each other out of the way to get in to flick through the poster-sized prints. Whoever it was who suggested it might be busy here was right.

The man who has purchased the painting is trying to

prise it out of my hands, but I'm gripping too tight. I'm watching her. *CeeCee*. She is scanning the aisles. She looks anxious.

'Thanks,' the man says, pulling at the painting until finally, I let it go.

I snap out of the trance that has engulfed me. 'Hope she likes it,' I say, but it's too late. The man has gone.

'How much is this one?' A short woman in a red bobble hat has pulled one of the prints out of the display reel. They aren't supposed to pull them out of the reel. 'Is it buy-one-get-one-free?' she says.

A surge of hot rage comes over me. A fiery wave that threatens to spew out of my mouth like magma. 'Sorry, I'm closed. Come back tomorrow.' I snatch the print from the woman's hand, and watch the faces of the small cluster as they slide from interest to disbelief to anger. There are several mutters of 'rude' and 'I won't be coming back to this stall again' as they disperse.

I don't care.

I'm fed up waiting. 'Hey,' I call. Waving an arm like an over-enthusiastic schoolboy. I realise what I'm doing. Drawing attention to myself. But it's too late. It's worked though. She's seen me. Her puzzled face turns into a beaming smile as she rushes through the dwindling crowd towards me. The rage cools. The lava sets. For now.

'Let's go,' I say, before she can say anything to me.

She helps me pack up. It doesn't take long. 'I thought you'd have been here earlier,' I say. *Weren't you desperate to see me?* I think.

I stack everything onto the little trolley. I bought it

yesterday, on the way here. I'd seen hers and realised how useful it might be. Especially now, when I want to get out of here as fast as possible. It feels like the walls are shrinking inwards. That someone is taking away the air.

We walk outside, where the storm has brought the first proper snow. It's already lying on the pavements. Not deep, but it looks like it's going to stick.

'I did . . . sorry. I got down to the hall at a good time this morning, but then Hilda wanted to chat and I felt bad for getting her to pack up all my stuff yesterday so I had to stay for a bit. Then I popped home again and Simon was at home. My son. We had a row—'

'What about?' I have a sudden wash of paranoia. Has she told her son about me?

'Oh, you know. Just family stuff. I don't want to bore you with it.'

She's lying. The snow is hitting me in the face and I feel the anger threatening to resurface. I am wasting too much time on this. We need to be indoors. 'Let's pop in for a drink?' I take her elbow and guide her into the nearest pub. I have no idea what it's like, but as soon as I open the door, a warmth gushes out at me and I immediately feel better.

I tell her to sit in the corner and I go to the bar for drinks. Buy us a bottle of red. Not the cheapest, but it has to be half-decent at least. I need her to drink it. She has to open up and I don't want her to drive home. Besides, the storm is picking up properly now. I'll keep her here all afternoon then I'll tell her it's not safe. Suggest she gets a room.

She looks more comfortable now. The anxiety has left her face. Her cheeks are flushed from the cold then the warmth of the pub. She sips her wine. 'I shouldn't really . . .' she says. But she will anyway.

'Please,' I say. 'Tell me what happened. I know you're not happy. You said as much the other day. I'm sorry if I seemed a bit distant. I've got a lot on my mind right now.'

'Tell me then?' She lays her hand over mine and I have to fight not to pull it away. I can't do it. The physical contact. I want to, but it's so hard to disassociate it from the other stuff. When you've choked the life from someone, watched their eyes lose their light, it's hard to imagine being intimate with another person ever again.

'I can't. Not now. Tell me about your husband. You said he didn't want to have children, is that right?'

She sighs. Takes a mouthful of wine. Looks at a place over my shoulder, as if gathering her thoughts. Trying to work out the best way to tell me this complicated story of hers. I admit, I am genuinely interested in this. I'm hoping it might help me to understand a few things.

'It's not that he didn't want children. It's more that he didn't want them with me. I trapped him. I'm not even denying it. He was too good a man to let me be a young single mother. My parents were horrified, of course. Pretty much forced him to marry me. Do the right thing. He drew the line at joining the family business though. Did I tell you my father comes from a long line of sweet makers? His great-grandfather set up Collins' Confectioners back in 1875. Dad wanted Eddie to take over the Horsham plant. He'd be set for life. We both would. But he was intent on joining the police—'

Bingo.

'So he's a policeman, your husband? Eddie, is it? That must be difficult. For both of you, I mean. I imagine it's a very demanding job . . .'

She takes another mouthful of wine and I lean over to top up her glass.

'He's working on a murder case at the moment. Multiple murders, actually. He doesn't really tell me much about work, but I think he was letting me know that he might not be able to make it to my parents' for Christmas. Well, unless they've caught him by then.'

I have to force back a smile. I pat her hand. It feels easier to touch her this time. She really has no idea at all. 'How awful. Do you know if they have any leads? Are they close to catching someone?'

She shakes her head. 'Like I said, he doesn't tell me anything. Probably for the best though, isn't it? I mean, can you imagine? He's spending all day searching for a *serial killer*?' She whispers it, as if she can't quite believe it to be true. Good old Eddie. DS Carmine. He's back there now, fighting the good fight. And I'm here, sitting next to his wife, getting her drunk. I can't stop staring at her. A single tear runs down her cheek, and she turns away.

I gave you a chance, Eddie. I tried to involve you . . . I thought you were the right man for the job, but I was wrong, wasn't I? You might notice this time though . . . You might get it now. You might understand how it feels to lose someone you love. Because I know you love her, despite what she says . . . you don't stick by someone for all these years without some kind of love, do you?

I rub my thumb across the back of her hand. 'Shocking,' I say. 'Perhaps you should stay here tonight. The weather is awful. It'll be dark before you know it. I don't like to think of you driving in the dark when you're so upset.' I let it hang for a moment. Give her another smile. 'Besides, I've already booked a room. You can have the bed, I can take the sofa . . .' I pull the key out of my pocket, dangle it in front of her. One of those leather fobs with the embossed gold lettering.

Room 12.

On the twelfth day of Christmas, my true love gave to me . . .

'If you're sure it's no trouble?' She looks at me so gratefully, with such desperation in her eyes, that I *almost* feel sorry for her.

I *almost* change my mind.

'Right then.' I stand up. Give her another of my best smiles. 'Shall I get us another bottle?'

37

She trips as she exits the lift, bumps into a flowerpot. 'Oops . . . that was a silly place to leave that little tree, wasn't it?' Giggles.

He steers her by the elbow. 'Come on, it's just around this corner.'

She leans into him as he unlocks the door. She can feel the heat coming off him, oozing through his jacket. That smell of leather and sweat and just a hint of his body spray – something heavy with musk. That's the thing that deer give off, isn't it? When they're trying to attract a mate? She takes a deep breath, breathes him in.

Feels that tingle down below.

He opens the door and leads her in. The air in the room is cool, the aircon left on full blast, and it wakens her, hits her with a blast of sobriety. He wasn't making it up about the sofa. There's a three-seater leather one, and a matching armchair, placed around a long glass-topped coffee table. Behind the sofa is a dark wooden cabinet, crystal decanters on a silver tray.

'This is a bit posh, isn't it?'

'It was the only room they had left,' he says. He drops the key next to the silver tray and looks away, and she can tell then that he's lying. Did he book this just for her? The fanciest room in the place, trying to impress her?

She blinks away her drunkenness, tries to focus. He's gone to a lot of effort. The least she can do is give him some effort of her own.

'I'm just going to freshen up . . .' She doesn't wait for an answer. She slips into the bathroom, trying to keep upright and avoid stumbling into anything else. Her whole body feels heavy with tiredness and alcohol. She tries to keep any thoughts of what she is doing to the back of her mind.

She pulls down her skirt and knickers and falls heavily onto the toilet seat. The lid crashes against the back with a clatter.

'Everything OK in there?'

'Fine, yes. Just a sec . . .' she says. She can see herself in the mirror. Sweaty red face, bloodshot eyes. Her hair is dishevelled. 'What are you doing, Carly?' she whispers to her reflection. She shakes her head.

She can hear the sound of clinking glass, a chair being moved, cupboard doors opening and closing. Something that sounds like plastic being ripped. She is suddenly very aware that the man in the room outside is a stranger, and something – she doesn't know what, because it's not the first time she's put herself into a risky situation like this and lived to tell the tale – something, suddenly feels wrong.

She thinks about Eddie. About the children – and even though they are no longer little kids, they are still her children and they deserve better than this. She splashes her face with water, pats it dry. Hangs up the hand towel.

'I was starting to think you were in there for the night,'

he says, smiling. He is sitting on the sofa, which he has pushed further towards the cabinet to create more space. The coffee table is further away now, too, and he has his legs stretched out in front of him, crossed at the ankles. His shoes are off, and he is 'wearing plain, dark-coloured socks and she has another flash, to Eddie, and his penchant for brightly coloured socks – often non-matching because he likes the freedom of refusal to conform on such a trivial matter as socks.

His expression changes to one of concern.

'Carly? What's the matter? I poured you a drink . . . He gestures towards the cut-glass lo-ball tumbler, with an inch of amber liquid at the bottom, sitting there on a slate coaster, waiting for her expectantly. She detests whisky, assuming that's what it is. An honesty bottle in the decanter, she assumes. Unless he has also arranged this especially for her.

He stands, offers her the drink, and the smell of it is enough. She throws a hand over her mouth and turns. Lurches back into the bathroom and manages to make it to the toilet just in time. Hot, acidic vomit splashes into the pan and she is vaguely aware of him crouching beside her, pulling her hair back from her face. Muttering something soothing. Stroking her cheek. She grips the sides of the bowl and stays there until she is sure she's not going to throw up again. Her head is pounding. Her face burns.

Then he is there again, a cold flannel pressed against her forehead. 'Here, can you manage now?'

She presses her hand over the flannel and he pulls his away.

'Thank you . . .' she manages. He has already disappeared back into the bedroom, leaving her to sort herself out. Her mouth tastes sour, of old wine and something disgusting that has found its way from the pit of her stomach.

She attempts to sluice out her mouth with repeated sloshings of water. Uses the wet flannel to wipe rings of eyeliner and mascara from under her eyes.

She stares at herself in the mirror. She looks small and pale. Embarrassed. Tries several of her winning smiles. Mouth open. Mouth closed. A hint of a pout. Tries to look seductive and wonders if she can still pull it off. 'Come on, Carly,' she mutters to herself. Pinches her cheeks, trying to get some colour back into them. 'He wants you.'

She walks slowly back through to the bedroom.

Tuesday

FIVE MORE SLEEPS

38

EDDIE

Eddie is drying his hair with a towel. Almost bumps straight into Simon, who has one hand scrolling his phone, the other rooting around in his pyjama bottoms.

'Morning,' Eddie says. 'Found anything interesting?'

'Fuck off, Dad,' he says. 'Where's Mum?'

'Language, please. She's not here. I got a call from her last night, saying she was stuck in Godalming because of the weather. She'll be back later, I suppose.'

He snorts. 'You don't sound too concerned.'

Eddie looks into his son's face, still sleep-lined. Crusty bits at the corners of his eyes. He smells of boy duvet, which is one of those smells that just exists. It can't be defined. He might be an adult, but he'll always be Eddie's boy. Carly will always be his mum.

He sighs. 'Sorry. But you know, she's a grown adult. If she wants to stay out all night, I'm not going to stop her.'

'Do you even know who she's with?'

Eddie shakes his head. He walks into the kitchen, throws his towel into the laundry basket. A cereal bowl and spoon are rinsed and lying on the drainer. His son might look like a slob, but he never leaves a mess. He was like that from a young age, Eddie remembers. Always lining up his shoes, folding his clothes neatly. He would never want his supper in bed because he hated getting crumbs in the sheets. Eddie has no idea where he gets it from. The one thing that he and Carly have in common is their ability to leave mess in an empty room.

'She was pissed the other day, you know. I came home at 2 p.m. and she was crashed on the couch.'

'What were you doing home at two?'

'For fuck's sake, Dad! It doesn't matter. Things are quiet. Too many bloody promos going on in that new bar next door. The manager asked me to sort out some stuff for the new menus, said it was fine to do it at home. I think he's going to promote me. Anyway, that's not really the issue here, is it? I put three bottles in the recycling bin. Left her some water. I sat and watched her for over an hour, just to make sure she was breathing.'

Eddie drops down into a kitchen chair. He feels too heavy, as if he might push the chair right through the tiles, through the floorboards, fall into the dark, mouldy basement and never come back out.

'I'll sort it,' he says. 'Try not to worry.'

Simon's bedroom door slams so hard it rattles the whole house.

Eddie sighs. Once this is over, he needs to spend more time with his kids. Get them back onside. Especially Simon.

Becky is in the office when he arrives. He admires her ability to function this early in the morning. Most of the others need several coffees and a kick up the arse to get going before ten.

'One of the builders from the site near Chris Hardy's house handed in a brick. He went to open a new pack and saw that someone had beaten him to it.' She peers down at a scribbled Post-it. 'An Ibstock Facing Brick in Golden Buff, in case you're interested.'

Eddie frowns. 'And? What was so exciting about this particular brick that he decided to take time from his busy schedule and bring it down here?'

'Jesus,' Becky says. 'Someone fell out of the wrong side of bed this morning.'

He rubs a hand over his stubbled chin. 'Sorry. Go on . . .'

'Builder's name was . . .' she pauses again to read the note, 'Mark Fitzgerald. He noticed that the polythene had been ripped and one of the bricks was lying on the ground nearby. Said it just looked odd. Stuff like that is usually well secured. Anyway, he picked up this brick and saw it was stained, which was also odd, as they're pretty universal in colour. He's read online about the Hardy murder and had a hunch.'

'Interesting hunch. Everyone's a detective these days, eh? Stained with what?'

She frowns. 'Not sure yet. It's being analysed now. I just called for an update and they said at first look, it seems that someone has recently treated it with bleach.'

'Definitely sounds strange. Good of him to bring it in. Do you think our murderer is playing with us now? Why bleach it and put it back?' He thinks about the other things. The advent calendar. The conversation in Ealing. If he's playing a game, he's making up the rules as he goes along.

Becky seems to read his mind. 'I don't think we're dealing with your *Average Joe* here. Oh, speaking of Joe . . . DC Dickson has found the names you mentioned.' She hands him the DVD.

'What's this?'

'*American Gothic*. A supernatural crime horror TV show from the nineties. Lucas Buck is the devil, Caleb Temple is his son . . . there's a sister too. Merlyn. She's dead. I think Colin and Chrissie watched this programme. I think Colin's taken on the persona of Caleb . . . he's trying to avenge his sister's death.'

'Jesus,' Eddie says. 'Colin Thacker is Caleb Temple? That where you're going with this?'

'Could be. Not enough yet. I want to speak to his dad again.'

Eddie nods. 'Abby came back to me. No Colin Thacker on the list of crime scene photographers. She's coming back to me on who was working Judy Dorringer's scene. I got a warrant for the other stuff. Colin is registered with the Press Association as a freelance photographer. Deborah's getting on to them. Seeing if we can get hold of his photo credits. Find out what he might have been covering, and when. I want to place him in London this time ten years ago.'

'Right . . . and hopefully match him to the other locations too? There was another thing I was thinking. Maybe he sells photos other ways too. I can't find anything online, but maybe he was doing it old school. Markets, fairs – that sort of thing. Another reason for him to be travelling around a bit.'

'Carly does Christmas markets. Did I tell you that? She's a potter. Makes bowls and vases and that sort of thing. When she can be arsed . . .' he says the last sentence under his breath. Becky doesn't react. 'I'll ask her if there's anyone at hers selling photographs. I mean, there's bound to be. Probably a waste of time. She might've noticed something strange, but it's probably a long shot.'

'Sure,' Becky says. 'I might pop back in that one in the church hall. I went the other night, but I hadn't really put it all together then. There's been something else bugging me too. Weird Christmas decorations . . .'

His phone beeps. Voicemail. He frowns. Doesn't remember turning the call volume down. Maybe the brief sojourn down the toilet last week had affected it after all – despite the night in a bowl full of rice. The phone, that is. Not him.

It's a message from Nick, asking for an update. The higher powers are getting anxious now. Two murders and no leads. Not to mention the advent calendar deaths. They know it's not a hoax now, that's for sure. But it's still an issue that they haven't found a link – other than the fact that it is clearly the killer who has sent it. Nick told him that plans for a press conference were underway and that Eddie had better come up with something decent by then. Or else. He didn't specify what the 'or else' might be, but it was unlikely to be good. His DI is good at pretending he doesn't give a monkey's, when in fact, he knows exactly what is going on at all times. That's what makes him a decent DI. And the slow progress and lack of tangible results might be a hint as to why, when Eddie and Nick are the same age, with the same number of years in the force, Eddie is still wearing his sergeant's stripes. And now, of course, he has Carly's antics to deal with too – at the worst possible time.

'Everything OK, Ed?'

He sighs and sits down. He's doing a lot of that lately. 'Just a bit of hassle at home. Nothing to worry about.'

'Do you want to talk about it?'

He considers this. Part of him does. But he'd tried to talk to someone about it once before, and that hadn't gone as planned at all. Abby seems to be OK with him now, but for a long while, visiting her office required thermal underwear and a hip flask of brandy. He should go and see her now, ask her about Thacker. Who knows, he might be on her list somewhere. Abby has lots of lists.

'Maybe later,' he says. 'Fancy another trip to see Rob Thacker?'

'Yep . . . just a little something we have to do first.'

He frowns. 'What?'

'Secret Santa.'

39
BECKY

The front door opens before they've got out of the car. 'Hello again, Mr Thacker,' Becky says. She picks up the blue and white carrier bag from the footwell and walks up the path.

'Rob,' he says. 'I told you that last time.'

'Of course. Sorry.' She raises the bag, offers it to him. 'Told you I wouldn't let you down.'

He peers inside. 'Fondant Fancies. Not what I'd have chosen myself . . .'

'Nice to have a change sometimes, isn't it?'

Rob turns and disappears inside. She follows him in, Eddie close behind.

'I've already boiled the kettle,' Rob says. 'Must've sensed you were coming this morning.' He pauses, looks at his watch. 'Still morning, isn't it?'

'Just.' Becky smiles.

'I'd half hoped that you wouldn't bother. I told you everything the last time . . . and on the phone. I don't know what else I can do to help you.' He bustles off into the kitchen without catching their eyes.

Eddie is staring at the framed photographs. 'It makes sense, now. What you said.'

'Hmm?'

'CT. See? In the bottom right. Colin Thacker. Caleb Temple. His alter-ego.'

'It's one of those weird things. The initials being the same. One of those coincidences that seem just too good to be true. The thing about the dead sister. Merlyn. I wonder if he killed her, so that she could play that part in his own version of the show? Or was it just that he loved watching it, and after Chrissie died, he felt like it was saying something to him. That he was Caleb. Like I said before. Trying to avenge his sister's death?'

'So you're saying he did kill her, or he didn't?'

She frowns. 'I don't know. We don't even know for sure that Colin *is* Caleb, do we? I just think it's a distinct possibility now, with the link to you and Ealing as well.'

Rob enters the room with a tray. Clears his throat. They stop talking. 'Tea for you both, right? I see you admiring the photos again, Detective Carmine? I was never really sure if they were that good. Maybe I just liked them because they're exotic. Take me away from this place. Mind you, it did lead him to do that course after—'

'A photography course?' Eddie sits on the couch and leans forward to pour milk into his tea. 'Where did he do that?'

'The university. Thought I'd said that last time. Did I not? I didn't see him much after that, actually. He used to travel all over the place. He still does . . . I mean, I assume he does. That's why he's never here.'

Becky tries not to look at Eddie, but she can see him in her peripheral vision. His look. That disbelieving frown that he does so well.

'When did you say you last saw him?' she says. She makes a show of looking at the photographs again.

'I'm not sure. Can't remember,' Rob says. 'A while ago.' He opens the box of cakes and takes his time choosing between brown, yellow and pink. He goes for yellow. Lays them on the table. Eddie picks up pink.

Becky glances at Eddie again. Scribbles in her notebook. *I think he knows more than he's letting on . . . have someone watch the house?* She looks up and notices Rob staring at her. She smiles.

'Would it be OK if I went and had a look at Colin's old bedroom? I won't touch anything, I promise . . .'

'I don't know why you're so obsessed with Colin.' Rob slams his mug back onto the tray; tea slops out over the sides, pooling on the tray. 'I told you. He wasn't even here when Chrissie died.' He leans forward, drops his head into his hands. When he sits up again, his eyes are tinged with pink. 'It's the first left, at the top of the stairs. You won't find anything. I've left it as it was. Chrissie's is next door, if you want to look in there too. It's the same as it always was. I dust them both every week. Hoover too. Gives me something to do.' His voice breaks.

Eddie gives her a hard stare. A warning. *Don't fuck this up.* She nods. Leaves them in the room. As she walks up the stairs, she hears Eddie's voice. Something about football. The universal male language.

The layout of the house is similar to her own. Slatted-wood banister at the top of the stairs. Plain wooden doors, flocked wallpaper. She pushes open the door at the left of the stairwell. Single bed, narrow wardrobe. A chest of drawers. The walls are covered with a mixture of art posters and a few framed photographs. Landscapes. Trees. The duvet is blue and white striped, the bed neatly made, corners pulled tight.

On the chest of drawers, a mirror printed with a beer company logo rests against the wall. Hanging off the corner, a selection of medals on different-coloured ribbons. Images of boys with footballs engraved onto the surface.

Next to it, one photograph. Black and white print in a silver frame. Two smiling teenagers, a boy and a girl. The girl has her head back, mouth wide, laughing. The boy is smiling. He is looking at her side on. Gazing at her intently. He is round-faced and light-haired. She has a mop of wild curls. Is this Colin and Chrissie? She looks familiar, from the photograph on her file, although she is not looking straight at the camera, and her hair is wilder than Becky remembers. She realises now that she has never seen a photograph of Colin. She has no idea what he looks like. Something familiar about him though. A similarity with the girl, nothing striking. Just a hint that they are from the same blood.

She takes out her phone, snaps a picture. Then she picks it up. She will ask Rob if they can borrow it, unless he has another. Something more recent. This photo of his children must be twenty-five years old. Behind the frame, lying on the top of the unit is a small plastic ziplock bag. Inside, dried flowers. She lifts the bag, unfolds it. Sees what is inside. A daisy-chain. Pressed and preserved, for all this time.

A heavy wave of sadness lands on her shoulders,

crushing her with its weight. She folds the empty end of the bag back underneath and lays it back down. Catches a glimpse of herself in the old pub mirror. The sadness is behind her eyes.

She closes the door quietly behind her and goes back down the stairs.

Eddie and Rob are in deep conversation. Something about Arsene Wenger, about whether he should stay or go.

She coughs, and they both turn towards her. Rob sees her holding the photograph and his face falls.

'I was wondering if you had a more recent picture of Colin that we could borrow?'

Something flicks across his eyes. She senses that Eddie has duped him. Lulled him into a false sense of security. A dark cloud, flickering. Anger? Fear?

'I told you,' he says. 'I haven't seen him.' He sighs. 'He does call me, though. Once a week. To let me know he's OK.'

'When did he last call you, Rob?' Eddie says.

'That's the thing . . . it's usually every Sunday, eleven o'clock, without fail. Doesn't matter where he is or what he's doing. Even if it means he has to get up in the middle of the night to make sure he gets me at the right time. But he didn't call me this week. And last week he said something strange. I didn't think much of it at the time, but now—'

Becky sits down beside him, puts a hand on his arm. 'What did he say, Rob?'

Rob looks up at the photograph of Purple Mountain.

'He said, "I'm sorry, Dad. It'll be over soon." And I asked him what he meant . . . I assumed he meant Christmas. We both hate Christmas. You can understand that, can't you? But he wouldn't say any more.' He pauses, lets out a long, slow sigh. 'When he hung up, I was sure that I heard him crying.'

40

EDDIE

Becky waits until they're in the car before she shows him the photo.

'Is this him? The guy from Ealing?'

Eddie frowns. 'He wasn't as round-faced, but there's something familiar. Yeah. I think this is him. Definitely could be.' He feels the familiar fizz of excitement run up his arms. Goosebumps. They need to call Nick, tell him what they have. That means telling him about the meeting in the pub in 2006 though, and he's still a bit confused about that. About missing the clue. If it was a clue.

Becky reads his mind. 'Should we call Nick?'

Eddie pulls out of the quiet street and back onto the main road. 'We haven't really got anything yet, have we? It's all circumstantial. You know what Nick's like. He likes it by the book. Hard evidence, no hunches. Let's see if we can find him first.'

'I think Rob's lying about having seen Colin lately. There was a can of deodorant on the window ledge. Lynx. It's one of the new fragrances. I know, because I bought some for Gary the other day. I suppose it might have been Rob's, but why would he leave it in there? It was on the bit of the window ledge that was covered by the wardrobe. You know what these bedrooms are like. Barely enough space to swing a cat. Rob might go in there every week to clean and dust, but he could easily have missed this, where it was . . .'

'Well spotted, Miss Marple,' he says. 'We'll go back later. Pile on a bit more pressure. I think we left it right for now. I don't want to spook the old man any more than we already have. He might well be lying, but remember this is his son. I think he's terrified. We don't want him warning Colin off, if they are in touch. Do we? Maybe we should send someone round to keep an eye on Rob's house, in case he comes back. I'm not sure Nick'll go for it though, not yet.'

'Hmm. Yeah. I'm sure we'll get told there's no resources anyway.' She falls silent. Then, 'Oh balls!' She smacks the hand-rest on the door. 'I forgot to ask him about Chrissie's craft box. We're going to have to go back.'

'We will. I already said that. Just relax, will you? What is it about the craft box that's bothering you?'

'I don't know,' she says. 'There's just something niggling at me.' They barely speak for the rest of the journey. She's scrolling through her phone. He's concentrating on the road. Thinking about too many things. This case. His life.

Bloody Christmas.

He sends himself happy thoughts. Imagines himself on a beach, somewhere hot. That photograph from Rob Thacker's living room, giving him ideas. A pile of books and a supply of cold lager for company. He's smiling by the time they arrive at the campus.

Eddie always enjoys visiting the university. It's one of the old ones, with the grand buildings and the smell of olden times. He imagines people rushing around in their black capes, heading to banquets in the long hall. Or maybe he's just getting it confused with Hogwarts.

Nowadays, it's more likely to be full of students who look like they are barely out of nappies, rushing around carrying folders, or sitting outside, when the weather is nice, philosophising. He's heard their conversations. He's always amazed by their deep thinking, although it's more analytical than he feels comfortable with.

Today, it's quiet. The students have already broken up for the Christmas break, except for a few stragglers that are staying behind for a few more days, finishing off things that can't be left until January. Plus, of course, the staff. They don't get the same holidays as the students. He'd always thought they were like teachers, getting weeks off at Christmas and Easter, the whole of the summer to do what they liked, but from what he understands, the lecturers here work a full calendar year, supplementing their standard teaching time with research and extra-curricular activities. They do get to take holidays outside term time, though, so he hopes that the person they want to see is still here. Becky had tried calling ahead, but after five minutes of 'Jingle Bells' on a loop on loudspeaker, he'd told her to hang up. No one needs that kind of torture. It had threatened to take him out of his happy place.

Becky is trailing behind him, stopping to read the various notice boards that line the corridor.

She catches him up. 'I kind of miss this place,' she says. 'Even when you're doing practical subjects, there's a nice feeling of unreality about studying. You know that last terrorist attack in London? I heard one of the officers saying they were able to cope with it because it felt like an exercise. They disassociated themselves from it, in a way, so that they could carry on with all they had to do, without letting their emotions get in the way. That's what it was like when I was here, doing my degree, then the police training modules. I felt detached.'

'And now? How do you feel now? With all these real people involved?'

'I still feel kind of detached. But it's like I'm forcing myself to feel that way. I want to do my job. I want to find the person responsible for all this . . . mess. I don't want to start thinking too much about the victims, or their families, because I'm scared that if I do, I won't be able to keep doing this job.'

He stops, turns to face her. 'Rob Thacker got to you. Don't worry, Becks. It's normal. Everything you're describing is normal. You have to distance yourself, but you're only human. You'll be affected. If you need help dealing with things, I can sort that out for you, you know. You only have to say.'

She gives him a small smile. 'Thanks. It's just . . . well, if this *is* Colin Thacker. If he's done all this . . . I just feel sick thinking about it. Poor Rob. He's already a broken man—'

'We'll make sure he gets all the support he needs. Look, we don't know anything for sure. Not yet. Let's find Colin, OK? That's all we can do for now.'

The photography department is housed in a turret, up a winding stone staircase at the far side of the main building. Eddie has been here before, when they've helped out with things in the past. He sometimes imagines himself giving up his job and becoming a student here, so he can photograph the creepy gargoyles and drink coffee with other students, hanging around in the turret all day. Staring out of narrow windows like he's trapped in a castle. His imaginary life is far more appealing than his real one right now. By the time they get to the top of the stairs, he feels slightly out of breath. He needs to get back to the gym.

The room at the top is deceptively large, the turret having a bit of a Tardis effect. There is a circular desk in the middle of the room. All around the periphery walls there are shelves filled with photography equipment. Cameras, lenses, tripods. Chairs are stacked, only pulled out when required. There is a small spiral staircase across the room, leading up to another level, which Eddie knows, from previous visits, houses their darkroom. This is not the only teaching room that the department has – there is also a large classroom on the ground floor, but the circular room is where they do tutorials, and where the head of department spends most of his time.

He's currently sitting with his feet up on the desk, scrolling through his phone, which is attached to a small speaker. Eddie recognises the song that's playing. The unmistakable voice of Ian Brown. 'Love Spreads' is one of his favourite Stone Roses songs, although he is perhaps in the minority. It appears that Henry Richards shares his love.

'They should've just left it at that album, don't you think?

The whole reunion thing is a bit embarrassing, although I have to admit – I did go and watch them in Finsbury Park and they were pretty good. I wasn't too keen on the bottles of piss being launched around the crowd, though. I suppose some of their fans never really grew up—'

'Eddie!' Henry takes his feet off the desk and lays his phone down next to the speaker. He turns it down a few notches, but leaves it playing. 'Long time no see.'

'Henry, this is DC Becky Greene. She's working with me on a whole bunch of shittery.'

'Keeping you on the straight and narrow, eh? Hello, Becky.' He comes round from his desk to shake Becky's hand. Eddie watches her reaction. Henry looks more like a Hollywood actor than a photography lecturer. A bit of the Tom Hiddlestons about him. He's never seen a woman resist his charms. He'd gone out for a drink with Henry a few years ago, after he'd helped him with a case. Although Henry had seemed oblivious, they'd spent a large portion of the night being approached by women. Eddie had forgotten about it until now, having not seen the man for a while, but it seems that he's lost none of his charm. Becky flushes pink, as Henry grips her hand for just a second longer than is necessary. He turns back to Eddie. Winks.

'You know me, Henry,' Eddie says.

Henry perches on the edge of his desk. 'Coffee? Tea? Have you got time? I'm guessing this isn't a social call, although we should do something about that soon, don't you think, Ed? It's been too long.'

Eddie is counting the days in his head. Get the case done. Sort things out at home. Then yes. Definitely yes.

'We will. For sure. Just wanted to pick your brains about something first.'

'Go on.'

Becky is walking around the room, looking at the equipment, the prints hanging on the walls. She glances up the small staircase.

'Darkroom's up there,' Henry says to her. 'I can show you if you like.'

Becky shakes her head. 'It's OK. Thank you.' Her voice is clipped. She keeps walking. Eddie makes a mental note to ask her about this later. She'd said something about the darkroom back at the station, but they'd been interrupted and she never finished what she was telling him.

Henry raises his eyebrows. Eddie gives him a tiny shake of the head.

'Do you remember a student called Colin Thacker? It'd be a while ago. Sometime between December 1997 and December 2007.'

Henry frowns. 'Are you sure it was here? I can't say the name is ringing any bells.'

'We think he might've studied here, then gone on to work freelance, possibly as a press photographer.' Eddie already knows that he was registered with the Press Association but he doesn't want to lead Henry into anything.

'Have you got a photograph?'

Becky hands him her phone, already open at the photo she took from Rob's house. She's zoomed it into Colin's face, cutting Chrissie out of the image.

'Hmm,' Henry says. 'He does look kind of familiar, I think. Long time ago though. And I don't think his name was Colin. Hang on.' He hands back the phone and goes to his desk. He slides a thin laptop out from a concealed drawer and flips it open. He starts typing. Clicking. He sits back. 'We've got a new system. It stores everything from the year dot. Quite handy, actually. That name . . . it's coming to me. Give me a minute.'

Eddie wanders over to a collection of prints hanging near the spiral staircase. Black and white. Close-ups of faces, showing all the lines and shadows. Sadness in their eyes. He wonders if this is how he appears to others. No one else sees what you see in the mirror.

'Got it,' Henry says. He sounds triumphant, as if he has just solved the case before Poirot. 'I was right. He started in the autumn 1997 term. One-year course. He's not called Colin. He's called Caleb. Caleb Temple. Funny, that name sounds familiar too, but I don't know why . . .'

Becky throws Eddie a look. *Bingo!* it says. *We're getting close.* 'Just wondering, Henry – did they do all the usual identity checks on people's names and stuff back then?'

Henry laughs. 'Back in '97 when dinosaurs ruled the earth? Actually, it's a good point. There would've been checks, but if someone had appropriate ID, the admin would take it. They wouldn't dig any deeper.'

'So if someone had a fake driving licence, for example?' Eddie gives her an odd look.

'I was just thinking about Colin . . . about Caleb's travel. Asia. My dad's told me stories about his travels back in the day. Said you could buy anything you wanted on the Khao San Road in Bangkok.'

Henry nods. 'He's not wrong about that.' He winks at Eddie.

Eddie rolls his eyes. 'Spare us,' he says. 'Anything in that database that might actually help us find him?'

Henry sits back, crosses his arms. 'If you're asking me, I assume that means you've exhausted all other options. There's an address on here. I'm sure it's OK to give it to you as it's nearly twenty years old . . . It's 47 Blackstone Road—'

'Fuck,' Eddie mutters. 'That's his dad's address. We've already been there. He hasn't lived there for years. Dad reckons he doesn't know where he is. Becky, can you show Henry the photo again?'

Becky scrolls through her phone, hands it over.

'Bugger,' Henry says. 'Hmm. Yes. He was a bit of a chubster though, come to think of it. Much bigger than in this photo. Kind of inflated looking, you know what I mean? Like someone who'd put on a lot of weight quickly. There's something about his eyes . . . Hang on.' He clicks a few more times. 'Hmm, interesting. This is definitely ringing a bell now. He was tutored by Andy Mortlake. He was a crime scene photographer too. If I remember rightly, Caleb . . . or Colin, or whatever his name is, was a bit obsessed with Andy, from what I recall. He wasn't interested in most of the course curriculum, actually. He was more intent on quizzing Andy about his work. He made note of it. Says here . . . "Caleb seems to favour the macabre." Ha! Bit of an odd comment, don't you think?'

'Any idea where we can find this Andy, then? Does he still work here?' Becky says.

'He gave up photography years ago. He told me the crime scene stuff really affected him. He got quite depressed for a while. Got involved in drugs. I don't know if he's clean or not now, but I know where he works. He's trying to reclaim his youth, I think. Just like the Stone Roses.' He smiles at Eddie. 'He's a DJ at the Union. Quite popular he is, from what I hear. Calls himself DJ Mortal . . . I know, I know. Give him my regards, will you? He's a good sort, Andy.'

Back in the car, Becky asks if they are going to the Union tonight. If she should text home to let them know she's going to be late.

'Let's leave it until tomorrow, Becks,' he says. 'I think we could both do with getting home at a decent time tonight.'

'Oh good,' she says. 'It's lasagne night, chez Greene.'

Eddie feels a stab of envy. He would love a home-cooked meal. He texts his wife. He's not sure if he cares what she gets up to any more, but he's prepared to have one last meal with her at least. He might as well get it over with, if only to avoid the sham of Christmas Day at his in-laws'. Besides – he wants to ask her if there's been anyone strange hanging round at the market.

41

BECKY

Traffic is backed up on the roundabout near the station. Eddie drums his fingers on the steering wheel. 'Come on,' he mutters. 'What's the hold-up?'

Becky winds down her window and a blast of cold air whacks her in the face. She leans out, trying to see what is causing the jam. She sees two men dragging a bedraggled Christmas tree across the road. The car in front creeps forward. 'I think Storm Hannah's tried to claim herself a tree.'

Eddie sighs. 'Those sellers have been moved on twice already, but they still come back. Stupid place for them to set up, even if they did have permission.'

The traffic starts to move again and as they pass by, the two men are trying to tether the trees to the lamppost in the centre of the roundabout with a rope. A van is parked, on the roundabout, the back doors wide open. A sign next to it displays the prices of the trees listed by height, a special offer of a box of decorations if you buy two trees. At the bottom of the sign, a naïve drawing of what looks like it's meant to be Mary and Joseph, or maybe it's Mary and Jesus. It's hard to tell.

Becky frowns. Strains her neck twisting around to look at them as Eddie drives off the roundabout and up into the station car park. As they walk into the building she says, 'Did you notice anything about those figures drawn on the price list?'

'What figures?' He pushes open the door. He's scrolling through his phone, clearly distracted.

She leaves it until they are back in the office, his phone back in his pocket.

'Sorry,' he says. 'I had a couple of missed calls from the wife. She was stuck in Godalming last night. She freaks out when there's a bit of snow on the road.'

Becky walks across to the whiteboard and picks up a pen. She draws the two figures on the board. Tries to remember them as they were on the price list, merges them in with what else she remembers. The male figure has a halo. Or is it a crown? 'I've seen these a few times recently,' she says. She lays the pen back on the desk near the board and the pinned-up notes of the cold and current cases. Chris Hardy's and Linda Hollis's smiling faces. She looks away.

'Oh yeah?' Eddie says. 'Go on . . .'

'In Linda Hollis's living room, on that sideboard with the ornamental dogs. There were two of these figures there. I didn't think anything of it. It's not exactly uncommon to have home-made decorations lying around. Grandkids maybe? I saw them on Chris Hardy's coffee table too. Slightly different, but same idea. I remember thinking then that they probably weren't home-made after all. They might be the kind of thing you get in Ikea or Tiger. I'd forgotten about them until I saw the crude attempt at a drawing of them on the Christmas tree price list. I read about them . . . I'd been starting to think that Caleb might've been using them as a way in—'

Keir Jameson walks into the room as she is thinking it through. He stifles a yawn. Glances at their murder board and Becky's drawings. 'Ah, you've seen these things too, have you? Popular this year, it seems. Apparently they found a couple on that body in Godalming early this morning—'

Eddie pulls his phone out of his pocket again. 'What body in Godalming? Who found it? Has it been identified?'

Keir takes a step back, holds up his hands. 'I don't know the details, sorry . . . you'll need to ask Nick. He went down there earlier . . .'

Becky sucks in a breath. Feels a trickle of ice run down her spine. She turns to Eddie. 'Didn't you say Carly was in Godalming last night?'

42

BECKY

Eddie drives too fast, but she doesn't say anything. Just holds on to the sides of the seat and hopes he doesn't get them both killed.

'Try and calm down, Ed. We don't know anything yet. It might be something totally unconnected. Just because Carly was there—'

'She's not answering her phone. Here, you try.' He pulls it out of his pocket and tosses it into her lap. 'Call Nick, too. Get an update. If it happened this morning, they'll at least be able to tell us if it's a man or a woman . . .'

'Nick knows Carly, doesn't he? He'd have called you if it was her.'

Eddie sighs, hits the indicator so hard he almost snaps it. 'I've got missed calls from him too.'

Becky says nothing else. Hits redial on Carly's number, then Nick's, but neither are answering. Surely if this was something to do with their case, they'd have been contacted by now?

They pass the university and Becky has a brief flash-back to their meeting with Henry. If she wasn't happily with Gary, she'd be asking for more information. Maybe a bit too old for her, but there was something intense about him that she couldn't quite shake off. Some people just had that effect. A magnetism. She watches Eddie from the corner of her eye. Eddie has it too. Just maybe a bit less obvious. Seeing him now though, it's clear he still feels something for his wife, despite what he's told her.

And she *is* happy with Gary, isn't she?

They turn off the dual carriageway and onto small winding roads. He slows down, finally, as they pass Charterhouse. A posh private school that Becky can't even imagine attending. It's the kind of place that politicians' children go to. Rich foreigners based in the City. She has no idea how it has come to be that Eddie's youngest daughter is there, and she's not going to ask. Scholarship, maybe? She must be one hell of a bright girl.

As they reach the edges of Godalming, she spots the blue flashing lights through the trees. They turn into the car park, stopping at the raised barrier so that Eddie can show his warrant card and get them signed in.

'Park on the left, don't drive past the cordon,' the uniformed officer states. Following up with a 'Thank you, Sir,' when Eddie gives him one of his looks.

It's a large car park, fenced off from the neighbouring fields. There are no cars, except for the response team and the CSI van. The rest is blanketed with thick snow, ruined, mostly, by the many footsteps that have trudged over it overnight and through the day. They've erected a tent and cordoned off the central area. Becky assumes that the body has already been removed. Outside the car park, media vans sit in silence.

They get out of the car. The snow has stopped now.

They've missed the worst of it. The CSIs must've had a tough job working through it.

'DS Carmine, nice of you to join us.' The man looks from Eddie to Becky. He looks familiar, but it's hard to place him when all she can see is his face; the rest of him is covered in a white hazmat suit and hood.

'Tim,' Eddie says, and they nod at each other like they are about to start sumo wrestling. 'This is DC Greene. Becky, this is DS Tim Jones. Tim leads the follow-up investigations team. Not sure what he's doing here, exactly . . .' he lets it hang. He seems to have switched his earlier mood from shock into anger.

Becky's not sure if this is banter or some past feud. One of the things that she's noticed the most since joining CID is how territorial the sergeants are. Everyone wants to be the first to know everything.

'Keegan called. Reckoned you were busy with your advent man.' A smirk.

Eddie ignores the dig. 'Is Keegan still here?'

'Left ten minutes ago. He's got a press conference to prep for. You might want to give him a call . . .' Another smirk.

Becky can tell by the way that Eddie is balling his fists that he is fuming. He's trying to keep it in check. For her benefit?

'Why didn't someone call me earlier?' He kicks a fresh patch of snow, spraying it into the air. 'Never mind. Bring us up to speed, will you? It's fucking freezing.'

Tim walks them across to the scene. Banter over. If that's what it was. 'We haven't ID'd him yet—'

'*Him?*' Eddie says. His shoulders slump forward.

Becky blows out a puff of white air.

Tim looks confused. Blinks. 'Yeah, young man. Late teens, early twenties maybe. He's gone for his post-mortem. We found a couple of things though. I'm guessing that's why you're here . . . doesn't really make sense, it being your man, but you never know when these crazy bastards are going to flip—'

She watches as Eddie recovers from the shock and relief by going straight back on the defensive. 'You mean "escalate". We don't know that he's crazy. If this is him, he's acting out of frustration. He's had enough.'

'Oh yeah, I forgot you went on that "serial killer course".' He makes air quotes. 'I suppose it's coming in handy now though, eh? You know Mari, don't you?'

One of the white-clad CSIs turns around. Mari Ramone. Becky's seen her before in the canteen, but they've never properly met.

'We found these things on him. The note in one pocket, the tree decorations in the other.'

Becky reaches out for the two neatly labelled and sealed evidence bags. In one, there's a note, a crease line from where it's been folded. Written in blue marker pen. Twelve. In the other bag, two small figurines. They might well have been Christmas tree decorations, but Becky knows they aren't.

'This is what I was talking about in the station, Ed. They're Jesus and the Virgin Mary. I read about them in those online articles on Victorian folklore. They called them the "advent images". Women would make them and go around the houses, asking for a penny. There was a little rhyme that went with them. One of those things that sounded creepy and innocent at the same time. Apparently, it was considered bad luck if you made it to Christmas Eve without being visited by women selling the advent images. I think that maybe Caleb uses them to get people to answer the door. They'd think 'it was a cute Christmas idea. He'd have told them it was for charity, probably. Then they'd leave the door ajar as they went in to get some money . . . not everyone does this now. People are more wary of people coming to their doors. But what if he visited loads of houses – not just the ones where he killed someone? It's a perfect cover.' She touches them through the bag. They are handmade. Perfectly drawn faces, neat little clothes.

Becky is sure now. Chrissie made them.

43

THE PHOTOGRAPHER

Disgusting bitch. Drinking herself into a stupor. Throwing up like that. I should've strangled her with that dressing gown cord there and then while she lay draped over the toilet bowl heaving up her guts.

But I bottled it. Maybe I do still have a heart, after all.

I left the room before she came back out of the bathroom. Turned up the heating in the van and tried to decide what to do next.

How could I have let this happen? She was never supposed to get under my skin. I don't care about her. I wasn't *supposed* to care about her. How was I supposed to know how damaged she is? How she is so like me, in many ways . . . all she wants is someone to love her. Love her like she loves someone else. Someone she can't have. Her marriage is a sham. We were never meant to be together. I don't love her. I could never love her. Carly had a lucky escape. She'll realise that soon. She'll realise that she should never have tried to tempt me. She should never have tried to love me.

Merlyn loved me.

I know she did. I hope she still does. I hope she knows that I've done all this for her. Because I love her. Because I miss her. Because there is no point in my life without her.

There is no point in being Colin Thacker.

Colin Thacker is a sad, weak man. Colin Thacker has nothing. His mother died from a stupid fucking mistake during an operation that should've been over in a couple of hours. His father is pathetic, refusing to challenge the error. Refusing to take the idiot doctors to court and get justice for the woman he said he loved. Colin Thacker is half an orphan and an only child.

Caleb Temple knows what he is doing. Caleb Temple does everything in his power to avenge the death of his sister, and the devil inside him helps him to do it.

I miss her so much.

Watching that TV show had been a highlight for both of us, those last few months before I never saw her again. That opening . . . the creepiest thing I'd ever seen . . .

Someone's at the door. Someone's at the door. Someone's at the door.

'I can't believe they made Midnight Caller into the devil,' Chrissie said. She was curled up under a blanket, a bowl of popcorn on her lap. Salted and sweet. Yin and Yang. Like us, brother and sister, opposites in nature. Best of friends.

'What I like is that the devil lives in such a backwater town. It's perfect for him to have complete control over the place.'

'That's because he's the sheriff. He'd have control anyway. It's kind of a ridiculous concept, but I like it. Caleb is so cute. All he wants is to help poor Merlyn.'

'Would you haunt me if you died?'

'Of course I would, you knobber. I'd never give you a minute's peace. Especially if someone killed me and no one knew who'd done it.' She mimes someone stabbing her in the neck, then falls forwards dramatically into her bowl of popcorn, spraying it out all over the couch and across the floor.

I couldn't stop laughing at her. Her perfectly timed comedy dramatics. 'Look at the mess! Dad's going to kill you.'

Dad's going to kill you, Chrissie . . .

'Who killed you, Merlyn? Why do you never reply? Why?' Tears prick at my eyes and I wipe them away on my sleeve.

I've done this. I've killed these people.

And why?

Why?

All I wanted to do was get their attention. Get them to notice the other murders, make connections, re-open Chrissie's case. I've let her down . . . I thought that Eddie could help, but I was wrong, and I couldn't even bring myself to punish him.

Nothing has gone to plan.

I've achieved nothing. I am nothing. It would be simplest just to end it all now. I will write them a note. I will explain. I can use the last of Chrissie's notepaper. I will let them have the figurines. I will apologise to my father. It's not his fault. None of this is his fault. I hope he realises that.

The box with the notepaper and the figurines is in the back of the van. I step out of the driver's seat and into the darkness. There are no other cars parked in the car park now. They will leave me a ticket, telling me to pay them an overnight parking charge, but I won't pay it.

I don't even sense that anyone is there until it is too late. I close my eyes. Remembering . . .

The figure appears behind the van. Hood up. A glint of metal tucked into his jacket. 'What you got in the van, mister?'

A lone wolf. An opportunist. A chancer.

I have to admire his entrepreneurism. 'Nothing that you'd want,' I say. I am not in the mood for this. I'll let him puff his chest for a little longer, then I'll show him what's inside. He'll want money then. I'll give him the cash.

Might as well have a little fun with him. Now that Carly is no longer an option.

He takes a step closer. Too close to me now. His face in my face. 'Open the fucking van, smart-arse,' he says. Rancid spittle hits my cheek.

Rude. I just can't abide people being rude. I was quite willing to give him what he wanted and let him go home, but he has irritated me now, with his bad breath and his baby-gangster swagger. If he has accomplices, I'd have seen them by now. It's only him.

Him and me.

I open the rear doors of the van. Take a step back, waiting for the little thug's reaction.

'What the hell's this? You living in here or something?'

The mattress has thrown him off guard. He was expecting something in a box, I think. Something that he could sell.

'I sleep in here from time to time, yes,' I say. At the far end of the mattress, I've fashioned a little box shelf with a battery-operated light, and various other bits to make it more homely. My duvet and pillows are stacked to one side. There are various bits of clothing on the other side. I hadn't put them away before going to the market in the morning.

'Anything decent in there?' he says. He leans inside.

I don't want him touching my stuff. I don't want him in my space. Blood starts rushing, making me itch. We're alone now, but I don't know how long it will stay that way. If he's hanging around here, there may be others. I have to act quickly. The fact that I hadn't planned this makes the thrill of it even greater than I could have imagined. Something in my head starts to fizz.

I pounce.

Just as he's pulling back out of the van. Using all my strength, I slam one of the doors into him, and he gets the full force of it on the side of his head. He drops to the ground with a muffled *whumph*.

Easier than I expected.

I crouch down to get a better look at him.

'Bet you wish you'd just gone home now, don't you?'

He groans, tries to roll over. I put a knee on his back, pressing him into the dirty tarmac.

'People like you make me sick. Disgusting little opportunists. What were you hoping for? Did you think I had a vanload of Christmas shopping? Games consoles and iPads. New flat screen for my mum. Designer clothes, maybe? You little bastard.'

I press my knee down harder, but he doesn't move. I ease back a bit, lift his head. It is indented with pockmarks from the loose gravel that I have pressed into his face. I pull him back by the hair. He's still breathing. Just.

You could say I have two choices now. I could finish the job, or I could leave him like this, maybe call an ambulance on the way.

Why should I?

No one called an ambulance for Chrissie. No one made the right choice there. If this little bastard had felt like sticking a knife in me to get what he wanted, he'd have done it. No questions. No hesitation.

I'm hesitating now. Why?

I blow out a long slow breath, watch it puff into a dense white cloud in front of me. If it's not me, it will be someone else. I'm doing society a favour. I'm still holding his hair with one hand. With the other hand, I reach around, pinching his nose and covering his mouth. In the semi-conscious state he's in, it won't take long. He probably won't even know it's happening. A mercy killing.

The rage comes back, forcing its way through my veins. Fizzing and prickling. A roar in my ears, like a stormy sea. A gust of wind, carrying icy droplets of fresh snow.

He doesn't deserve my mercy.

I take my hand off his nose and mouth, and I slam his head down onto the tarmac. There is a crack. I pull it back and smash it down once again. A crunch, muffled a little, the soft skin of his face being macerated on the ground.

That fizzing in my head again. Buzzing. Screeching in my ears.

I let go of his head and it hits the ground with a soft thud.

When I sit back, I realise that things have changed now.

I have become something else. There is no coming back from this.

That choice again. Take him somewhere, dump his body. Or leave it here, and hope that the snow covers him overnight. Leaving him to the elements, and to chance.

My muscles ache. I feel like I could sleep for a thousand years.

I scribble on a piece of Chrissie's notepaper. Twelve. Then I push it into his left coat pocket. In the right pocket, I place two figurines.

I'm not playing games any more.

44

CARLY

Her mouth is dry and sour and she has vague memories of being sick but not a lot else.

Oh God. Caleb.

She rolls over, and is relieved to find that the other side of the bed is cool and unruffled. She has not shared her bed with anyone, it seems. She turns back onto her back and stares up at the ceiling. Stays still, trying to stop the room from spinning.

Oh God. Eddie.

She has a cheek to be annoyed with Eddie. To her knowledge, Eddie has never had as much as a sniff of an affair. Not even a bit of harmless flirting, or a one-off meaningless drunken kiss. Of all people, she would have said he had more right than anyone to do any of these things. Have a proper affair if he liked. In some ways, it would have made life easier. Imagining that he might be happy, even if it was with someone else, but still coming back to her and the children.

In the beginning, she'd imagined that he would grow to love her, eventually. How could he not, when they had such beautiful children, a perfect home? He enjoyed his job, but he didn't have to do it if he didn't want to. Her mum and dad would have helped them to work things out. All they had ever wanted was for her to be happy.

She grows bored of the peeling paint on the cornices. The shadow of dust on the lightbulb. She closes her eyes. She's made such a mess of things. She knows that. But sometimes things just can't be fixed. Maybe it will be better if Eddie does leave them. She'll cope. The kids will cope. They've been coping long enough as it is.

Is it any wonder that Noelle is staying on at boarding school for an extra week of additional study, rather than coming home to her family? She'll be eighteen soon. She'll be finished school in five months. Carly knows that she won't see her for dust. She's not the only one that's been waiting for this day to come.

Of course, her grandmother has already planned the party. They'll be seeing in 2017 as their youngest daughter turns eighteen, and if there's a person in West Surrey who hasn't been invited, Carly will be extremely surprised. No expense spared for precious little Noelle, always her granny's favourite. Carly is sure that her daughter had sensed from the minute she was born that she was a result of a drunken mistake, just like her brother and sister. There was a gap, yes. There had been a brief time when Eddie had seemed happier. She'd imagined for a little while that maybe they could start again. But then it had fizzled out to nothing. Except for the pregnancy, of course. To his credit, he had never as much as hinted at them not going ahead with it all. That's not something he would ever think, never mind say. But it had crossed Carly's mind. Did she really want to put herself through it all again? Plus, it meant she wouldn't be having any sex for a very long time. Even she drew the line at hook-ups when she had a visible bump . . . and afterwards, she was out of bounds until the milk disappeared and she could convince Granny to let her go on a night out. Eddie wouldn't babysit for that. He wasn't a complete pushover. She'd hoped the older kids might have been interested in helping out with their little sister, but once the novelty had worn off, they were back to their own self-absorbed ways.

Carly hates herself most of the time. For allowing this to happen. For letting her children become spoilt and indifferent. For letting her husband down, day after day. The drinking was inevitable. But it has to stop.

She drags herself out of bed. The alarm clock says it's 12.30, but how can it be? Wouldn't they have called her and told her to check out? It's not even her room . . . She glances over and sees the phone off the hook. Groans. She should get ready for the market. She needs food. Something greasy.

There's a white towelling bathrobe lying on the sofa. Plastic wrapping half-stuffed under a cushion. The cord is uncoiled on the floor, like a bored snake. She has no recollection of taking the robe out of the bag. Did Caleb do it?

She can't face seeing Caleb again. She doesn't want him to remind her of what she might have said the night before. Or done. Just because it didn't happen in her bed, it doesn't mean she didn't have sex with him. She's blacked out a sexual encounter before. Sometimes she's wished she could black one out. Things didn't always work out as she wanted them.

She's in the coffee shop next door, waiting for her double-shot Americano and her microwaved bacon roll, wincing at the irritating Christmas tunes being piped through the speakers, when she remembers that she called Eddie the night before, told him she wasn't coming home. She can't remember exactly what she said, or what he said back, but she can still feel the waves of disappointment that made their way down the phone.

'Pull yourself together, Carly,' she mutters. The woman standing next to her, pouring sachets of sugar into her drink, gives her an odd look. Carly ignores her. She takes her coffee and her roll into the corner of the café. Hopes that her hands will stop shaking soon so that she can drive home.

The house smells of slow-roasting beef, rosemary, garlic and tomatoes. She thought about baking some dinner rolls, but she realised too late that she'd run out of yeast and there was no time to get any. It had been a surprise – a nice surprise – to get Eddie's text saying he was going to be home for dinner, so could she pick up something on her way back? Assuming she *was* coming back, he'd said. There was a subtext there that she chose to ignore, deciding instead to imagine that her husband might want to spend some time with her. She'd texted the children, asking if they wanted to eat too, but Fiona had already made plans and Simon didn't bother to reply. If Noelle was home, she would have enjoyed sitting with her mum and dad for dinner. It hadn't happened for a long time – partly because Noelle spent most of her holiday time staying with her grandparents, and also because of Eddie. When he did make it home, he went straight to his study and often stayed in there all night.

But not tonight! Tonight, he is coming home. So she's making sure that she is cooking his favourite meal, and that everything will be perfect.

Now that she's back home, in the comfort of her own kitchen, she is thinking twice about confessing her intentions towards Caleb.

Nothing happened.

Lucky escape there, she thinks. After all, she hadn't known anything about him. He'd seemed very interested in Eddie's job, once she'd let it slip that he was a detective. But when she'd told him how little she actually knew, he'd been disappointed.

Shit! A thought hits her. What if he was an undercover reporter? What if he was using her to get information from Eddie . . . something to do with his case? Was this what Eddie had been asking about on the phone when he'd mentioned photographers? He didn't take any photos of her. She can't even remember seeing him with a phone, never mind a camera. Wait though – hadn't he said something right at the beginning about not taking photos 'any more'? Well, so what. She'd told him nothing.

She opens the oven door and lets the aromatic steam fill the kitchen. Then she takes a bottle of red out from the cupboard and uncorks it. She considers having a glass before Eddie gets home, but no. She's going to use all the willpower she possesses not to do anything to ruin this evening.

'This is delicious,' Eddie says. 'When I said I fancied dinner, I didn't mean for you to go to this much trouble.

Becky mentioned she was having lasagne and it got my stomach rumbling.'

They are sitting at the small table in the kitchen. She has laid it with their decent plates and their nice cutlery. A thick white candle on a plate, decorated with holly she plucked from the bush outside.

'I thought it would be nice to make an effort.' She smiles at him, lays a hand over his. She's showered and changed into a casual green dress that he's always liked, although he hasn't commented on it tonight. They lapse into silence, only the sound of cutlery scraping on plates and the occasional distant sound from the street outside.

It takes her a moment to realise he has rested his cutlery on the edge of his plate, put his elbows on the table – his hands steepled together. He is staring at her. She can't read his expression.

'So anyway,' he says, 'what were you doing in Godalming?'

This is what she has been afraid of. She hasn't come up with a decent lie. 'Oh, that. The market in town was poor this year, actually. A lot more tat being sold. Far fewer people around, and the ones who are seem to want this imitation rubbish. Cheap crap instead of a few quid extra for actual home-made crafts. I still did OK, but it just didn't have the atmosphere . . .' She spears a piece of broccoli with her fork and smiles. 'One of the stall-holders said that Godalming was the place to be this year, so I thought, why not? No one needed me round here—'

'The kids needed you. Simon was worried—'

She waves her fork. The broccoli is still on there, like a little flag. 'Oh come on. They're only here when it suits them. Then suddenly they expect me to be at their beck and call?'

She wants to suck the words back inside. She regrets drinking the glass of wine. Even just one. She's topping up from the consecutive days of caning it. She knows that she drinks more than all of her children put together, but it's not her fault that they don't like partying.

She shudders at her own thoughts. What the hell is wrong with her? Well it's obvious, really. She's acting up, because she is terrified. Everything is coming crashing down around her and there's nothing she can do.

'Who were you with then?' He tries again.

She can see that it is a huge effort for him to remain calm, when he (quite rightly) is bubbling away inside.

'No one . . . I went myself.'

He slams his knife down on the table.

'Don't bullshit me, Carly. I'm not an idiot. When did you ever disappear off somewhere on your own, eh? Who is it? Who is he this time? Just some random you met somewhere and started pouring your heart out to? That's your usual type, isn't it? I assume you've been fucking him? While I've been run ragged, chasing after a fucking serial killer. You know someone was murdered in Godalming last night? Until a couple of hours ago, I thought it might've been you.'

He drops the knife onto his plate. Puts his elbows on the table and lets his head fall into his hands.

She feels the wine burning in her throat. 'Was it your serial killer? He was in Godalming? Oh God . . .'

'I tried calling you,' he says. His voice is flat.

There's no hope for them now. She thinks about Caleb. Thinks about all the other meaningless flings over the years, and wishes she could turn back the clock.

Wednesday

FOUR MORE SLEEPS

45

EDDIE

He dresses in his most photogenic suit. A dark grey with a smart matt finish. It'd cost a few quid, but that was a few years ago and he kept it in good condition by almost never wearing it. The text message from Nick Keegan had been brief.

> *Get your glad rags on.*
> *We're live at ten.*

This was it then. The bit where Keegan took over, putting on his public face. Would he mention Eddie? He assumed so, unless he was just meant to sit there like a plum.

Gemma, the eternally enthusiastic Press Officer, bounds up to him the minute he arrives in the office. 'Oh great, you're here. Pre-briefing is just starting.'

Eddie follows her into Nick's office.

All eyes are on him now. He swallows back his irritation. He and Becky were all over this. They were closing in on Colin Thacker. Yet now, after his late-night call to Keegan telling him everything they'd uncovered, it is being pulled away from them.

Maybe it's better this way. Eddie prefers to get on with the job, rather than spout and spin and flash his teeth at the cameras. He is also slightly consoled that Keegan has had to postpone his holiday. He'd be throwing everything he has at this now, aiming to get Thacker behind bars before Christmas.

'Eddie . . .' Nick gives him an open-armed greeting from behind his desk. He's also dressed in his finest, although to be fair, Nick generally looks the smartest in the whole department. Probably because he spends more time schmoozing in meetings rather than getting his hands dirty or his trousers creased from sitting in a car. 'Great work on Thacker. We're going with a bit of a risky strategy, but the powers that be have decreed it.'

'Oh?' Eddie says. 'What's happening then?' He's starting to feel his irritation bubbling over into anger. Why hasn't he been consulted on their media strategy? He's been leading the investigation, albeit not as the SIO, officially, but to all intents and purposes . . . 'I wasn't expecting this just yet. We're almost there. Thacker is a key person of interest, but we don't have any evidence yet. Nothing that will stick. We need to find him first. I told you this last night—'

'Yes, Ed. That you did.' He claps his hands, rubs them together. 'As you said yourself, you can't find him. We don't have a recent picture of him. But we think he's nearby, right? We've discussed this . . .' he nods at Gemma, 'and we feel that the best thing to do is try and draw him out. Lure him into the spotlight. What do you think?'

'What if you scare him off? If we're right about this, he's been murdering people for twenty years. Picking them off at random. No one's seen him before or after. He's been floating around the suburbs like a ghost.'

'Exactly. So, we've had his photograph aged. There are four versions – one where he looks the same, just older. One where he's a bit thinner, then another two with a bit of facial hair. A small beard, as is common these days. We're hoping at least one of them might trigger something. Of course we could've gone further, done one with hair, one bald. But the main thing is, we're going to name him—'

'Wait, hang on . . . you're going to name him on national TV? I told you, we don't have anything to pin on him yet, other than circumstantial stuff – him being a photographer, being related to the first victim, and the fact that he's gone entirely off-grid . . . and we do think his father knows something. We're still working on him. I'm not sure that naming him is the right move.'

'Relax, Eddie. We're not saying he's a suspect . . . but the fact that he was the crime scene photographer on the Ealing case does cast a certain shine on it all, don't you think?'

'Person of interest though, right? Everyone knows what that means.'

'Have you considered why he might be doing this, Eddie?'

Eddie balls his hands into fists. This is what he hates about this job. This. Exact. Thing. He was the one who was sure there was something going on when they received the advent calendar. He was the one who led things with Becky . . . they'd spent a lot of time talking about Colin Thacker, and what his motives might be. Particularly around the Judy Dorringer case. Approaching Eddie in the pub, trying to get his attention. If Eddie is right, this is what it was all about. He doesn't believe he killed his sister. He's shared his theory with Nick already. Is he supposed to repeat it now, like a performing monkey?

'I've told you my theory, yes.' He glances around the room. Nick, with his patronising half-smile. Gemma looking at him like he's a cute little pet that won't go back into its cage. Becky trying to give him her best approving look. The DCI has his arms folded and a face that suggests he's unimpressed. Some of the others are just waiting for him to fuck things up. Then there's Joe, looking back and forth between him and Nick like he's watching the men's singles final at Wimbledon. 'I don't think he killed his sister. I think he's trying to avenge her death, somehow. He's been trying to get our attention for twenty years, because no one knows who killed his sister . . . and that's destroyed his life.'

A few murmurs around the room. He knows that Becky isn't quite convinced yet. The rest of the team is split in two.

'It's pretty extreme though, isn't it? He's violently bludgeoned or stabbed eight people, strangled six, smothered six and now he's battered a teenager to death using his own face and a car park floor—'

'We know he's escalated. Something has triggered that, and yes, the last murder was particularly brutal. We're linking it based on the note and the figures left by the body, even though it doesn't follow the pattern. Basically, he's snapped. He's now completely unpredictable. Also, it's highly likely that he wants to be caught. He's had enough. He's got our attention . . . but he's not finished

yet. I'm worried that naming him will drive him under-
ground.'

'I'm with you on most of that, Eddie. I think we're all
in agreement that he's flipped. The thing is, we'd rather
catch him before he manages to destroy anyone else's
Christmas. Wouldn't you agree?'

'You don't think this is revenge though, do you?'

'I told you earlier that I thought it was extreme. Most
revenge killers operate over two to three years, max – if
they're targeting victims based on their disgruntlement with
an organisation – which is presumably what you're
suggesting here. That he's pissed off with us for not catching
his sister's killer? I'm not buying that entirely. Not yet. It
would be very unusual for a revenge killer to lie dormant
for eleven months of the year, then just pop up before Santa
comes to batter a random stranger in their own living room
. . . and do it again every year for twenty years.'

'I agree with Nick,' DCI Carmichael says. 'He wants
our attention. He wants us to stop him. I think he killed
his sister. He enjoyed it. So he kept going. But now it's
got out of hand and he wants us to finish it for him.'

Murmurs of agreement float around the room.

Eddie feels outnumbered. He also knows there's nothing
he can do, if this has been sanctioned by Keegan's super-
iors. If the DCI is behind it, then that's it.

'Thing is, Eddie – we've already decided all of this. If
it backfires, it won't be your neck on the line . . . and we'll
be happy to accept your "I told you so" when it comes.'

Eddie nods his assent. What else can he do? 'Fine,' he
says. 'Let's do this.'

Keegan claps his hands and rubs them together. His signature move.

Let's just hope this plan of theirs doesn't leave them all looking like fools. He really doesn't want to see another crime scene before Christmas.

46

THE PHOTOGRAPHER

It's a strange feeling, watching it all unfold in front of me. Everything I've done, everything I've felt – removing myself from society. Has it been worth it?

I think so.

For one thing, I won't have to spend any more time in this filthy squat. Or any of the others that I've frequented over the years. To be honest, I will miss the van – the mattress was the most comfortable I've ever had.

I don't have much time.

It was a mistake, driving so aggressively out of that car park. I expect they will have picked up my number plate on the ANPR system now. Thankfully, the number plate is from a burned-out 1992 Ford Fiesta and I expect it will take them a little time to unpick the trail.

It's strange, watching them on TV, talking about me like this. I hadn't expected them to name me. I suppose they think it's their best hope of ferreting me out. They don't quite get it yet though, do they? I want them to find me. I've always wanted them to find me. I'd thought I was leaving a trail of breadcrumbs for someone to follow, but I know now that I was too clever.

Oh the irony! I left school with two O-levels. Both Cs.

Music and carpentry. Neither of them have got me where I am now.

I shuffle back onto the stinking mattress in the corner of the main room. The others are asleep. The sounds of their breathing and the stench in the room suggests it is alcohol related.

Bunch of losers.

I could kill the lot of them right now.

But I won't.

I have other plans. They came to me while watching the press conference, as it happens. I didn't really listen much to what the smug-faced DI Keegan had to say. I know he's not the one who's been truly working this case. It's all bureaucracy and bullshit now, is it not? Carmine and Greene are the ones who've done all the work. I know that, because I've been watching them.

I've been close to them so many times. Overheard their conversations. Seen them in my own bedroom, of all places. The hidden camera worked. I did notice that Greene had clocked my can of deodorant on the window ledge. Smart girl.

Perfect.

I'm glad they haven't focused too much on the advent calendar in the press conference. Yes, I know there are two numbers left. Eighteen and twenty-two. But that's fine. I don't need to use them both. The last one can stay empty, and leave them wondering. They might think they saved someone's life. Thwarted my final act.

After the next part has come to fruition, there will only be one door left.

Number eighteen. My birthday.

I wonder when they're going to realise that the final act is me?

47

They spend the rest of the afternoon and most of the evening wading through the piles of notes that have been left for them by the other members of the team. Hundreds of leads. Most of them completely useless. After the press got hold of the serial killer theory, it had sent all of the other forces into a spin. Eddie wishes they'd taken more of an interest earlier on, but there's not much he can do about it now. Becky has spent most of the drive to the Students' Union taking calls.

The girl at the front desk is about the same age as his daughter but it's hard to tell what she would look like without the piercings. Didn't it used to be illegal to stick pins all over your face or was that just tattoos? He remembers the thing in the news from a few years back. Belgium. Tattooist did a bunch of stars on the cheek of a teenager who was not only too young but most likely drunk. Sure, there are lasers, but her face would never be the same again. Pin-face smirks at them, looks like she's about to comment on their ages or their clothes but before she can say a word, Becky has pushed the warrant card into her face and silenced her.

She nods to a man standing just outside the safety of her Perspex box. A man who doesn't look like he needs to be protected by plastic. He holds out a hand and gestures for them to do the same, before wordlessly stamping them with a small ink stamp. Eddie is about to say something about the ink running out, when he shines a penlight torch over them and the ink lights up into a bright violet.

HappyTimes! ☺

'Cheers,' Eddie says.

He turns to Becky and rolls his eyes. 'Shall we?' They push through the metal swing doors into the club. The noise and the heat almost knock them back. Not to mention a strange chemical undertone that could be cleaning products or cheap perfume. They take a few steps inside and the music becomes clearer, the pounding bass that hit him in the chest lessens, and the smell takes on more than a hint of sweat.

The place is packed. Girls and boys, young men and women. A few older. Squeezed close to each other, shouting into ears. Writhing as a mass on the jammed dance floor. People snaking through the crowd, drinks held high but still slopping out of plastic cups. Blues and reds and greens and something he assumes is beer, if beer is similar to dirty dishwater.

'Where's the bar?' he shouts towards Becky. She's moving slightly in time to the music. Something that sounds vaguely familiar about rocking a baby, a song that doesn't deserve the airplay it gets, in Eddie's opinion. He doesn't get modern music. Anything past 1999 and you might as well wear ear plugs.

He watches as Becky slithers her way through the crowd with ease. He spots the bar. Thinks there's no way she'll get anyone's attention there, when miraculously a gap opens as if she is Moses parting the Red Sea. Her age and her sex have got one over on him this time, that's something he can't change.

He stays close to the side of the room, trying to take in what's going on. He feels old and grumpy. Wishes he had taken off his suit. He feels ridiculous. Wishes he was at home. Then a song comes on that makes him grin. Becky appears at his side, clutching two cold cans of Coke.

Miraculous. Maybe he can cope with this a bit longer after all.

'I love this song,' she yells in his ear. It's Dario G. 'Sunchyme'. One of his favourites too.

'You know the original song it's sampled from is much better,' he shouts back. '"Life in a Northern Town".'

'What?'

'Dream Academy.'

'What?'

'It doesn't matter. You're too young to know what I'm talking about.' He doesn't bother to shout this, because she can't hear him anyway. He pops the ring on the can and downs half of it in one. Runs the cold can across his forehead. Why didn't he leave his jacket in the car?

She leans in close, talks loud, right into his ear. He feels a slight shiver at her breath, chilled from the cold drink. 'Barman told me to go through the back . . .' She nods towards a door marked 'Private'. 'Says DJ Mortal will be stopping for a break at ten.'

Eddie pulls his phone out of his pocket. It's almost ten now. Things are looking up. A suited bouncer with that generic bouncer stance that says 'I don't actually care what you say or do' puffs his chest at them as they try to push through the door. Becky flashes her warrant card at him with a look on her face that tells him exactly what she thinks. He raises an eyebrow and opens the door. He saves his glare for Eddie.

'Who you looking for?' His voice echoes into the dimly lit corridor behind.

'Him,' Eddie says. Tilts his head towards the DJ booth. 'Make sure he comes in for his break, OK? I take it there's an office down here?'

'Last door on the left.'

The door to the club swings shut behind them and they can hear themselves think again. Only the vibration and thump of the bass escapes through the door. The strip-lights cast a purple hue. They flicker and buzz, and the whole effect is not unlike something from a horror film. Eddie shivers. The heat and the sweat are turning quickly to a chill without the body heat of a couple of hundred others to keep him warm.

Becky has disappeared into what he assumes is the office. He finds her sitting at the far side of the small room on a fabric swivel chair that has seen better days. There is a bank of four CCTV monitors, each image flipping from one camera to another. There is very little air in the room, and what there is of it smells of mouldy cheese.

'There's eight in total. They change every four seconds.' The man sitting next to Becky leans forward and presses a button. 'You can flick them manually too if you want. See?'

'Thanks,' Eddie says. He throws Becky a look, and she shrugs in reply. 'Sorry, who are you?'

'Stuart Elmer. Part of the security team. You'll have met my colleague, Al?'

'Ah yes. The charmer. Listen . . .' Eddie lifts a chair from a stack in the corner. Plastic dining-room chairs. Nothing special. 'We're not here about security—'

'Although it seems like you're doing a great job.' Becky beams.

'Right,' Eddie says. He throws her a look and she pretends to study a poster about Health and Safety that's been taped to the wall next to where she's sitting. 'We just need a quick word with your DJ. Andy Mortlake? It won't take long.'

Stuart lets out a long, slow breath. Shakes his head. 'Aw man. I warned him, you know. He said he'd stopped that shit . . .'

'What shit's that?' Becky says, swivelling round to face them again.

'Yeah, Stu, what shit's that?'

Eddie turns at the sound of the voice. It hadn't been obvious when he was behind the box, but the DJ is reed thin, with the heavily lined face of someone who has spent many years abusing their body. 'Andy Mortlake,' he says. 'At your service. I don't know what Stu-pot's been telling you, but—'

Eddie holds up a hand. 'Relax. We're not here about drugs. Although . . .' he pauses, 'you might want to think about sorting that out, and being as cooperative as you can, then we might not need to bother calling the drugs squad – what do you say?'

Andy Mortlake grins. Unsurprisingly, his teeth are mostly yellow. 'What can I do for you?'

Becky stands up. 'Colin Thacker, aka Caleb Temple,' she says. 'Any idea where we might find him?'

Eddie tries to read Mortlake's face, but it flashes through a range of emotions so quickly, it's impossible to know whether this is a natural tic, a genuine reaction, or the result of whatever it is he's taken to get him through his set.

He leans against the door frame, going for casual. Looks up into the corner of the room. Looking for the best lie. 'Jesus, there's a name I haven't heard for a while. What's he been up to?'

'We were hoping you might be able to tell us that, Andy. We spoke to Henry in the photography department. Says you two used to hang out. That you were Colin's mentor, or something.'

Mortlake snorts. 'Not sure I'd go that far. It was a long time ago. I'd done some freelance work. Caleb . . . Colin was interested.'

'You still taking photographs now?' Becky says.

He shakes his head. 'Nah. Left that all behind years ago. It gets to you after a while. You get desensitised. Then they start to come to you in your dreams.'

'Who do?' Eddie says.

'The victims. The corpses. I'm talking about crime scenes, man. You know what it's like, right? But getting that close. Taking their pictures—'

'When did you stop?'

Mortlake scratches at his stubble. 'Must be fifteen years now, I think. Early 2000s. Work was drying up, actually. Most of the forces don't use dedicated photographers any more, do they? CSIs just do the lot. It's a different skill, if you ask me. But anyway, I couldn't do it now. I'm fine here with my happy dance tunes and a bit of cheesy pop.'

'When did you last see Colin?'

He scratches at his scraggy beard again. Looks down at the carpet. 'I can't remember. Long time now. Yeah. Long time.' He looks up. 'Did he ever start doing crime scenes, do you know? I gave him a few of my photos. Probably shouldn't have. I meant to ask for them back, but then I forgot and we lost touch—'

'I don't suppose you know which photographs you gave him, do you Andy? I know it's a long time ago, but this could be important. We're trying to find him. No one seems to know where he is. No one seems to know what he's up to these days.'

Mortlake closes his eyes. 'I gave him a photograph of his sister, OK? It was me who attended her scene. But I think you already know that, don't you? Or else why would you be bothering me? I think he knew that when he started hanging around after the class, asking me questions. It was like he was working up to it. I don't know why he wanted to see it. I told him it was a bad idea—'

'It's OK. You don't need to worry about any of that now. But if you know where Colin is, please, just tell us. We really need to speak to him.'

Mortlake nods. Shakes his head. Looks away. 'Sorry. No. I've no idea.'

Becky speaks before Eddie can lose his rag. 'If you think of anything, maybe you could give me a call?' Her voice is gentler than Eddie's.

They push their way back out of the club and onto the street. 'I meant to follow up with Abby on who was Chrissie's crime scene photographer. I assumed she'd have contacted me if there was anything significant, but how would she know what we were looking for?' He kicks a bin and a cascade of polystyrene boxes fall out, scattering chips and limp lettuce leaves. 'But you know – this just backs up my point – that he didn't kill his sister. Because if he did, he wouldn't need the crime scene photograph, would he?'

He feels a stab of guilt as Becky bends down and starts trying to scoop up the debris. She stuffs the boxes back into the overflowing bin, wipes her hands on her jacket. Pulls a face. 'Maybe . . . but he didn't do the photography course until after his sister was killed. What if he didn't take a photograph at the time, but then decided that was going to be his plan, so he tracked down Mortlake and managed to get hold of Chrissie's photo—'

They open the car doors in unison. 'So he could complete the set?'

'Exactly.'

Eddie sighs. 'Come on,' he says. 'I'll take you home.'

48

BECKY

'Hey . . . this is a nice surprise! I thought you'd be flat out at work with your big case?' Gary grabs her around the waist, pulls her into him. He kisses her hard and she responds with as much energy as she can muster. Which isn't much.

'Eddie told me to get an early night. Reckons it'll all kick off tomorrow. Keegan will have the whole station involved, not to mention the others who've got a vested interest. I'm expecting a call any time, telling me I need to go back in—'

'So maybe we should take advantage of this time then, hmm?' He starts to nuzzle her ear, and she pulls away. He looks hurt.

'I'm sorry . . . really. I just . . . I'm knackered. I probably stink. Plus, I am absolutely starving.'

He pushes her away, playfully. Sticks out his bottom lip into a poor attempt at a pout. 'Want me to cook? He takes her hand and pulls her through to the kitchen. 'Look – I even went shopping.' A supermarket carrier bag stuffed with several other carrier bags is sitting on the worktop next to an unopened loaf of wholemeal bread and a six-pack of Diet Coke. Next to it, an open bottle of Shiraz and a glass with a hint of red at the bottom.

'I'm hoping you got more than that?'

He pouts again. 'The fridge is full, your majesty. Your wish is my command.'

'Surprise me,' she says. She pours wine into the used glass, takes it through to the living room, bending to lift her bag from where she'd dumped it in the hall a few minutes ago.

'Make yourself at home,' he calls through, 'don't worry about me.' There is such happiness in his voice. She realises how much she's been neglecting him.

'Bring us something to nibble, will you?'

He appears beside her just as she is pulling off her boots. Lays a bowl of crisps on the side table next to her. 'What did your last slave die of?'

'Not doing what he was told.' She kisses his ear before he straightens back up.

'Half an hour for food, OK? I'm doing a quick sausage casserole with green beans.'

'Perfect,' she says. She holds out the DVD that she's taken from her bag, flutters her eyelashes at him. 'Pretty please.'

He rolls his eyes. Walks over to the TV and slides the disc into the slot at the side. He turns the box over in his hands. 'This looks interesting.'

'Research. Cheers, babe.'

He tosses the remote into her lap and disappears back through to the kitchen. 'That'll be me dismissed then,' he mutters. 'Get back in your box, Gary.'

She smiles. Things are so easy with him. So comfortable. She doesn't really need excitement, does she? She's got work for that.

49

EDDIE

After last night's argument, he doesn't really want to go home. But he's exhausted. He's barely eaten, and despite all her faults, Carly is an excellent cook when she's in the mood. Hopefully she's kept last night's dinner in the fridge so he can heat it up and have it in his office. He closes the door quietly, walks carefully through to the kitchen. He doesn't want to talk to anyone right now. He needs time to think things through. Like Colin Thacker, and where he might be hiding. Is Nick's tactic of trying to draw him out by naming him on the news going to blow up in their faces?

'Eddie, is that you?'

Carly's voice drifts through from the living room. He notices then that the TV is on low. He hadn't noticed it when he came in. Assumed she'd be asleep. He ignores her, walks through to the kitchen and drops his car keys on the table. Opens the fridge and the bright light makes him wince.

'Eddie? I saw the news. I need to talk to you.'

He sighs. 'Not now. Please. I'm knackered. Is there any of that meat left from last night?' He rummages on the shelves, moving packs of cheese and tubs of yoghurt out of the way. 'Did you go shopping?' he asks, surprised. The fridge has been a sorry sight for days. He turns to face her. She's dressed in a velour tracksuit, her hair freshly washed and pulled back from her face. She looks clean, fresh. Smells floral. He realises with further surprise that she hasn't been drinking. He takes out a pack of ready-cooked chicken drumsticks and rips the cellophane away from one corner.

'I know the man from the press conference,' she says, pushing the fridge door shut. She waits for him to react.

He takes a bite of chicken. Tries to swallow but it is too dry and he feels his throat start to close up. He coughs, and she hands him a bottle of water.

'What do you mean?' he says. He drops the chicken back into the plastic tub. The hunger that had been gnawing at him slips away. 'Which man? Keegan? Of course you do—'

'No,' she says. 'You need to listen to me, Ed.'

He looks at her properly, then. Sees the fear in her eyes. He sits down. Gestures for her to do the same. 'Go on . . .'

'The photofit. I mean, it's not great. But something about the eyes. He has very striking eyes—'

'Who does?'

'Caleb . . . it said on the news that he was called Colin, but he's not. He's called Caleb, he's—'

Eddie stands up too fast, feels the room spin. 'How do you know him, Carly? Do you have his number? Do you know where he is? Did you . . .' He pauses, the realisation hitting him. 'Did you sleep with him, Carly? Is this who you were with in Godalming?' He watches in horror as she starts to tremble. Tears flow down her cheeks. She shakes her head.

'No. I . . . I wanted to. I did. But something changed. I don't know. I drank too much. I was sick. When I came out of the bathroom, he was gone.'

'Which bathroom? Where did he go? Think, Carly. Think! Did he give you his number?'

She shakes her head again. 'No. But maybe you could call the hotel. He might've given it to them. It was the white one on the High Street, you know it. I can't remember the name . . .'

The thought hits him, and he has to fight the urge to throw up. He can taste the chicken at the back of his throat, threatening to reappear.

He's been there all along.

Thacker has been fucking with him all along. He's spared Carly – this time. But the pattern is so messed up now, Eddie has no idea what might happen next. He puts his hand over his wife's and tries to stay calm. 'Which room were you in?' he says.

She turns her hand over and takes hold of his. Clings on as if trying to stop herself from falling. He can see now, how desperate she has been for some human contact. Remorse crashes inside his skull. All this time, all she's wanted was his affection . . . and it was the one thing he couldn't give her. Too busy fighting off the ghosts of his past. But it's too late now. Too much water under the bridge.

'Which room were you in, Carly?' he says again.

'Twelve,' she says. 'I remember because it was one of those big leather fobs . . .' her voice trails off.

He pulls her towards him, onto his knee, and he holds

her there. Buries his face into her hair. Feels the wetness on her cheeks as she presses her face to his. She will have to go into the station, make a statement. But it can wait until morning. For now, she is safe . . . and Eddie realises that he wants to keep her that way.

Thursday

THREE MORE SLEEPS

50

BECKY

Becky is impatiently tapping her fingers on her desk when Eddie arrives. 'Morning,' she says. 'I've got an update you might like—'

'I've got one too,' he says, cutting her off. 'But you probably won't like this one.'

'Oh?'

'I've just left Carly in the Sunshine Suite. Joe and Keir are interviewing her.'

She stops drumming her fingers and stands up. 'What's going on, Ed?'

He sighs. 'Carly's apparently been hanging out with our man at her Christmas market . . . she went to Godalming with him—'

'Wait, what? With Colin? Where is he now?' She runs a hand through her hair, pulls on it, pricking at her scalp. Trying to waken herself up a bit. She can't really take it in. 'He's been right under our noses the whole time?'

'He's played us for mugs, Becks. And aside from that, Carly's lucky to be alive.'

'Fucking hell . . .'

'Yeah. Well I'll probably be off the case in a bit so might as well get cracking while she's still being interviewed, eh? What've you got?'

She feels a fluttering in her chest. It's all coming together now. 'I got a call from Andy Mortlake this morning. He apologised for not telling us last night, but said he needed time to think . . . said he couldn't believe that Colin might be a killer, but then he caught the press conference on the all-night news and had second thoughts. He reckons we might find him at a squat on Hamilton Avenue. Although who's to say he'll still be there, if he saw the press conference himself?'

'Oh he'll have seen it, all right. It's exactly what he's been waiting for. All the attention. Let's go.'

'Don't you want to wait for Carly—'

He shakes his head. 'Come on, Becks,' he says. 'Let's go.'

She tosses a pound coin into the swear box as they walk out of the office.

The address that Andy Mortlake has given them is on a Victorian terrace just off the town centre. It's a place where homes have been owned for decades and in many cases fallen into disrepair. Dotted in amongst the houses with front gardens full of rubbish and window frames with flaking paint are the increasingly apparent renovations – painted boards with the names of the building firms erected around the front doors and windows, blocking the view from the street.

Number seventy-seven is not a renovation.

It's mid-terrace, on the side of the road where most of the houses are in serious need of repair: their stonework stained dark from damp, front walls either removed or crumbling into the paths. The number of wheelie bins usually determines the number of flats or bedsits that the house has been partitioned into, but at number seventy-seven there are only bags of rubbish, some overturned and already providing a simple hunting ground for rodents.

Only a single doorbell. No intercom.

Becky knows of a couple of places like this in the town. The elderly owners have died, leaving the house to someone who was either difficult to track down, or not sufficiently interested to claim the property. In some cases, the person who it's been left to has let the house be turned into a squat, because they couldn't be arsed to deal with cleaning it up.

She rings the bell, but she doesn't hear any sound coming from inside. They wait. No one comes.

'We might as well go in,' Eddie says. He's standing with his hands in his pockets, shoulders hunched against the wind. He's moving from foot to foot. Cold and impatient. He puffs out a cloud of white breath, then steps past her.

The door opens easily. Left on the latch. Eddie tries to click the locking mechanism back out, but nothing happens. 'It's buggered,' he says. Shrugs.

The house smells of rot. That damp, fusty smell of old carpets and unopened windows. Something else too. Stale alcohol. Bins. Unwashed bodies.

The hall is dimly lit, the light coming through the glass pane at the top of the door from the dull sunlight outside.

She shudders.

She has a bad feeling about this place. About the people who might be in it. Lurking in the shadows. Waiting. The thing with squats is that someone always has to be there. Leave it empty, even for a short while, and the council can claim possession, on account of it being uninhabitable. She clicks the light switch. Nothing happens.

'No bulb,' Eddie says. She follows his gaze up to the high ceiling. 'Even if they do have any electricity. Which is doubtful, unless it's owner-occupied.'

Becky wrinkles her nose. 'Surely no one who owned this place would want to live in it like this?'

'You'd be surprised. Drugs. I've seen it when the house has been left to an addict, and they've moved all their mates in. Usually gets them a good deal on their gear, when they have a place for people to sleep . . . to sort out their transactions off the street.'

Becky feels a bit sick, but mostly she feels sad. She always feels sorry for people who've ended up in a life like this. She's not one of those who believes that addicts are the cause of their own downfall. Addiction is an illness, just like any other. Sometimes it doesn't take much for someone to fall down the rabbit hole.

The door to their left is ajar. Eddie pushes it open, sticks his head in. 'Hello,' he says. 'Anyone in there?'

No answer.

'Kitchen. Although it's covered in so much crap, it'd be hard to tell if it wasn't for the sink and the units.' He walks in, holds the door open wide. 'Hello?' he says again. Still nothing. He kicks at a lump on the floor, but it turns out to be a pile of filthy clothes. The movement releases a greasy, salty stink. He backs out into the hall. 'Let's try upstairs.'

She lets him take the lead. The stairs are bare boards, some of them rotten. Luckily, he has a small torch, and he shines it on every stair before stepping on it. You can't be too careful. She follows close behind, gripping the banister but also keeping close to the wall, just in case the rickety rail comes away in her hand.

At the top of the stairs, a small bathroom is straight ahead. The door wide open, the old white toilet and sink coated in black. Limescale, mould and general neglect. Flies are buzzing around the toilet. The small frosted window has a top pane that flips down, and it is open, letting in the freezing air from outside.

Eddie pushes open the door to the left, and she can't help her curiosity about the bathroom. She steps inside, sees brown murky water in the pan, a darker brown rim lined above it. At least there is water in there. At least they can flush. Hanging above the bath is a filthy plastic shower curtain, also stained with mould, but inside, it looks like someone has recently used it. Droplets of water are still there on the filthy tiles. The thought of having a bath or a shower in there makes her want to throw up.

She follows Eddie into the room. He's standing silently, just inside the door. She walks in on tiptoes, not sure why she is doing it, but the floorboards creak anyway.

'Wakey wakey,' Eddie says. He claps his hands.

What she'd thought was another pile of dirty clothes, in the far corner, suddenly moves. A slow roll to one side. A face appears from the top of what she can now see is a sleeping bag.

'Fuck off,' the man in the bag says, predictably.

This room is also lit by the muted sunlight outside. She peers around, letting her eyes adjust to the gloom.

In the other corner, balanced precariously on a pile of wooden fruit crates, is a flat screen TV.

She almost laughs at this absurdity, but it's always the way. The size of a person's income seems to be inversely proportionate to the size of their TV – except for all the so-called 'normals' who also have normal-sized TVs. So they do have electricity then. She glances up to the ceiling. Just no bulbs.

'Where's Colin?' Eddie says.

'Fuck off,' the man in the bag says again. But he does pull himself up into a sitting position. 'What time is it?'

'Gone eleven,' Eddie says. 'This your house?'

The man in the bag snorts. 'That's right, mate. I'm the lord of this manor.' He pulls himself out of the bag, like a fat pupa emerging from a cocoon. 'Whatever you're looking for, it ain't here.'

'Did Colin watch his press conference here then?' Eddie says. He nods towards the TV. 'Nice bit of kit. Bigger than mine.'

The man laughs, and it turns into a hacking cough. Once he's done, he roots about in his pockets, pulls out a packet of tobacco. He takes papers out from inside and starts rolling himself a thin cigarette. 'No Colin round here, mate,' he says.

'Caleb then? Seen him?' Eddie walks further into the room. 'And I'm not your mate, or else you'd have offered me a cup of tea by now.'

Becky notices the camping stove in the corner, close to where the man is sitting. A couple of stained mugs next to it. He's looking down, concentrating on making the cigarette. Avoiding eye contact.

'Police, are ye?' Becky can't work out the man's accent. It's some sort of mix of London and Irish, maybe. Or maybe he just picks and chooses how he speaks, depending on his audience.

'Right,' says Eddie. 'So no Colin. No Caleb. What about Lucas?'

The man drops the tobacco into his lap, stares at Eddie. 'Who's asking?'

Eddie pulls out his warrant card. 'DS Carmine. This is DC Greene.' He nods towards her. 'So, this Lucas—'

The man frowns, seems to be considering his options. Decides that he doesn't really have any after all. He obviously doesn't feel any loyalty to the man who calls himself 'Lucas' – the name that Colin (assuming it was Colin) had mentioned in Ealing.

'You just missed him. He took all his shit. I don't think he's coming back. Which is a bit of a shame, as it happens, because he usually brought decent stuff with him. Kept the rest of us from starving to death, you know. Don't suppose you've got anything to leave us, have you, guv?'

'Any idea where he went?'

The man shakes his head. 'Nah. He's got that van though. He sleeps in that a lot. Only comes here now and then. Especially when it's cold. Not that it's much warmer in here, mind.'

'Let's go,' Eddie says. Impatient.

'I'll bring you some things . . . tomorrow,' Becky says. 'I won't forget. OK?'

The man grins. 'Merry Christmas, darlin'.' He lights his cigarette.

51

He is not waiting at the door for them this time. No doubt he is sick of the sight of them, but there's nothing they can do about that. The old man is lying. Yes, he is protecting his son – Eddie knows that he would do the same – but he must also be pretty sure that his son has not killed anyone. Or if he isn't, he's done an excellent job of covering it up. He opens the door, gives them a look that says 'please, no more'. They follow him inside.

He tilts his head towards Eddie. 'Saw you on the telly. Thought you'd have been the one doing the talking, mind. Do you want a drink?'

It's OK,' Becky says. 'We won't be long. I promise. There were just a couple more questions we wanted to ask . . . well, I wanted to ask, actually. About Chrissie.'

Rob sits down on the chair. Becky and Eddie take the couch. It feels like a well-rehearsed routine now, except for the tea and cakes. They've gone past the point of tea and cakes, sadly. Rob crosses his arms. He's trying to sink into the chair. Make himself smaller. He doesn't want any more interrogation. He's scared that he can no longer keep up the lies.

'Did Chrissie like making things, Rob?' Becky asks.

'Like what?'

'You know, arts and crafts – that sort of thing.'

'I already told you she did, didn't I?' He scratches his head and Eddie notices that his hand is shaking.

'Did she ever make little figurines? Like these?' She leans across and shows him the picture on her phone. Jesus and the Virgin Mary.

Rob drops his head into his hands.

'I'm sorry,' he says. His voice is thick with tears. 'I'd lost my wife. Then my daughter. You can't blame me for protecting my son, can you? He's all I've got left. I hoped that you were wrong. I didn't want to believe he could do any of this . . . hurt those people. He was always such a gentle boy—'

'Where is he, Rob?' Eddie's voice is hard.

'I don't know. I swear. He called round yesterday. He was different . . . he said he wouldn't be coming back. Said I'd never see him again. He said he was sorry—'

'Do you have any of those figurines,' Becky says. 'Are they here?'

Rob nods and gets up from the chair. He seems to have aged ten years since they first met him. He disappears from the room.

'What're you thinking, Becks?'

'Evidence. I want to make sure. If he has others, we can get forensics to match them against the ones we have from Godalming. I've asked Joe to take one of the CSIs back to Linda Hollis's and Chris Hardy's houses to collect the figurines from there too. We're lacking in anything concrete to get him on, in case you hadn't noticed.'

She is still pissed off with him for not telling Keegan

about Ealing straight away. He'll sort it. But not right now.

Rob comes back into the room. He's got the deodorant can inside a transparent freezer bag. He holds it aloft. 'This is his. He must've left it the other day. You might need it for prints . . .'

'Christ,' Eddie says. 'You do realise you've been aiding and abetting a murderer, don't you, Rob? You do understand that, don't you? If you'd told us before, you might've saved another family from the Christmas heartache that you've had to deal with all these years. Or maybe it's all a bluff . . . maybe you even helped him cover up the fact that he murdered his own sister. Your daughter—'

'No! You've got it all wrong. He loved Chrissie. He'd never have hurt a hair on her head.' He starts trembling. The bag containing the deodorant falls from his hands. He bends down to pick it up, lets out a strangled sob.

Becky gives Eddie a look. Eddie shrugs.

'This is really helpful, Rob. Thanks,' Becky says. 'Any luck with the figurines?'

'Sorry.' He stands up, hands her the bag. Shakes his head. 'They were in a box in Chrissie's room. In the bottom of her wardrobe. He must've taken them. It's gone.'

Eddie puts a hand on Rob's arm. 'We'll make this as painless as we can for you, Rob. But if there's anything else you can think of . . . anything else that Colin might've said that could help us find him?'

Rob wipes away a tear with the cuff of his sweatshirt. 'I think it's too late, Detective Carmine. The way he said goodbye to me – it felt final. I think . . . I think he might have gone somewhere to kill himself.'

Back at the station, things are in full flow. The place is buzzing. More officers have been assigned, every one of them bursting with nervous excitement.

'Ah, there you are.' Keegan pops his head out of the office. 'Briefing in five minutes.'

Eddie balls his fists. Opens his mouth to say something, but Becky stops him.

'Come on, Ed. It's still our baby. We've brought it this far.'

He nods. She's right, but it doesn't mean it doesn't piss him off. If there's one thing this case has done, it's that it's awoken his ambition. He'll enquire about doing the Inspector's exam after this. He's got a new burst of life, in his job, at least. Home might take a bit more to sort out.

He walks over to the wall of faces. Spends a moment looking at each one of them individually, giving them the time they deserve. All twenty-two of them. They are not just victims. They are people who had lives and families and jobs and children. People who went Christmas shopping, looked forward to too much turkey and Christmas pudding and sherry. People whose lives were taken before they got the chance to tell anyone that they loved them. He re-reads all of their names.

Chrissie Thacker. Dave Connolly. Rhian Cummings. Kevin Tumnell. Sally McGee. Kate Steele. Jack Thomson. Albert

Hemming. Brian Cowley. Judy Dorringer. Stephen Jackson. Clare Jones. Fran Davies. Laura Davis. Lydia Simms. Jason Smythe. Victoria Moon. Lewis Kane. Sam Brown. Linda Hollis. Chris Hardy. Aaron White.

He runs his finger across the last one. The hoodie in the car park who was in the wrong place at the wrong time. Who took the brunt of Thacker's rage after he left Carly alive.

Carly Carmine. His wife.

'OK,' Keegan says. He claps his hands. Eddie turns around and blinks. The office is full of people. He'd been so engrossed in the photographs that he hadn't heard them all come in.

Joe steps forward and hands Eddie a pile of newspapers. The headlines scream at him.

CHRISTMAS KILLER STILL AT LARGE
ADVENT MAN KNOWN TO POLICE
POLICE NO CLOSER TO CATCHING KILLER

Eddie sighs and lays them on the desk. Nods a thanks at Joe.

Keegan notices and sighs. 'As you can see, the press are having a field day with this. The press conference was a success. We've had lots of information fed in. Lots of useless stuff, obviously, but not everyone is a time-waster. There have been sightings of Thacker both near his family home and near the squat at Hamilton Avenue. We've got people watching both properties right now.' He pauses, glances at Eddie. 'Due to a key witness coming forward, we also have an updated photofit . . .' He points at the board. 'Tasks are on the board. We're closing in on this guy, and we're going to make sure that we get him. Aren't we, team?'

A few nods and murmurs.

'Aren't we, team?' he says again, louder.

A chorus of 'Yes, Sir's' ripples across the room.

Keegan claps his hands again and the crowd starts to disperse. Eddie is reading the list of assigned tasks when Keegan appears at his side. 'A word, Eddie?' He nods towards his office. Becky gives him a tight smile as he walks away.

'Right,' Keegan says. 'We have a couple of issues here, Ed, don't we?'

Eddie opens his mouth to speak, but Keegan silences him with a hand.

'You should've told me about the Ealing thing earlier. Obviously it was significant. That he was fixated on you. Right?'

'It's obvious *now*,' Eddie says.

'Yes. Yes.' Keegan waves a hand. 'Then there's your wife . . .' He pauses. Shakes his head. 'So you had no idea she'd been seeing this man? Seeing Thacker?'

Eddie balls his fists again. Under the desk, where Keegan can't see. 'Of course I didn't,' he says. 'She didn't know who he was either. Why would she?'

'The photofit suggests he's quite a handsome man these days. A bit different from the tired, puffy image we had put in our heads from before, hmm?'

'Are you taking me off the case?' Eddie says.

Keegan steeples his fingers together. 'I've thought about that. Discussed it with the DCI. We think it's better to keep you on. Keep you visible. We don't know what Thacker is planning next, but having you removed might unsettle him. We'll justify this if we have to.'

'I'll tell you what's he's doing next, Nick. There are still two empty doors on that advent calendar. Eighteen and twenty-two. I don't think he's planning on leaving them blank, do you?'

'No, I don't,' Keegan says. 'And what's more, I'm worried about his deviation from the pattern. He chose your wife, then spared her. The Aaron White killing was pure rage. He knows we're on to him. He's in a different zone now. We need to throw everything we've got at this, Eddie.' He pauses, his voice softening. 'And don't worry about Carly. She's been a star witness. We've offered her counselling, if she needs it.'

Eddie nods. 'Right,' he says. 'Let's find this bastard.'

Eddie leans back in his chair, yawns. He's been through all the newspapers, looking for any insight and clues that the press might've picked up on. They've spent hours chasing leads and dead ends. It's dark outside, and he's tired. They all are. 'Look, Becks, I'm going to take you home. We've done enough today. I suspect Keegan's going to have us on a full manhunt tomorrow. They've traced the plates on the van – fake, obviously, but they're looking into how he ended up with the Fiesta plates on there. Might be he just bought them somewhere dodgy, but there might be a chance that there's some link. We'll know in the morning. I don't think there's much else we can do tonight. Forensics are checking the deodorant can. Hopefully we'll get his prints. We've got Rob's to rule him out. Unless Colin used gloves when he left that letter and the dolls in the teenager's pocket, I reckon we can get him with his. It's something, at least. Finally. Obviously we have to hope he's going to confess, because we haven't got much else. Come on. Let's go.'

Becky barely speaks throughout the journey. He pulls into the kerb outside her house, leaves the engine running.

'Is there something else bothering you? You were right about the figurines. Obviously Colin has those now. Anyway. Get yourself indoors. We can't second guess what Thacker's going to do next, because he's past any chance of us predicting his actions now. All we can do is wait and see . . . and hope that he's finished his current spree. We *will* find him. You know that. Besides, maybe Rob's right. Maybe he'll top himself and save us the bother of having to take him to trial.'

Becky opens the passenger-side door and a cold blast of air hits her. 'I hope not. I'd like to see some justice done here, wouldn't you?' She sighs. 'You're right, Eddie. I could probably do with an early night. See you in the morning.' She gives him a little wave as she closes the car door. It's not properly shut, and as he leans across to close it, he spots a CD case in the footwell, leans down to pick it up. It's Pearl Jam's *Ten*. He feels a stab of irritation that this is lying on the floor like this. It's one of his favourite albums. He didn't even realise that Carly had it in her car.

When he comes back up, Becky is gone.

He spots the number on the door. She lives at number eighteen. One of the last two numbers in the advent calendar. Another one of those odd coincidences. Should he text her, just in case? Tell her to be careful?

He's being stupid. Why would Thacker target Becky? He shakes his head, dislodging the thought. Overactive imagination. They're not in one of those far-fetched TV dramas. Thacker's not after Becky. It's him that Colin wants to rattle. *Idiot.* He cranks the heater up full blast, turns the radio onto that channel that always plays the decent indie stuff. Chrissie Hynde is singing the sad song about her band's dead guitarist. Eddie's never been sure if it's 2000 miles to heaven or hell, but either way, it's the least cheerful Christmas song he can think of, and it's perfect. He's humming along to it as he pulls away from Becky's house.

She is safe.

Now he needs to get back to his own family. This is no time for arguing. There's a killer on the loose and Eddie is certain that he hasn't finished yet.

52

THE PHOTOGRAPHER

I've left the van parked in the bit of wasteland behind the police station. I couldn't help but laugh at it all. I wonder if they've already spotted it? But it's dark, and there are two other white vans parked in there, so it might be a while before they do. I should flash up on the ANPR though, I think. But I don't know if it will lead them in there. Who'd have thought that a white van was the best way to appear invisible?

I've enjoyed using the scooter. One of the benefits of having my whole life in the van. Plenty of space for the scooter at one side, and still enough room for my mattress.

It was risky going back to Dad's, but I made sure to stay hidden until their surveillance was over. I knew they wouldn't be able to have someone sitting outside the house full time, but I had expected them to be there more than a couple of times a day. Anyway, they never bothered to check the back garden. The gap in the fence hidden by Dad's laurel bush giving me my own secret doorway to the rear.

The young detective has gone now, as has her partner. He thinks she's safe, but in fact, at this point, no one knows where she is. I do though. She's gone to that boyfriend of hers. She goes round there more often than not. Why she doesn't just move in with him, I don't know. I listened to her talking to him on the phone the other day, saying no, that she didn't want to. Not yet. I think she's trying to keep him at arm's length. Maybe he's not The One.

I have a dilemma: go round there now, make sure she's there, or make the call, then go there. There's no risk, not really. It probably makes more sense for me to wait a bit, give her time to relax before things kick off. On the other hand, I need to keep an eye on things. I need to know if he's going to go down the road for an Indian takeaway, like he does at least twice a week, or if they're both going to stay in. I open up my rucksack, admiring the clean metal, the sharp blade. The handle fits perfectly in my hand. It should do, the price I've paid for this thing. Last of my cash. Just as well I won't need it any more. The woman in the shop had gift-wrapped the carving knife so beautifully when I'd told her it was a Christmas gift for my mother.

I decide to wheel the scooter round. Take my time. I step out from under the tree that sits diagonally across from Becky's house. I blow on my hands, trying to get some warmth back into them. I should wear gloves, I know. But I want to feel things, tonight. I want to feel everything tonight.

Because after this . . . everything will change. Again.

He only lives a few minutes' walk away. I stop at the end of his street, kick out the stand and leave the scooter parked at the kerb. How long will it be before anyone notices it? There are no parking restrictions around here.

The benefit of being just a little too far from the centre of town.

I stare at the house. Waiting. Finally, someone pulls the curtains shut across the bay-fronted living room. I can't see if it's him or her. The light inside is dimmed, shadowing them.

I reverse the scooter round the corner without turning on the engine. I'm still thinking. Still mulling over the options.

Who's it going to be?

I take the phone out of my pocket. I took it from that fat loser, Derek, at the squat, after he got the call from Mortlake to say that the police had been to see him at the Union. Good of him to tip me off. I'm sure he won't mind doing me one final favour.

I dial 999. The operator's voice is crisp and clear. A woman. Sounds young. I wonder if she will enjoy this moment. 'Which service do you require?'

'Police please . . . it's urgent.'

'Can you tell me your name please, sir?' She sounds calm. Efficient. She deals with urgent calls all the time. I need to do more to rattle her. I hold my breath, letting the carbon dioxide build up inside me. I have never been very good at holding my breath. Getting rid of hiccups has always been problematic. I feel my throat start to constrict, panic starts to set in.

'Sir, are you still there? Please can you tell me where you are?'

I take the phone away from my face. I gasp for air. My chest tightens as I gulp in lungfuls of the freezing night.

'Please . . .' The panting is real now. This is what panic sounds like. Call me a method actor.

'It's Colin Thacker . . . he's just called me. Says he's going to kill that detective . . .' Breathe in more air. Pant it back out. 'You have to help me.'

'I will help you, sir. Can you please tell me your name and I'll get you put straight through to an officer who can help you.'

Does she think this is a joke? Why is she still so calm?

'It's Andy Mortlake. I'm a DJ at the Students' Union. Detectives came to see me, said they're looking for Colin Thacker . . . now he says he's going to kill one of them . . . you need to hurry!'

'Mr Mortlake, I'm going to get someone to help you right now. Can you tell me where you are? Did Colin Thacker tell you which of the detectives he was planning to target?' I hear a slight wavering in her voice now. I've got her. She hasn't dealt with this kind of thing before. She'll have called over her supervisor. They will be trying to locate me.

'Please hurry,' I say. 'He's going to their house right now!'

I end the call. Drop the phone on the floor and crush it to pieces, then I kick it down a drain. I check that the knife is still securely strapped into the side pocket of my backpack.

I flick up the stand and give the scooter a couple of revs.

I've made my choice.

53

She sits down at the table in the centre of the kitchen, watching him as he starts to prepare dinner. For the second night in a row. She could get used to this, and yet she doesn't want to. She feels wired; the only thing that's keeping her awake is adrenaline. She takes a lemon out of the fruit bowl. Rolls it around in her hands. 'Are you going to be totally pissed off if I say I really, *really* fancy a curry?'

He sighs theatrically. 'I go to all this effort . . .' He lets the sentence hang. She can tell by his voice that he's just as happy as her to have a curry, even though they've been eating more takeaways than real food lately. Living near such a good takeaway is a double-edged sword. Exercise is definitely on the agenda for January.

He picks up his phone.

'Hang on, I don't know what I want yet—'

'Chicken tikka bhuna, lemon pilau rice, garlic naan and an onion bhaji.'

'Actually, I was thinking of something a bit . . .' she pauses, sucks in her stomach, 'lighter? Tandoori chicken, maybe? That comes with a little salad . . . you just get your usual and I'll have a bit of your rice.'

She lets him phone in the order. He'll walk along to

collect it in twenty minutes or so. She goes through to the living room. An episode of *Emmerdale* has been paused. She loves it that he watches such crap TV. It's one of the things she loves about him. He has a normal job, a normal life. Nothing outrageous, but everything is steady. That's what she needs in her life. Someone to make things normal, when she spends her days doing the least normal things – especially recently, with the attack on campus, and now this. Colin Thacker. She lies down on the couch, the cushions already in perfect position from where he was obviously lying earlier. Her head fits into the same indentation on the cushion. The blanket that's been thrown off fits perfectly over her body, the edges tucked into the bottom and sides of the couch, the way he always cocoons himself in.

Yes, all very safe. A nice little routine. He keeps telling her how much he would love to look after her. So why is it that she keeps turning him down?

She does love him. Doesn't she?

She closes her eyes. She's been pretty spooked recently. The university thing had brought back painful memories. She'd even thought that Paul in tech had been a potential threat. Eddie had told her that he was known for his wind-ups, and she'd accepted that, although the way she'd felt in the darkroom with him – scared, vulnerable. It didn't really seem like it was OK. Anyway, it was past now. There were bigger fish to fry.

'Back in five,' Gary calls through from the hall. The front door slams shut.

Her eyes have grown heavy. Itchy. She closes them. Feels

herself drift off. Not fully asleep, as she can still hear the sound of the TV that she had flicked over to the news. The occasional *clip clop* sound of shoes, people walking past the window. She feels herself drifting further away, like she is sinking into the couch. Just five minutes. A power-nap. Then dinner, then bed.

She jolts awake at the sound of banging on the door. Her heart leaps. What the hell? Then she remembers. Gary has gone to collect the food. The doorbell has been broken for weeks. She pulls herself upright, staggers slightly as she wanders through to the hall, feeling drowsy. Overtired. Desperate for a full night's sleep.

'Why didn't you take your key, you muppet?'

She's smiling when she opens the door.

54

He's on his way home when the call comes in. He answers on hands-free, his phone already connected through the plug-in car system.

'Detective Carmine? This is Peter Greene, Becky's dad. She left your number pinned to the fridge, you know, for emergencies. I hope it's OK to call? I . . . have you heard the radio, I'm sorry, I—'

Eddie feels like a sliver of ice has fallen down the neck of his coat. 'Whoa, calm down, Peter.' The man sounds distressed, words tumbling out on top of each other. Eddie pulls in at the side of the road. One more street and he'd have been home. 'Take a deep breath. Tell me what's happened.'

'It's Becky . . . she's not here, and—'

'What do you mean she's not there? I dropped her off ten minutes ago.'

Silence.

'Peter?'

'Sorry. I don't know. She must've changed her mind, gone round to Gary's. He only lives around the corner. She's done it before.'

'Without telling you where she was going?'

'She's twenty-eight, Eddie. Is it OK if I call you Eddie

. . . I know we haven't actually met, but Becky talks about you a lot . . .'

He is rambling now. The panic is still in his voice.

'Just tell me what's happened. I'm in the car. I can go wherever you need me to go, but first you need to tell me what's going on.'

'It was on the radio . . . the police radio, I mean. I've got an old scanner set up in the spare room. I installed one of those scrambler things. They say you can't pick up the frequency now on Airwave, but you can do anything if you know how. Becky's told me off for it before, but, well . . . I don't *do* anything with it, I just like listening to it sometimes.'

Eddie drums his fingers on the steering wheel. 'It doesn't matter now. Just tell me what you heard.'

'Didn't you hear it then?'

Eddie stares at the console, at the wires connecting the hands-free kit, his Airwave handset . . . He'd turned it off. He was sick of the buzz. If someone needed him, he had his mobile. He glances down at it where it sits in the cradle and notices the message bar at the bottom of the screen. Four missed calls.

Shit . . . why hadn't he heard it? He picks it up, presses buttons on the side. The ringer volume is at zero. He has no recollection of doing this. Second time it's happened recently. There's definitely something wrong with it. *Fuck*.

'They said that you and Becky were in danger – they'd had a call – something to do with Colin Thacker? He's going to target one of the police . . .'

Shitting shit! Thankfully he has no swear box in his car.

'What's Gary's address? I'm going there right now. Have the officers arrived at your house yet?'

'No, not yet . . . hang on, there's a car pulling up outside.'

'No blues and twos?'

'Sorry?'

'Sirens and flashers?'

'No. No . . . there's a uniformed officer getting out.'

For fuck's sake, Eddie wants to shout. He needs to know what the message said. Presumably there will be a car sent to his own house, too. They'd suggested protection after Carly had left the station, but stupidly Eddie had told them not to bother. That Colin wouldn't come after her now, not when he'd had the perfect opportunity in the hotel in Godalming.

'The address, Eddie?'

'Yes, sorry. Go on.'

'The house is called Maple Lodge, it's on Longford Road, about halfway along on the right-hand side if you're coming from the shops end.'

'Doesn't it have a number?'

'It might do . . . I only know it by its name. Hang on, that's the door . . .'

'Go and get it. But Peter, check the ID first. Can't be too careful tonight. Don't answer the door to anyone but a police officer, OK?'

He hangs up. What now? Call Carly, to tell her that there are officers on their way? Try calling Becky, to find out if she's OK? Call Keegan? Dispatch – to get the details of the call?

He's dropped the ball on this, but he can catch it again. First things first – check that Becky is OK. If someone's already on the way to his house, then that's covered. Keegan can phone him and bollock him later. He can listen to the call transcript at Dispatch later . . . one thing he needs though, and he needs it fast . . . Becky's house is number eighteen, but she's not there. Gary's house is called Maple Lodge, but there will be a number on record, the Royal Mail keep these things stored for postcodes.

He scrolls through the numbers on his phone. Thinks about who will answer the quickest and who will find what he needs without asking questions. She answers on the first ring.

'Eddie . . . I was wondering if you were going to call—'

'Abby, sorry – not now. This is not a social call—'

'What do you need?'

'House called Maple Lodge on Longford Road. I need the house number. Can you get it now?'

'Hang on . . .' He hears the sound of her typing. She's still at her desk. Thank God. 'Right . . . it's number thirty-four. Is that all you need? I can—'

'Thanks Abby. I'll call you properly soon. I mean it.' He hangs up. Fires the ignition, and pulls out into the street. Forgets to check his mirror, and a car swerves and beeps at him. The driver winds down the window and gives him the finger. Eddie hasn't got time to care. He has to get there before he's too late.

Number thirty-four isn't even in the calendar. It's a red herring. Trying to throw them off the scent.

There are two doors left . . . eighteen and twenty-two.

Number eighteen is Becky's house, but Thacker's not going there.

He's going to number twenty-two.

Eddie's house.

He slams his foot on the pedal and screeches into the road.

She's been lying on the couch since they brought her back
home, dozing on and off. Exhausted. Trying not to think
about what she's done. How stupid she's been. The police
who interviewed her had been calm, patient. They probed
her to remember details and she gave them all she could.
It all feels very unreal. How close she came to being killed.
Would he really have killed her? The police think so. She's
not so sure. She shudders, pulls the blanket up further.
A noise is shuttling around in her head. A jangling,
insistent whine. She closes her eyes. Thinks about Eddie.
How he was with her when she told him about Caleb.
How he wanted to protect her. Is there still a chance for
them? After all this? She feels herself drifting off again
and it takes her longer than it should to work out that
the noise she can hear is the doorbell being pressed inces-
santly and not something from the TV, not something
imaginary. She blinks, trying to keep her eyes open.
Shuffles through to the hall. She doesn't bother to check
the spyhole before opening the door, even though Eddie's
told her countless times to be careful, especially at night.
Especially when she's not expecting anyone. Especially
after everything that's just happened. But she's not really
thinking straight. She can't get Eddie's face out of her

mind. The look he gave her when she told him about Caleb . . . what had almost happened. She wished that the man they had named at the press conference was another man, not Caleb. It scares her to think that her judgement could be that impaired. She stifles a yawn, talks to the closed door. Her voice is thick with sleep.

'Did you forget your key?'

She pushes her hair behind her ears, rubs away the tears that are drying and itching on her cheeks. She's expecting to see Eddie standing there on the doorstep, a different look on his face this time. One that says that despite it all, he still loves her. Wants to sort things out. Wishful thinking. She struggles with the locks, turns the top one too far and hears it click. Turns it back again. Sighs. She pulls open the door.

'Sorry, I—'

It's not Eddie.

'Uh . . . ' Confusion swirls around her head and she staggers back slightly, bumping into the sideboard and sending a crystal vase of past-their-best orange poppies crashing onto the tiled floor.

Two men stand on her doorstep. Neither of them are her husband.

This is the thing that all policemen's wives fear. Always. That knock on the door, or the ring of the bell, late at night. Unexpected. After an argument – always after an argument, in her head, at least. Although Eddie had been so lovely the last time she'd seen him. The argument pushed away by fear and relief. Relief that she hadn't been murdered. Why did Caleb spare her? If he wanted to get to Eddie, why not take his chance? What was he going to do next?

'Mrs Carmine? Carly? Are you OK?'

The uniformed officers step inside. She doesn't stop them. She knows them. Has met them at a summer BBQ or maybe a christening or something, somewhere. Eddie's colleagues. Their names have dissolved inside her head. She wonders why these two, though. Wouldn't they have sent someone from CID? Someone of higher rank? Someone whose name she wouldn't have to pull from the depths of her muddled brain.

'What happened?' Carly manages. She stands up straight, glances at the broken vase shattered on the tiles. 'He's dead, isn't he?'

The officers cast a quick look at each other. 'Shall we go through to the living room? Maybe you should sit down . . .'

'I don't want to sit down. Just tell me what's happened to Eddie!'

The younger of the two officers lets out a breath. 'Carly, Eddie is fine. This is not about Eddie—'

'But I thought . . . Oh God.' She puts her hands over her eyes, slides her palms down her face. 'It's one of the kids, isn't it? Eddie doesn't even know yet, does he?'

'No . . . no.' The officers look at each other again. 'Carly, please. Sit down. Nothing has happened to any of your family, OK? Everyone is fine.'

She drops down heavily onto the sofa. 'Then what are you doing here? Do you need me to come back to the station? Have you found Caleb?'

The younger one has his phone in his hands, texting something.

The older one opens his mouth to answer, just as his mobile rings. 'Eddie. Yes. We're with her now. She's fine . . . Yes . . . OK—'

Carly stands up, tries to grab the phone. 'Is that Eddie? Can I speak to him?'

The officer shakes his head and ends the call. 'He can't talk right now, Carly. We just needed to make sure you were OK. We're going to stay with you for a while. Make sure things are OK.'

Things start to swirl around inside her head again. What a mess. What a horrible, horrendous mess.

56

THE PHOTOGRAPHER

I lunge forward, knife pointing straight towards her in my outstretched hand, as if I am fencing – my rapier-like sabre held out in front of me. *Allez!* I wish I'd worn a mask. It would have created that final, menacing touch.

She looked tired earlier, but there's no sign of that now. It's incredible what a burst of adrenaline can do. I can feel it myself, fizzing through my veins. It makes me feel ten feet tall. She tries to slam the door in my face, but she's too late. I shove it hard towards her and her eyes flash with fear.

She turns. Runs up the stairs.

Oh Becky . . . That was a pretty stupid move. Unless she has some means of escape, I have her cornered now. Has the girl never watched any horror films?

I close the door behind me, lock it and pull the chain across. On the off-chance that her paramour is not completely unconscious at the foot of the small patio garden, I don't want him coming in and interrupting us.

'Becky . . .' I call from the bottom of the stairs. 'Where aaaaare you?' I draw out the 'are' and add a little sing-song rhythm to my voice, contributing nicely to the horror movie feel. I hadn't planned it like this, but it seems to be coming out of me naturally.

It's OK. I do realise that I have completely lost my mind. I have turned into that psychopathic madman that I tried to convince myself I wasn't. I was doing this for Chrissie, wasn't I? It's me now. It's Colin. Caleb Temple has disappeared back into his fictional world. I am here now, in the real one. I can do what the hell I like. There is no plan any more. There are no rules.

I walk up the stairs. I don't rush. This is the last time I'm going to have any fun, so I might as well savour it. Give her longer to sweat, make her more likely to reveal where she is. I'm used to waiting. Making sure that the last sparks of the electrical charge that is life has ebbed away, before taking the perfect photograph and leaving them behind. I regret leaving my camera in the bag now. It would've been nice to have one final memento of my struggle.

It being one of these standard terraced affairs, I know the layout instinctively. Bathroom at the top of the stairs. A bedroom either side. The stairwell protected by a waist-high slatted banister, the same colour wood as the doors. The walls are a pale grey; the carpets are some sort of matting. Berber. Is that what they call it? Generic art prints on the walls. Becky's boyfriend is not very imaginative.

'You might as well come out, Becky. I can stand here for as long as you like, but the longer I wait the more bored I will be . . . I don't like being bored. It makes me angry.' I stand still, trying to focus my hearing. It's almost completely silent, except for the ticking of a clock somewhere nearby. I glance around, see that it's one of those replica station clocks, hanging on the high wall above the stairwell.

I turn back to the rooms. All three doors are closed.

Which one do I choose? It's like *The Adventure Game*. I stifle a giggle. Then I feel my shoulders slump, and I sigh. I am so tired now. I want all this to be over. I could end it now. Turn the knife on myself. Plunge it into my stomach and let myself fall down those stairs. Some say that suicide is the act of the weak. I disagree. There is a braveness in attempting to switch off your own light.

I kick open the door in the middle. I was right, it is the bathroom. I yank the shower curtain across, push the door back as far as it will go. She's not in there. I hadn't really thought that she would be.

'Come on, Becky. Let's just get this over with, shall we? I'm sorry if I scared you. I only want to chat . . .' I cock an ear towards the bedroom on the right. Was that the sound of something banging on the floor? Maybe she's hiding, and she'd knocked something over.

I try the other room first. Kicking open the door, keeping my knife arm outstretched. It's been set up as an office. Sofa bed at the far end of the room, desk at the side with one of those chunky padded chairs pushed right underneath. Filing cabinets. World map on the wall.

Nowhere to hide.

I step back into the hall. Hear another faint sound, like scraping.

'I'm coming in now, Becky. I need to tell you something.'

I kick open the door, scan the room. Double bed – one of those ones on a frame – plenty of space for someone Becky's size to slide underneath. I smile. Too obvious. I lift the duvet with the tip of the knife, peer underneath. Nothing.

On the same wall as the window that overlooks the front garden, there are two chests of drawers. In the middle, a fancy-patterned armchair strewn with clothes.

The far wall, the one I am looking straight at, is lined with fitted wardrobes.

'Come out, come out, wherever you are . . .' That sing-song voice again. I stand still, waiting again for the slightest noise. She's very good at this. I can't even hear her breathing.

I walk around the bed; slide open the first wardrobe door.

57

BECKY

He hasn't spotted it yet.

She can't see him, but she can hear the creak of the floorboards as he creeps around the room, taking everything in. He will have checked under the bed first. But they both know that would have been a useless place to hide.

It's quite incredible how her fear of the dark dissipated when it became a life or death situation. That episode in the darkroom had been a blip, nothing more. The therapy sessions have done their job. She hopes she doesn't have to be here for long though – a new phobia is developing, and it involves spiders and other crawling nightmares that she can't currently see.

She's thought about shuffling as far back into the eaves as she could, but if for some reason he did manage to get up here beside her, she really would be trapped. Besides, there is more chance of her slipping off one of the beams and falling through the ceiling as she tries to avoid all the crap that Gary has stored in his loft. She thanks her lucky stars that her boyfriend is rigorous about keeping things in the right place. The stick with the hook to grab onto the hatch had been in its usual place, clipped to the little brackets he'd made for it on the window side of the largest chest of drawers. How she had managed to get the hatch open, the ladder down and scramble up there without him catching her had been nothing short of a miracle.

Maybe this isn't her time, after all. She's a strong believer in fate.

She sits with her knees pulled up to her chest, the stick gripped in both hands, held out in front of her. If he manages to open the hatch without it and somehow gets hold of the ladder, she will stick the hook in his eye without giving it a second thought. It's the first rule of self-defence. Go for the eyes. They can't attack you if they can't see you.

She hears the scrape of the metal runners as the first wardrobe door slides along the rails. Coat-hangers rattle as he forages inside, looking for his prize.

Her phone vibrates in her pocket.

The rattling of the coat-hangers stops.

Is he looking around now, for the source of the vibration? He must've heard it, when everything else is so quiet. She pulls it out of her pocket and switches it to silent.

She has reception! There was one flickering bar when she tried it before, but maybe it's because she's closer to the front of the house now. Out of the way of the cross-beams. She's about to start typing a message to Eddie, when a message pops up.

> *Becks, I assume you're with Gary and that you're OK. Don't open the door to anyone you don't know, tonight. Eddie is coming round to see you. He was a*

bit annoyed because he
thought you were here
with us. They had a call.
There was something on
the radio, but don't
worry! Love you, Dad xx

She wants to laugh. This is her dad's way of warning her that Thacker is on his way. He's trying not to worry her, and if it wasn't for the fact that she was already cowering in the attic, trying not to attract the attention of the murderer who is only a few feet below her, skulking around Gary's bedroom, then she would've phoned him and shouted at him for scaring the shit out of her. Eddie must be fuming. He told her to go home, and stay there. He was trying not to freak her out, too, after Keegan had told everyone at the press conference to be on hyper-alert, not to open their doors to strangers.

She holds her breath. Hears the sound of the next sliding door being dragged along the runners. The second one is stiff, it sometimes comes right off. She crosses her fingers and hopes that it falls on top of him.

'Oh Becky,' he says again, in that horribly creepy way of his. He seems to be enjoying himself, which is at odds with what Rob had tried to convince her of, the loving brother who'd been driven to this through grief. Maybe it was killing the teenager in the car park that had finally made him flip. He is more unpredictable than ever, now. She's trying to push the fact that he knew where she was tonight out of her mind. She was stupid not to have told Eddie when she'd felt that someone was watching her.

What's that saying? Just because you're paranoid, doesn't mean they're not out to get you.

She grips the end of the stick between her knees and starts quickly typing a message to Eddie.

> I'm in the loft space
> above the bedroom. I
> don't think he can get to
> me, but I'm not sure.
> Please hurry!!!!

There's a *phthump* noise, as if someone has taken a large pile of clothes and thrown them into a heap on the floor. Coat-hangers clatter together.

The third door is slid open. It's shelves in that one. She closes her eyes.

'Where the fuck are you?' His voice has lost its melody, turned hard. She can hear the anger. Another flush of adrenaline hits her and she can hear the *thump thump* of her own heart, as if it might burst from her chest.

'I'm getting a bit bored now, Becky. I told you before . . . I really don't like being bored.'

The floorboards creak as he walks around the bed again, towards the door. Then he stops. She holds her breath again.

He starts to laugh. 'Oh that's wonderful, Becky. Absolutely wonderful. If only I'd looked up at the ceiling before . . .'

The floorboards creak again. Then the noise stops. She can hear him breathing, long, loud breaths. He's right beneath her.

He's spotted the loft hatch.

58

EDDIE

He's driving too fast down these residential streets but what choice does he have? He calls the station, barking the command into the hands-free. He gets the duty sergeant, Keegan's phone forwarded. Fuck!

'Sergeant O'Keefe . . .'

'Bill, it's Eddie . . . what's going on? My radio's fucked. Has someone been despatched to my home address? Is my wife OK?'

Bill O'Keefe manages to keep his cool in all situations, from Saturday night abusive drunks clogging up the foyer, to the wailing mothers of missing children. It's going to take more than the threat of a serial killer at a colleague's door to rattle him. 'Calm down, Eddie. Sergeant Shaw and PC Devlin are there now. Devlin texted to say all was clear.'

Texted? 'Thanks, Bill.' He ends the call and immediately barks 'Shaw' into the system. He answers on the first ring.

'Eddie. Yes. We're with her now. She's fine—'

'Make sure she really *is* fine. Don't bloody leave her on her own, OK? I'm going round to check on Greene. She's with her boyfriend. Has anyone been sent?'

'Yes, they're on their way—'

'OK. I'll get round there myself. Call control. Tell them I'm coming.'

'OK—' Sergeant Shaw hangs up and Eddie bangs his hands on the steering wheel as he keeps driving too fast, hoping he's not too late . . .

The text flashes up a few minutes later – it's from Becky . . . he catches the end of it as it scrolls across the screen.

Please hurry!!!

He slams the steering wheel again. He's put Becky in danger. He left her at home but didn't see her go in. He should've checked she was OK, instead of heading home to his when he knew there were officers en route. He's been sure that Becky wasn't the target. Thought it was all about him. But of course, that's why Colin has gone after her, isn't it? Another go at destroying Eddie, and this one is all his own fault.

59

He's stopped laughing, and there is silence again, except for his heavy breathing and the continued thumping of her heart.

'I'm impressed,' he says, finally. 'It's my own fault for taking it so leisurely, I suppose. I'd thought it would be fun to draw things out a bit, but I gave you enough time to get yourself barricaded up there. It's a shame though. Because now I'm going to have to put in the extra effort, and to be honest I'm feeling quite tired.'

She starts counting in her head, a technique she learned to deal with stress. She needs to calm down. She squints in the semi-darkness, looking for a more substantial weapon. She is no longer sure that the stick with the hook is enough, now that she has lost the element of surprise. She's surrounded by boxes, crates and bin-liners full of old clothes. Maybe she'll wait for him to open the hatch, then just start launching things at him. If she had a torch, she might have a chance up here. Maybe there was a way to get into the loft space next door, a partition wall she could stick her foot through. But in this dusty darkness, there's little she can do but wait.

More creaking down below. Scraping. *Thump thump. Thump thump.*

What is he doing?

Oh no . . . She realises her error. It's far too late now, but she could've bought herself a lot more time. She should've dragged that chest of drawers across the room and barricaded the bedroom door with it – but there was no time – and she'd been trying not to let him know so easily which of the three rooms she might be hiding in.

She should've gone into the office and jumped out the back window. A broken ankle would've been a better option, now that she's trapped in here like a hunted animal, waiting to die.

She can hear his breathing, closer now. Panting with the exertion of dragging the chest of drawers from the side of the room, positioning it under the hatch. The other dragging sound had been the metal legs of the bed. That's what he's using to enable himself to climb up onto the chest of drawers.

Fuck.

She should've known that he would find her eventually. She'd just hoped that Gary would've come back first . . . found the door locked and raised the alarm. A thought stabs her in the side of the head. Where is Gary? She has lost all track of time. The fact that he is not here, and neither is Eddie, is not a good sign.

Oh please don't let him be dead. She's been questioning if they are truly meant to be together, but either way, she would still very much like for him to be alive.

This is her fault.

She has brought Thacker here to Gary's house. Lured him with her own naïvety. Why was he always one step ahead of them?

Because he's been watching them the whole time.

There's a squeak of the hatch as it flips open. She instinctively pulls her knees closer to her chest. Blinks at the sudden flood of light into the space where she has adjusted to the darkness.

She doesn't think.

She just launches herself towards the hatch, stick in her hand. He hasn't had a chance to grab hold of the ladder, which is folded on the floor. She trips over it. It all happens too fast, in a blur. Then she's falling through the hole and she's screaming and there's a crunch as he falls back, hanging half off the chest of drawers as she lands flat on top of him.

There's an *ooomph*, and she knocks the wind out of him. But he's still holding the knife. She realises she's dropped the stick, but it's too late for that to be of any use. She tries to get up, and he grabs on to her top, grappling with her. She brings up a knee, doesn't quite get it on target, but close enough. He grunts, shoves her, but she's holding on to him.

They both fall onto the floor with a thump. He's half on top of her, dazed . . . but he is still wielding the knife. He swipes back and forth as if he is fencing and she has to tilt her head side to side to avoid it, but she feels the hot pain as it catches her on the cheek. The pain gives her another boost and she manages to roll away. He grabs for her ankle, but she's too fast. She bolts out of the bedroom, leaps over the banister as if it's a hurdle.

Stupid! Stupid! the voice inside her head screams, as she tumbles down the stairs.

60

THE PHOTOGRAPHER

She's got spirit, I'll give her that. There is a sharp pain in my chest. I think she may have cracked one of my ribs. I'd glanced up in time just to see her disappearing over the banister. It was kind of comical, actually. It's incredible what the mind tells you to do in that fight or flight situation. She managed to make it a combination of both. It hurts as I pull myself off the floor. Definitely a cracked rib. The pain is excruciating, and I wonder if I can stop myself from passing out. I take it slowly. Finally get to my feet. I walk gingerly across the landing and peer over. I was half expecting to find her lying there, broken. But she is not going to allow herself to give in. I admire that. She is an impressive young woman.

I'm not sure I want to kill her any more.

She's knocked the fight out of me, quite literally. There was fire in her eyes – she reminded me so much of Chrissie.

Oh Chrissie . . . why did you have to leave me like this? I'm nothing here without you. I've destroyed everything now, and for what? It's not going to bring you back.

I hobble down the stairs. I still have the knife.

Pain sears through my chest.

It's over.

I've decided. I will hand myself in. I pause, just at the

spot where the stairs turn on an angle. There's a sound of sirens, growing louder. I can feel a faint trickle of cold air coming through the house. I think she's gone out the back. She should've done that in the first place. I half think she might've wanted that fight as much as I did.

I'm almost at the bottom of the stairs when I hear car doors slamming, muffled voices outside. A shout. Then a bang as the door splinters inward. Two officers dressed in their full fighting gear appear inside. I drop the knife.

'Where's Detective Greene?' the first one shouts.

'Are you Colin Thacker?' the other.

I step back towards the wall, raise my hands. I'm not worried that they might shoot me, but I'm actually terrified of being tasered. Especially with my cracked rib. I genuinely think I could die from the pain.

Eddie Carmine almost flies through the open door. 'Where's Becky? What have you done to her?'

I'm about to tell them I don't actually know where she is, when she appears in the hallway. Limping, slightly. One side of her face is smeared with blood. She looks crumpled. But she is OK.

'I'm fine,' she says. Her voice is hoarse. Probably from that screaming she did when she fell through the loft hatch. 'Gary, though . . . I don't know where he is.'

The two with the stab vests and the tasers come towards me. I don't protest.

'He's next to the bins,' I say. 'I don't think I killed him.'

Eddie gives me a look of fury. 'Wait here, Becks,' he says.

One of the officers cuffs me. They lead me outside,

where there are blue lights flashing and curtains twitching. People are outside their houses, hugging themselves against the cold. They are not ashamed of their blatant rubbernecking.

I watch as paramedics rush up the path. 'It's OK,' Eddie says. He's crouching down between the bins. 'He's alive.'

Becky comes running out of the house. She'll be fine. A bit of bruising, maybe. I'm actually sorry about the cut on her cheek. I hope it doesn't scar.

One of the officers pushes me into the back of a van, and the other climbs in beside me.

'I'm sorry,' I whisper. The van doors slam shut. I'm not sure if anyone heard me. Or perhaps I only said it inside my head.

Friday

TWO MORE SLEEPS

61

BECKY

They let her go home at 6 a.m. They'd checked her over thoroughly, X-rays, swabs, bloods – the lot. But he barely touched her. The bruising on her side, from where she had thrown herself over the banister, would fade. She was lucky not to have cracked ribs, or worse. Maybe that slight layer of extra fat she's carrying around there has done her good. There's the small scar on her cheek, but it looks worse than it is. Now that's it's cleaned and stitched, it will be fine. They've said it probably won't even leave a scar. There's another smaller cut next to it, but that only needed paper stitches. When they'd found her, her face had been covered with blood. She'd looked a mess. She'd seen herself in the reflection of the metal equipment in the ambulance. Thank God for her dad and that police scanner. If he hadn't been listening, no one would have known that she wasn't at home. That they were coming to save her in the wrong place.

The family is gathered around the breakfast table. No one looks like they've slept. Her dad had been with her in the hospital, but the others were told to stay home. They have sleep-deprived eyes, red-rimmed and half-shut. They have mussed-up hair, and there is a faint smell in the air, something she recognises from when she has visited the families of victims. It's like the aftermath of adrenaline. Release and relief . . . and fear. It's a smell that's hard to define. Metallic, slightly soily. Overlaid with sweat, and steam and over-stewed tea.

'I'm fine. You can all stop worrying now.' She's starving. Again, the aftermath of adrenaline. She has already eaten four slices of toast. Drunk too much tea. She's wired. Buzzing.

It's not everyone who gets held captive in the attic by a knife-wielding psychopath in their boyfriend's home while he pops out to collect a takeaway.

Gary is there too. He's in a worse state than her, but he barely lets go of her hand. His hand is large and clammy, and he grips her too tight. Her hand feels small inside it. Lost.

Her sister breaks the spell. 'So was it really scary? Like a horror film? Were you shouting at yourself inside your head after you opened the door without putting the chain on, you know, like we shout at stupid girls in those cheesy slasher flicks?' Allie's eyes are still red-rimmed, but they are bright, excited. She's also mainlining toast, buttering another piece as she speaks.

'For goodness' sake, Allie,' her dad says. 'Your sister's been through an awful ordeal. She needs a bit of care right now, not your mad ramblings about horror films.' He sighs. Shakes his head. 'Sorry, Becks. I'll run you a bath. Put that nice vanilla bubble bath in there, shall I? Then you can get some sleep. You must be exhausted!'

Becky swipes a piece of toast from her sister's hand. 'I'm fine. Really. You need to stop fussing. I'll grab a quick shower, then I'll get to work.'

Her dad almost jumps out of his seat. 'Work? Don't be ridiculous. You heard what Eddie said . . . take as much time as you need—'

She shakes her head. 'And I will take the time. After today, OK? It's Christmas Eve Eve! We've got a serial killer in custody. A man that I've been hunting down for the last week—'

'Who tried to kill you. Don't forget that bit,' Allie says. Her dad slaps her on the arm. Not hard, but hard enough for her to drop her toast, jam side down, obviously.

Just a typical morning in this house, she thinks. This is why I love them all.

Becky starts laughing. Can't stop. Allie starts next, then Gary, and eventually, her dad.

They laugh until snot runs out of their noses, and tears fall out of their eyes, and Allie makes a weird honking noise and croaks out, 'I can't breathe . . . I can't breathe . . .', which just makes Becky laugh even harder.

She's still shuddering with it as she leaves the table, walks upstairs. Her ribs do hurt a bit now. Probably more so from the laughing. She has painkillers, though. She'll survive.

She makes it into the shower before she starts crying. Huge, shuddering sobs. She crouches down and lets the hot water spike her, like needles. Careful to keep her face away from the spray. Don't get those stitches wet.

She's not sure if she's crying out of fear, or relief . . . or if it's the fact that it has dredged up a painful memory that she tries hard to keep hidden deep inside. Now replaying itself in glorious Technicolor on the inside of her eyelids, as she keeps them tightly shut.

62

THE PHOTOGRAPHER

The interview room is just as I imagined. Plastic chairs, cheap table with a top that is meant to look like wood but you can see from the chips around the side that it is only a veneer. Fake. Just like I am.

When they arrested me, it was as if I had finally woken up. The man that had been living my life for the last twenty years was not me.

I realised, then, that he was an imposter. Someone who'd inhabited my body and my mind. Someone who wanted to make an impact. Be noticed. For her. For Chrissie. For Merlyn, too, although she was nothing but a figment of my imagination. Maybe the only thing that had stopped me from killing myself, all these years.

Those people that they're saying I killed. The people in the photographs. It wasn't me. It wasn't Colin Thacker. Freelance photographer. Sometime artist.

It was Caleb. Caleb was born of the devil, and that was the only explanation there could be. I close my eyes. Try to imagine that the two detectives sitting opposite are not there. That the duty solicitor with the ill-fitting suit and the pock-marked face is not here to represent me.

It's not real.

It's. Not. Real.

'Do you really want to sit here all day, Colin?' DC Greene speaks. Her voice is tinged with impatience. An undercurrent of anger. She thinks I killed Chrissie.

'I didn't kill my sister,' I say.

The solicitor sighs. Under his breath, he says, 'I thought we agreed on no comment?'

I think about DS Carmine's wife. That little game I played. OK, I admit – that was me. That was Colin. I wanted to find a way to get close to him. I wanted him to help me. I wanted to know more about him. What made him tick. I tried, ten years ago, in that bar in the hotel after the murder in Ealing. I photographed that one officially, as well as taking my own photo at the scene. That was the only time. That's when I was sure I was going to be caught.

But he didn't get it. Too wrapped up in his own life.

I thought I'd made a mistake. I walked away. Carried on elsewhere.

Until I saw his face. Sitting in McDonald's, of all places. Eating breakfast. Staring into space.

I watched him when he spoke to that old tramp. Lady Margaret.

I decided to give him another chance.

His wife was the way in. Carly. *CeeCee*, she said her name was. Trying to trick me. Lure me. I thought she'd worked it out, that night in Godalming, when we almost slept together. That was the moment I realised it had gone far enough.

No more games.

'I didn't kill my sister,' I say again.

'And the others?' DS Carmine leans forward in his seat.

'Did you plan to kill DC Greene too? What changed your mind?'

'Of course I fucking didn't,' I want to say, but I stay silent this time. Say it in my head. She was collateral damage. My final swansong. I never really thought I would get away with it. In fact, it was nothing short of a relief, when they caught me.

'I think you killed your sister, Colin. It might have been an accident. A prank gone wrong. I used to muck around with my sister, you know. It's normal family stuff. It was an accident, wasn't it, Colin? You didn't mean to kill your sister. You didn't mean to kill Chrissie. All the others – they were nothing to you. You were punishing yourself, for what you did to Chrissie. Weren't you?' DC Greene is playing bad cop. I wasn't expecting that. But I am not going to bite. She thinks the amateur psychology will work on me. Keep repeating her name. Let me know that it's going to be OK. They can help me.

No one can help me now.

'I have advised my client not to comment on any of the allegations at this point.' The solicitor leans in towards me slightly. More psychology. I'm on your side.

He has to be on my side. He's been appointed to defend me, whether he believes a word I've said or not.

'It will be easier if you tell us the truth, Colin. We can help you—' DC Greene tries again. Changes tack. Just a little. I can't help but notice the small scar on the side of her face, a couple of those paper stitches stuck across it. Dried blood caught in the adhesive. I don't think it will scar. I hope not. She has such a pretty face.

'I didn't kill my sister.' I will keep saying it until they believe me. They have to believe me. I wasn't even in England at the time. They can prove this. I know they can. They are trying to break me. Make me confess to something I didn't do. They want it all sewn up so they can go down the pub and enjoy their Christmas.

'I didn't kill my sister.'

DS Carmine has been rolling a pencil between his fingers. Finally, it snaps.

'Interview terminated at 14:00 hours.' He switches off the tape. Pushes his chair back hard, until it crashes into the wall. Then he walks out of the room.

63

BECKY

They took a break, leaving Colin Thacker in the interview room with his solicitor for almost an hour. They were hoping the solicitor would talk some sense into him, get him to confess to everything.

As it turned out, he did. The victims from the crime scenes in the advent calendar, and the boy he left broken and bloodied in the car park. This one had affected Becky the most. The violence, and the callous way he had left the boy there on his own to die. The pathologist said it was likely he was still alive when Colin had driven away, but that his heart had given up, from the pain and the cold and the shock, less than twenty minutes afterwards. Just before the ambulance arrived. They'd identified the boy as Aaron White. He was only seventeen. Known to police for various stupid offences, burglary, mugging – he'd been in and out of young offenders' centres since he was twelve. Colin Thacker reckoned he was doing the world a favour, ridding it of vermin that was sure to become increasingly bold and feral with age. His actual words. No remorse.

His confession regarding his sister had been more reluctant. The solicitor had asked if a deal could be struck if he pleaded guilty to all, plus, it would save any lengthy trial and make things easier for the families of the victims.

Eddie still didn't like it.

They are in Keegan's office, drinking whisky from paper cups. Keegan went out and bought the bottle specially. Becky doesn't have the heart to say she hates the stuff. She is mostly a beer drinker. Preferably IPA. Nothing warm and flat. She pushes her cup towards Eddie and he knocks it back when Keegan is rummaging around under his desk for something. He reappears with a bag of chocolate pretzels. Splits them open and lays them on his desk.

'So,' he says. 'Good work. Both of you. It's been noted that the pair of you did the groundwork on this case, right from the start. Eddie – I want you to enrol on that SIO course ASAP. I need you in that role properly from now on. You're a good leader. A good worker. Becky . . . excellent investigational skills. You'll do well here. Cheers.' He raises his cup.

Becky and Eddie follow suit, and she pretends to take a sip. Keegan doesn't notice. He's busy tossing up pretzels into the air and catching them – his mouth clamping shut like a goldfish.

'I take it I can leave you to tie up the paperwork so I can get the last flight today? It's cost me a bloody fortune to change it, although I think that Mrs Keegan is happy enough to have a day there on her own without me. She'll have the credit card maxed on those designer shops before I can collect my suitcase from the carousel.' He crunches noisily on the pretzel. He lays both hands on the desk, looks at Eddie, then at her. Grinning. She wants to be annoyed with him for being so chipper when she is still feeling the effects of all that has gone on, but he is in holiday mode and his smile is infectious.

'Have a great time,' she says. 'We'll get finished up here. I've got the next few days booked off anyway. I think Eddie does too.'

Eddie lets out an angry humph. 'I still don't like this, Nick. He was pushed into that confession about his sister. A guilty plea for the lot will get him life several times over, a not-guilty for one murder gets him a drawn-out trial, *plus* life, and no doubt sent somewhere more shit.'

'He's never getting out of prison anyway, Ed. Why does he care about the trial, and where he ends up? None of it's going to be a luxury.'

'I told you. I don't like it. I want to double-check that alibi of his. I know it's not going to make any difference to him, but if he didn't kill his sister . . .' he pauses, raises a hand to stop them objecting, 'then someone else is still walking free for that. That's the bit I don't like. That's the bit that unsettles me.'

Nick frowns. 'Anyone else on your radar?'

'No . . . but I said already, we weren't finished yet. There were still a couple of lines I wanted to follow up on—'

'Eddie . . . Eddie. Listen. It's Christmas. We have our man. He's not ruining anyone else's Christmas, OK? I suggest you finish up here, then go home and get on with yours.'

Becky wants to cut in, help him out, but she doesn't know what to say. She's in agreement with Nick and the others on this. Colin killed Chrissie. It was an accident. They argued. Something went wrong. And he's been punishing himself, and others, ever since. He was trying to get caught, desperate for someone to stop him. He'd targeted Eddie, but Eddie had failed.

This . . . this was not something she was about to bring up in Keegan's office though. Because Eddie hadn't written anything in the case notes about what had happened in Ealing. That was between her and Eddie. And Colin, of course. And he had said nothing. Probably guessing that it wouldn't make much difference to where he found himself now. He was right.

'Let's go,' she says. She squeezes Eddie's arm. 'Joe texted me earlier to say everyone was meeting in the Wheatsheaf at seven. You up for it?'

Eddie sighs. 'Maybe,' he says. 'I need to go home first. I've got another scene to deal with there.'

Becky stands up, and Nick mirrors her. He comes out from behind his desk, shakes her hand. Waits for Eddie to get up so he can do the same.

She watches as the men make eye contact. There's a determination in Nick's eyes, despite the jovial pre-holiday banter.

'Drop it, Ed,' he says, still gripping the other man's hand. 'Have a good Christmas.'

They walk across the deserted CID office. The lights are still twinkling on Miriam's ridiculous pink tree. Becky bends down and switches them off at the wall.

Eddie mutters, 'Fuck it,' under his breath, and drops a handful of coins into the swear box.

Becky smiles, and follows him down the stairs and out of the building.

The sky is heavy with snow, and as she waits for him

to unlock the car, the first flurry starts to swirl and float down from above. She sticks out her tongue, just like she did as a child, to catch the perfect, cold flakes.

'Get in then,' he barks at her. Slams his door. Typical Eddie. Ruining the only bit of serenity she's felt in weeks.

She gets it, though. She knows he's going home for another battle. While she's looking forward to another family Christmas, with everyone she loves around her.

64

EDDIE

'I'm sorry for snapping,' Eddie says. 'It's just a bit . . .
ah, you know.' He puts the heater on full blast, doesn't
put the wipers on just yet. Let's the flakes land on the
windscreen. Sits there mesmerised. He turns the radio on
to one of the commercial channels that he tries to avoid.
The first few bars of Wham!'s 'Last Christmas' start up.
George Michael with that voice like honey. He loves
Wham!, actually. But he's not telling Becky that.

Becky crosses her arms. Her mood has changed. 'Look
at all those people that Thacker killed, and yet he gets
himself a nice cell with three meals a day, a library to go
to, courses he can do—'

'Have you actually been inside a prison, Becks? They're
not exactly five-star resorts.'

'Better than being dead though, right? Those poor
families. Christmas must be hell for them. It's times like
this when you do think that America's got it right with
the death penalty—'

'Bloody hell . . . this is a bit deep! Can we bank this
one for January, when everyone's even more depressed?'

'Sorry,' she says. 'Just pisses me off. The whole justice
system is—'

'Becky, stop. That's an order.' He turns on the wipers. The snow is already lying thick.

'White Christmas,' Becky says. 'I can't wait.'

He drops her off at Gary's. 'Are you sure you want to stay here? After what happened . . .'

'It's fine. I need to spend some time with him. He's been neglected enough as it is.'

'So you're not going to the pub later? I was half thinking I'd give it a swerve too. Nick's already on his way to the airport, so he's not going to notice if we ditch it—'

'I think we both need to go, Eddie. We need to cleanse ourselves of all this.'

He's laughing as she climbs out of the car. 'Don't get too ahead of yourself, Becks . . . there's a paperwork mountain bigger than an Alp to deal with. And I don't mean a Toblerone Alp.'

He tries to keep his mood up as he drives home. Even leaves the radio channel as it is. It's all going fine until Noddy Holder yells, 'It's Chriiiistmaaaaas!' He draws the line at that.

Carly is waiting for him in the living room. She has laid out a tray with cheese and crackers. Sticks of celery, a small jar of cranberry sauce. A bottle of red breathing next to two glasses.

'The kids are all out tonight,' she says. 'I thought we could have another chat . . . a calmer one this time. I'm sorry. About everything . . .' She is wringing her hands. A nervous habit that she seems to have developed lately.

He stands in the living-room doorway, runs a hand

across his face. He needs to shave. He's starting to get that itchy way that he hates. He blows out a breath.

'I'm sorry too, Carly. Things have run away from us, haven't they? I thought that everything was over. I was ready to throw in the towel. But when you told me about Thacker . . . and I started to think about what could've happened.' He shakes his head. 'No matter what's gone on with us, you've always been a good mother. You've brought up those kids well, even when I haven't been around much to help you. I've been selfish. I can see that now.'

She's sitting on the couch, a hand on the empty seat. She pats it. Smiles. 'How ironic that it takes a serial killer to get us talking to each other again,' she says.

She's trying to be brave, but he can still see the fear behind her eyes. He hopes she'll take the counselling that's been offered. She needs it more than she realises. Maybe he should have some too, all things considered. They need a break from each other. They both need to think about what they want to do next. He takes a deep breath.

'Maybe you should go to your parents' tonight, Carly. I think you should be around people right now. I'm going for a shower, and then I'm going out—'

'But . . . are you going to come over tomorrow? You said you were off – that we could have Christmas dinner together. It's been years since we've managed it without your work getting in the way . . . and you know it's Noelle's last one before she turns eighteen . . .' She leaves the sentence hanging. They both know what this means.

'You'll enjoy it better without me there, casting my dark cloud.'

'Eddie, please . . .'

He turns back to her. Sees the broken expression on her pretty face. 'Maybe I'll come round in the evening. Once everyone's in a food coma . . . I'm just not sure I can handle the rest of it right now.'

She smiles. Hope lights up her eyes. 'OK,' she says.

He walks out.

65

BECKY

She feels as if she hasn't cooked a meal in months, but it's really only a couple of weeks. She remembers making a Thai green curry the night before the attack on campus. Next day she was thrown into her biggest role within CID yet . . . and only a few days later, she was on a multiple murder case. Things have changed a lot in a short space of time. Is this why she's having doubts about Gary? Dependable Gary who had done nothing but make her feel loved and safe since the minute she'd met him.

She'd been coming out of her counselling session, struggling with her umbrella in the wind, and had walked smack right into him as he was making his way, head down against the sideways driving rain, into the pharmacy to buy ear plugs, in prep for a work team-building weekend where he'd be sharing a room.

It was one of those clichés that really happened. Their eyes met, and he'd hastily written his number on the back of a receipt. She was flattered, but still a little wary. Two years of counselling and she was only just starting to feel confident enough to think about going out with someone else. A stranger . . . well that would've been out of the question, had Gary not seemed so completely normal.

But then so had the last man she'd dated, and look how that had turned out.

Nine months later and she is getting itchy feet. Was there ever a way back, once your heart had started to make its journey elsewhere?

'I wish you would think about taking another job – there's loads of things you could do, Becks. Or move departments, at least. It's far too dangerous, what you're doing. You're not long out of therapy. Do you really want to go back there?'

This irks, and she wants to snap at him. But she keeps her mouth shut for now. After all, it is her fault that he's got a face that's still one and a half times its usual size and a black eye that a prop forward would be proud of. She loves her job. It's only just getting interesting! Plus, she knows she's good at it. Eddie and Nick both said so, and she's not going to argue with either of them. She knows she still has a lot to learn and she's looking forward to it.

The therapy comment had come across as a dig too, or was she just being over-sensitive?

She ignores his last comments, and leaves him to his paper. He's sitting at the kitchen table, while she snips parsley into the beef and mushroom stew. In a couple of days, they'll both go round to hers for Christmas dinner, with the whole family including her dad's latest girlfriend, who he has only been seeing for a few weeks but who seems like someone who might actually do her old man some good. It'll be Gary's first Christmas with them all, and she's been looking forward to it for weeks . . . but now? She closes her eyes and stirs the stew. Breathes in the delicious cooking smells.

Nothing has changed, and yet everything is different.

She doesn't want settled, content and dependable. She wants laughter and risqué jokes and garlic pizza bread and beer at lunchtime. She wants light-hearted arguments about music and debates about big issues.

She wants a bit of darkness in her life . . . like Eddie.

But it's not Eddie that she wants. Under different circumstances? Maybe. But he is her partner and she wants to learn from him, and she most definitely doesn't want to screw things up.

Spending time with Eddie has made her realise that she would rather spend time with him – or someone like him, at least – than she would with Gary. Plus, she gets the impression that Gary wants someone with less . . . what can she say . . . *fire* in them. Someone with a nice, normal job who works nice normal hours and likes to curl up on the couch afterwards and watch nice normal TV. That, Becky realises, is not her.

It's Christmas, though.

She can't dump Gary at Christmas. She will have to get through things as best she can, and then in the new year, they will have a chat and they will part amicably and she is sure that in no time at all, Gary will bump into the girl of his dreams and he will forget she even existed.

Becky, on the other hand, will be glad to be on her own – to have time to focus on work, to socialise with her colleagues without feeling that pang of guilt that she should be at home with a chili con carne and a soap opera on catch-up.

'You know what,' she says. The thought springs into her mind, pinballs around inside, switching on several lights. 'You should take all those old clothes in the loft to the charity shop.'

He looks up from his paper and smiles. 'Yeah, I know. One of those things I keep meaning to get round to. They've been up there for years. I don't even remember what's in those bags.'

She stares at the stew. Looks back at him, with his head straight back inside the paper. She was starving before, but her appetite seems to have disappeared.

'You mind if I go and get them now?'

She's off before he can protest. She hooks the hatch down, pulls down the ladder. Her ribs squeal with protest as she climbs up there, grabs the first couple of bags that she can reach and throws them down onto the bed. It doesn't really matter what's in them, does it? The recipients are hardly fashion conscious.

She marches back into the kitchen, leaves the bags sitting next to the front door.

'Becks, what are you doing—' He looks at her like she's gone mad. Even more so when she takes a large plastic box with a lid out from the cupboard near the sink, tips the entire contents of the pot of stew into it. She should've let it cool first, but she doesn't really have time.

'There's leftover curry in the fridge. It'll be fine. Listen, I'll probably just go home after, so don't wait up. I'll see you tomorrow, OK. We'll spend Christmas Eve together.

Watch some cheesy films?' She leans down and kisses him on the forehead.

'Becks—' he tries again, but she's already out of the front door.

She doesn't bother knocking. She knows that no one will answer. She drags the bin bags and the box of stew up the stairs and into the room on the left. It's dimly lit by various candles that have been dotted around. The man in the bag is still in his bag. He's rolling a cigarette. He sees her at the door, turns his mouth into something resembling a grin. The woman lying on the floor beside him jumps up.

'Hey, what the hell—'

'Pipe down, Rosie,' the man in the bag says. 'She's a friend.'

Becky walks into the room, drops the bin bags near the couple. Offers the woman called Rosie the box of stew.

'Careful. It's still hot.'

Rosie grins. She takes the stew and lays it on the floor. She grabs the first bin bag and rips it open, spilling out the contents.

'Mostly men's stuff, I think,' Becky says. 'I'm not really sure what's in there.'

Rosie pulls out a blue woolly jumper and holds it up to get a better look. 'Well, fuck me,' she says, grinning from ear to ear, 'you'd think it was Christmas or something.'

Becky can't wipe the smile off her face as she practically skips down the stairs.

She drives to the station, leaves her car in the car park.

The Wheatsheaf at 7 p.m., they said. It's only up the road.

The street looks beautiful now, with the twinkling decorations on the lampposts and the light dusting of snow. She opens the door to the pub and she's hit with a wall of heat, laughter and the familiar trumpet sounds of Jona Lewie's 'Stop The Cavalry'.

'Here she is, Queen of New Year . . . where have you *been*, Greene?' Joe is red-faced, swaying slightly.

'What time did you get here?' She laughs, can't help it.

He shrugs. Hands her a pint of something that was already sitting on the bar.

'Cheers,' he says. He clinks her glass, sloshing half of his own drink over his jumper, which is already looking worse for wear.

This is what I want, she thinks.

It's this.

66

She takes the biggest suitcase out from under the bed. It still has a tag from the last time it was used. A two-week holiday in Tenerife, where Eddie spent most of the time lying by the pool with his face stuck in a book, and Carly spent most of her time walking along the long promenade on her own, hoping for some excitement. She lifts it onto the bed, unzips it, flips the top open. A small pile of sand has pooled in one corner. There is still a faint hint of coconut sun cream.

'Moving out, are you?'

Carly turns around. Her eldest daughter, Fiona, is leaning against the door frame, one hip cocked and a hand resting on it. She's dyed her hair a deep red. Quite a change from the dirty blonde that she's had for the last few months.

She walks over to the door and gives her daughter a hug. 'The colour suits you. It really makes the green of your eyes pop. I don't know why you didn't do this before.'

'Thanks,' Fiona says. She flicks her long fringe away from her face. 'So are you going to tell me what's going on? That case is a bit big, isn't it?'

Carly avoids her gaze and walks across to the chest of drawers. Opens the top drawer and starts pulling out

T-shirts. 'I'm packing to go to Gran's. What do you think I'm doing?'

Fiona sits down on the bed. She peels apart the airline sticker and pulls it off the case. 'Mum, come on. I'm twenty-five not five. You don't have to keep protecting me.'

Carly pulls out the second drawer, starts rummaging through knitwear. Tears are pricking at the corners of her eyes but she doesn't want her daughter to see that she's upset. She was hoping to get to Broughton Manor before any of them twigged that she'd brought far too many clothes for five days at the grandparents', but it didn't look like she was going to get away with it now.

She turns back to the bed, her arms laden with clothes. 'Don't be silly, darling. There's nothing going on.' She places the pile of clothes into the case. She hasn't bothered to clean out the sand.

'Simon's already told me—'

'Told you what?'

'Come on, Mum . . .'

'If you're talking about the night I had a few too many and fell asleep on the couch—'

'Yeah, well there's that . . . but it's hardly the first time, is it? And there's the disappearing to Godalming . . .' she runs both hands through her hair. Sighs. 'What the hell were you thinking? I just don't get it. What's the deal with you and Dad? It's always been a bit . . . weird – you can't deny that, surely?' She doesn't wait for an answer. 'But lately . . . Jesus. Are you having a mid-life crisis or something? I'd ask Dad, but I've hardly seen him for weeks. You can't keep this up, Mum. You just can't.' She closes her eyes and flips back onto the bed. Lies there, staring up at the ceiling.

Carly climbs onto the bed, shuffles across until she's sitting beside her daughter. She strokes her hair, fanning it out across the pillow. 'He was never really mine, you know? I've tried to convince myself all these years that maybe he does love me. Even just a bit. But I just can't do it any more.'

Fiona pulls herself up onto one elbow. Her face is creased into a frown. 'What are you talking about? Of course he loves you . . . he married you, didn't he? What're you saying this for?' Her voice starts to pitch up. Anxiety pushing through. She sits up, leans back against the headboard. 'Mum? You're scaring me . . .'

'I'm sorry, darling. Ignore me. It's just a difficult time. We'll sort it out, we always do. Dad's busy at the moment, but he'll be coming over on Christmas night. We'll have a great time at Gran's. You could come with me now, if you like?'

Fiona sighs with relief. 'I was only popping in to see if you were all right. I'm meant to be going out tonight. I was going to come to Gran's tomorrow . . .'

'Then go out, darling. Please.'

'OK . . .' Fiona leans over and kisses her on the head, and for that moment, at least, everything is just fine.

67

THE PHOTOGRAPHER

You hear about people being put on suicide watch, but they don't tell you what this really means. What it means in my case is that they have taken away everything that I might be able to use to kill myself. Belt, shoelaces, those sorts of things. A police officer sticks his head through the little slot in the door every five minutes. I know it's five minutes, because I've counted it in my head.

One one-hundred . . . two one-hundred . . .

Five minutes.

Do they really think I wouldn't be able to kill myself in between their checks? Do they really think, having seen all the things that I've done, that I wouldn't be capable of smashing my own head off the floor? I'd only be able to do it once, but it would be enough.

That's only one of the options.

Over the years, I've gone through them all. I've compiled a top five. Oh come on. Hasn't everyone?

1. Jump off a bridge. Only problem is getting over the railings in time before someone spots you, when you're thinking about one of those seriously high bridges like the Clifton Suspension Bridge or the Forth Road Bridge. It's risky, as there are people watching for this exact sort of thing

nowadays. Seems like it's everyone's number one option. There's no surviving a fifty-metre drop, no matter which way you land.

2. Jump off a cliff. This would be joint number one, if it wasn't for the fact that cliffs are unpredictable. There can be hidden ledges beneath that you might land on and break your fall. Or you might get caught on rocks, smash yourself up but survive. The worst thing that can happen as a result of any suicide attempt is survival. Unless you're only after a bit of attention. Then survival is your ultimate goal.

3. Overdose on alcohol and pills. A good option if you can get the quantities right. Get them wrong and you'll wake up with a tube down your throat and bright lights shining in your eyes. Or worse, you'll wake up with the hangover from hell, but three days later you'll die in agony when your organs start shutting down, just at the point where you've decided that living might not be so bad after all.

4. Slit your wrists. Obviously you have to do it the proper way. Down the artery, not across it. Two reasons for doing it in the bath – firstly, the hot water will make sure you bleed faster. You don't want this to linger. Secondly, it makes it less messy for whoever it is that finds you. There will be a lot of blood. Baths can be cleaned. Think about it.

5. Auto-asphyxiation. Potentially the most fun option, if you can get it right. Dressing gown cord around your neck, hang off the back of a door and have a wank. Got to be more fun than just straightforward hanging, which, by the way, is rarely hanging. It's more often strangulation, and that can take a while and it sounds fucking horrible so you

might as well get something out of it. You know what I mean? I was going to set Carly's up to look like this. Shame I didn't get the chance.

Anyway . . . I'm not going to do any of these things. Not in here. I had my chance with that knife. I could quite literally have fallen on my sword. It would have been quick, and I'm sure it would've been relatively painless. I'd have passed out from the shock before I bled out.

I'm actually sorry for what I did. The young detective – that was a moment of madness. I lost my way. Forgot what I was trying to achieve. Manipulating DS Carmine's wife was my biggest mistake. I should've gone back to *him*. Reminded him of our chat in Ealing.

I know he remembers.

The teenager . . . barely so. Still a boy. A stupid, dirty feral little boy – but who knows, maybe there was a chance for him somewhere down the line? Maybe what he needed was a decent stretch in prison to consider his options.

I took all his options away.

The attack on him was brutal, born purely of frustration. I am ashamed of myself.

But the others?

I'm not ready to feel bad about the others. Not yet. Chrissie's killer didn't just take my beloved sister. He destroyed my life. My dad's life. We were already so broken from losing Mum . . . who would do that to us? Who would take everything we had, our last piece of hope, and stamp it into tiny, inconspicuous little pieces?

Who?

This is my biggest regret. I didn't kill Chrissie, and yet I've been coerced into saying that I did – to make things easier for the families of the other victims – to make the sentencing simple, so that no one has to be dragged along this path of broken glass.

This is my biggest regret – because now I will never find out who did kill her. I will never get the opportunity for the truest revenge.

I just wanted them to notice me. I wanted them to help me.

I wanted them to find Chrissie's killer.

DS Carmine knows I didn't kill Chrissie. I could see it in his eyes. Perhaps I'll let the dust settle. Await my sentencing. Move into my new accommodation – at Her Majesty's Pleasure.

Yes. That's what I'll do. I'll wait until everything is arranged, then I will send him a visiting order. See what he has to say.

After all, he owes it to the families of all the victims since 2006 . . . when I tried to enlist his help then, and he chose to ignore me. He still needs to find Chrissie's killer. I know he won't let me down again.

68

EDDIE

Eddie takes his drink and scans the pub hoping for a corner seat in a quiet bit, away from all the noise. No chance. Friday before Christmas, the last day of work for many. His second least favourite night of the year, after the disappointing carnage that is New Year's Eve. Amateur night. Pubs filled with the people who stay at home all year, making their way to the pub for a forced festive celebration, drinking more than they should and doing things they regret. No to mention the seasoned pissheads and binge drinkers who can't seem to stay away. Anyone who fancied their usual Friday night in their local is screwed, tonight.

'So how come you're such a miserable bastard, Carmine? Didn't you just get your man?' DS Jones has had too many sherberts and is clearly feeling brave. Eddie hopes he gets called out to something gruesome at 6 a.m. when his Christmas Eve shift starts.

'Shouldn't you be taking it easy, Tim? You're on morning clean-up, aren't you?'

Tim slaps Eddie on the back, causing Eddie to slosh drink over the carpet . . . a voiceover plays in his head, like one of those presenters from a kids' TV programme: *And that, science lovers, is why pub carpets are so sticky!*

'Sorry, man. I'll get you another.' Tim ambles off

towards the bar, leaving Eddie with his now half-pint of bitter, ignores his call saying it's fine, doesn't matter.

It really doesn't matter.

Eddie doesn't want a drink. He doesn't want to be in the pub at all, but Keegan had insisted they go. It was a big deal, catching Colin Thacker in time for Christmas. People would sleep easier now, no longer terrified in their own homes. Unable to open their front doors even to a bunch of harmless Boy Scouts for fear of being murdered in their living rooms. Thacker played a blinder this year, ramping up his campaign to mark the anniversary of his first kill . . . his own sister.

Maybe.

He scans the room, the drinkers of all ages, all professions. Cluster of his police colleagues hovering near the bar. Voices booming. Excited. They'd done well.

Thacker was in custody and he wasn't going anywhere anytime soon. He'd repeatedly denied killing Chrissie, insisting that this event was the trigger to his own madness. And then suddenly, after a chat with his brief, he'd done a miraculous U-turn. Told them that Chrissie was his first kill, but it was an accident. Keegan was delighted, but Eddie was wary. Colin would have to undergo a full psych evaluation, of course, but Eddie hoped that it would work in their favour. They didn't want him to get diminished responsibility – not for what he had done. He was sly. Calculating. Organised, but ultimately reckless. He'd tried to target Eddie through his own wife, for fuck's sake. These weren't the actions of a madman. These were the actions of a psychopath. It would all come out. His past. His reasons. He was too good at what he did. The consummate actor. He was still playing them now, trying to bullshit them about his sister.

Wasn't he?

Eddie's not convinced. He takes a sip of his drink and grimaces. He's glad that Tim seems to have forgotten to return with a fresh one. He just wants to go home, even if the place is going to be cold and empty. Just him now. That was what he wanted, wasn't it? Everything was going the way he wanted it, right?

'All right, boss? You're looking a bit . . . lost, there.' At some point, Becky has appeared at his side. She smiles at him, tips a bottle of brightly coloured drink towards his sad-looking pint. 'Want me to get you a drink? Something a bit less . . . shit?'

Eddie looks down at what's left of his drink. Shakes his head. Glances around. Still no tables. Not even a spare seat. People are squeezed into clothes that are too small, crushed into places that they barely fit into. Everyone is laughing, drinking. Knocking back shots. The odd screech here and there. The familiar bassline of a song in the background. He recognises the song. 'Birdhouse in Your Soul'. They Might Be Giants. Some weird band from the nineties. Where are they now? he wonders. What did that song even mean? Despite not knowing, he knows he can recite all of the lyrics without even thinking about it. He's not sure who his only friend is. Does he even have one?

'Fancy some air?' he says.

Becky knocks back the rest of her drink and follows him outside. As the door swings shut, the first few bars of Spandau Ballet's 'Only When You Leave' starts up. He smiles. Imagines a DJ playing the soundtrack of his life. They do that well on some of the soaps. Background music that you don't notice until you realise the lyrics are perfectly suited to the scene. He'd love that job. Matching the music to the misery.

'You OK?' Becky shrugs her shoulders up. She looks cold.

'Carly's taken the kids. Gone to her parents' for Christmas. Maybe longer. I don't know—'

'You could come round ours? It'll be chaos, I'll tell you that now. Gary's mum and dad were meant to be in Goa but his dad's got a heart problem and they had to cancel it, so we've got them now as well as the four of us, and Allie and I think Allie's new boyfriend, even though none of us have even met him and he'll probably have dumped her by New Year's Eve . . .' She pauses, eventually, asks, 'Eddie, what is it?'

He blows out a long, slow breath. 'It's Thacker. His story about his sister, how he suddenly changed his mind—'

'You're not falling for that, are you? It doesn't make sense. No one kills twenty-one people for revenge. To try to make the police notice. No one does that, Eddie. You know what happened. He killed his sister by accident, it drove him mad, he killed someone else as a cover-up, to make it look like another killer. Then it got out of hand. He couldn't stop. He got the taste for it . . .'

'He has an alibi for the night his sister was killed. He was in Scotland. The hotel has him signed in on their guest book.'

'He could've left during the night. Driven down then. We can check it again, of course we can. But I know he's lying. I just know it. He confessed, Eddie. What more do you need?'

Eddie frowns. 'I wish I had your resolve, Becks. I just can't help thinking that we've missed something. Someone. We never did manage to get hold of Tabitha Smart . . .'

'I'm freezing, Ed. I'm going back in. It's Christmas Eve tomorrow, for fuck's sake. We've got our man. Nothing is going to happen tonight. You need to go home, get some sleep. Take the day off that you're owed. If you still feel rattled about it when we're back in, we'll go to Nick together, OK? I'm your partner now, right? I'm sticking with you, even if just to be there when you realise we were all right all along . . .'

'You're remarkably chipper for someone who could've been killed the other night.'

'He'd never have killed me. It was the final scare. The final shake-up. He was handing himself to us on a plate.'

'Sure. If you say so.' Eddie can't argue any more. Not tonight. She's right. He needs sleep. Needs a day off. Maybe a solo Christmas isn't such a bad thing after all.

She turns back to him, says, 'Listen . . . my family broke up. My mum went off with a woman. My dad has a new girlfriend every month. But we make it work. You can sort things out with your lot. You just need to *talk* to her. 3 p.m. at ours on Sunday, if you're coming. We'll make a space for you.' She leans over and kisses him on the cheek.

'Merry Christmas, Eddie.'

'Merry Christmas, Becks.' He shoves his hands into his pockets and makes his way down the street, dreading the walk across town playing dodge the drunken reveller.

Maybe she's right. Maybe he's just thinking too much about it all, but he can't get the man's face out of his mind. His expression when they mentioned his sister. Broken. Helpless. Eddie imagined himself in his shoes. Thought, what if it was one of his kids? What would he do in that situation? Someone you love being taken from you in the worst possible way . . .

He's home before he knows it, barely noticing the light swirl of snow around him.

He stares at the black, empty windows, knowing there's nothing in there behind them.

It doesn't have to be like this though, does it? Maybe he will go over to Carly's parents for Christmas lunch. Maybe he'll wear a paper hat and get drunk on sherry and have a good time, for once. Maybe it'll be his last Christmas with his family.

Or maybe it won't.

As he sticks the key into the lock, a solitary snowflake lands on his hand. He smiles, as he watches it melt.

Saturday

ONE MORE SLEEP

He walks along the pavement, grit crunching underfoot. The edges are still heaped with the remnants of snow stained brown from the grit and dirt that's been sluiced from the mushy melt of the recent thaw. He slips on a patch of black ice and swears under his breath, irritated that he's wearing shoes with no proper grips on the soles. He should know better.

Coming here had been a last-minute decision. The wrong one, maybe. Probably. He pauses, briefly, under a dim streetlamp and lights a cigarette.

He could still change his mind. He could stop. Turn. Walk back into town to the station, jump on one of the fast trains to central London. Grab his stuff from the hotel on the Strand then get in a cab and to the airport in only a couple of hours. There's a flight at midday. He could still make it.

He sucks hard on the cigarette. It's been years since he's smoked, but something about coming back here has made him want to reminisce. He glances up and down the street. Notices how little it has really changed over the years. Maybe fewer bikes inside the front-garden walls. Wheelie bins now instead of overflowing lidless ones and stacks of stinking carrier bags, the fermented smell attracting cats and foxes. Rats. He has a sudden memory of taking the rubbish out late one night, lifting a bag and seeing those sharp yellow eyes peering back at him.

It was purely instinctive when he brought the heel of his boot down on the evil pointy little face. He shivers. The memory and an icy breeze wrapping around him.

He finishes the cigarette. Surprised at how much he enjoyed it after all this time. He crushes it under his formal black shoe and his mind flashes once more to the rat that he killed. He stares at the cigarette butt and all he can see are the yellow eyes. The pink strings of brain matter flattened and smeared into the ground around the rodent's head, like a raw hamburger halo.

He pops a mint from a small plastic dispenser and sucks on it. Carries on walking.

Number eight, number nine.

Number ten.

Outside the front window, a thick magnolia blocks the view. He remembers when they planted that tree. Not much more than a twig and a few bright leaves, but it had been flowering when he first visited this house, and bare when he left. Sudden hard frost had caused it to shed its leaves, leaving it exposed. He'd assumed it had died, but clearly he was wrong. Another mistake. These stupid fucking shoes. In this weather.

He wouldn't make another.

He pauses on the doorstep. Notices the new front door, expensive oak with a bright brass knocker. Not the cheap red-painted wood that he remembered. No doorbell now, either, and the frame is neat and fresh. There's no evidence of the winding ivy, the black mould growing in the gaps in the brickwork. It's been repointed, refreshed. Someone has spent money on the place. She must've got it for a song, after what happened. He'd always sensed that she was canny, that one.

Tabitha.

His hand is hovering over the knocker, but before he can change his mind, someone inside senses his presence on the path.

The door swings open.

'Sebastien . . . Jesus. What are you doing here?'

'Surprise!' he says. He tries to give her his best winning smile but it must look wrong, because she backs away . . . starts to slowly close the door.

'How did you know I still lived here?'

He laughs. 'You're a celebrity now, Tabitha! I looked you up . . . read about you staying on in your student house, being part of the re-gentrification—'

'Right. Of course . . .'

'You must've seen the news? I've been in town for a couple of weeks. Staying at a hotel in London. I'm heading home again – it was lucky I spotted it, really. I only happened to flick it on after I got back early from a meeting—'

She visibly relaxes. 'Oh, of course. They caught Chrissie's killer. You know, I never in a million years imagined her brother could do something like that. All those poor people.'

'So you're sure the police got it right? I just can't imagine that he'd kill Chrissie. All the others, yes. Clearly he is a very deranged man . . .'

Her shoulders tense again and she pushes the door closed a little more. 'I have to get ready for work now. It was nice to see you, Sebastien.'

He takes a step towards the door. Wedges his foot into the gap. Grins.

'You never did like me much, did you, Tabitha?'

He kicks the door back and it smacks into her face. She stumbles backwards, throws her hand up to her head. Blood slides through her fingers. He can see it in her eyes. Fear. And something else.

She remembers.

She remembers that he is really not a very nice man at all.

'You . . .' she says. 'You were here that night, weren't you? There was an empty can of Coors in the kitchen bin. I remember it. I remember it because no one drank that beer except you. I told the police but they said it was coincidence. Maybe Chrissie put it there. Your alibi . . . your parents said you were having dinner with them . . .'

'Of course they did, you stupid bitch. Parents always protect their children, don't they?' He kicks the door closed with his heel. Watches her slithering across the polished wood floor, trying to get away from him. He stares at her, feels a burst of adrenaline hit his veins.

He slides off his black leather gloves, revealing the white latex ones underneath.

He grabs her ankle and drags her to the foot of the stairs. She kicks and flails, but the floor is too slippery and she can't get any purchase. He bats off her attempts at blows as if she is an annoying fly.

He grabs a chunk of her hair, bashes her head on the floor. Hard. When she stops twitching, he drags her closer to the bottom stair, smears blood from the back of her head on the edge. He lets her go and she falls limp, like a ragdoll. He pulls off her shoes, throws them into the basket by the door.

Doesn't she know how dangerous it is to run down polished stairs in her stockings?

What a tragic accident . . . on Christmas Eve, too.

He glances up and down the street, but it is deserted. It's cold. People are wrapped up inside, watching crap holiday TV, eating cereal and ignoring what's going on just metres away from them in their street. Their good street in a good part of town. Used to be full of students, but not any more. Nouveau riche and people who cashed in on the last big crash. People like Tabitha, who bought their student house for peanuts and did it up like something from one of those glossy home magazines.

He walks away, takes it slow, normal.

Pops another mint.

Tabitha was the only one who could really link him back to what happened to Chrissie. She was the only one who might remember that he was there.

He smiles as he remembers Chrissie's advent calendar. Remembers her smiling face when he'd arrived that night, woken her with a kiss. Her beautiful face, so peaceful. So serene. She'd been so happy to see him . . . but it had quickly soured when he told her he was going back to the States. That he wasn't coming back. Her whining had annoyed him. He didn't have time for all that. He had another life to get home to. Another girl to get back for. If only she'd accepted that it was only ever meant to be a fling.

Poor Chrissie.

Poor Tabitha.

No more sleeps.

ACKNOWLEDGEMENTS

I never really planned to write a Christmas themed book, but meeting my fantastic editor, Ruth Tross, and discovering that she had a very similar take on the usual twee festivities led to the birth of a serial killer who had a very different use for an advent calendar. Massive thanks to Ruth, and to all at Hodder – especially Nick Sayers, Cicely Aspinall, Aimee Oliver and Rosie Stephen for all your hard work and massive support.

Thanks, as ever, to my champion agent, Phil Patterson and to all at Marjacq Scripts.

This book involved much more research than usual (for me) so huge thanks to all those who helped me with the police-y bits, especially Elizabeth Haynes and Lisa Cutts. Any errors or bends in the truth are entirely down to me.

As ever, there are many people in the crime writing community who have kept me relatively sane during the writing of this book – by cracking the whip, and providing tissues, gin and gossip. You know who you are.

Monumental thanks to my family, who have to put up with me being too busy to talk to them most of the time. I love you.

A colossal thanks to all my friends who have been a huge support from the start, and especially to Hannah Evans, who was very demanding about having a cameo appearance and is now immortalised as a violent disturbance of the atmosphere.

Finally, gigantic thanks, as always, to JLOH for keeping me in the manner to which I have become accustomed. Thank you for the tea, the hoovering, the washing, the cooking, the singing and dancing, and most of all, the love.

K

You've turned the last page.

But it doesn't have to end there . . .

If you're looking for more first-class, action-packed, nail-biting suspense, join us at **Facebook.com/ MulhollandUncovered** for news, competitions, and behind-the-scenes access to Mulholland Books.

For regular updates about our books and authors as well as what's going on in the world of crime and thrillers, follow us on **Twitter@MulhollandUK**.

There are many more twists to come.

MULHOLLAND:
You never know what's
coming around the curve.

HODDER